Evelyn in Transit

Evelyn in Transit

A Novel

David Guterson

W. W. NORTON & COMPANY

Independent Publishers Since 1923

For information about permission to reproduce selections from
this book, write to Permissions, W. W. Norton & Company, Inc.,
500 Fifth Avenue, New York, NY 10110

For information about special discounts for bulk purchases, please
contact W. W. Norton Special Sales at specialsales@wwnorton.com
or 800-233-4830

Manufacturing by Lakeside Book Company
Book design by Brian Mulligan
Production manager: Louise Mattarelliano

ISBN 978-1-324-11105-4

W. W. Norton & Company, Inc., 500 Fifth Avenue, New York, NY 10110
www.wwnorton.com

W. W. Norton & Company Ltd., 15 Carlisle Street, London W1D 3BS

$PrintCode

. . .

For Dawa Drolma, the Saint of Uncontrolled Energies,
and for the Ecstatic formerly known as Jan

And in memory of
Ane Chime Drolma and Dezhung Rinpoche III

Note on Tibetan Names and Titles

TIBETANS COMMONLY HAVE A two-part given name—for example, Tsering Lekpa.

Prominent Tibetan Buddhists are primarily referred to by titles instead of given names. "Rinpoche," meaning "precious one," is a term of respect for individuals recognized as reincarnations of significant teachers. It is sometimes the case that a prominent Tibetan Buddhist is referred to by a title with no elements of that person's given name retained. Thus Tsering Lekpa, on receiving his title, might be called, for example, Norbu Rinpoche.

Evelyn in Transit

Evelyn

. . .

———————————

. .

YOU CLIMBED ONTO A STUMP, AND FROM THE STUMP got hold of a branch, and from that branch caught a higher branch, and after that the branches were so close you could climb until the tree got wispy, and from there you could see the river, tracks, farms, roads, and a line where the earth met the sky.

The big view made Evelyn wary. A hollowness grew in her, and she wondered about it.

One morning, as Evelyn descended, a shudder went through her. She hurried to the lowest branch, let go, and, when her feet hit the ground, woke from her dream. 'I'm alive,' she said to herself. 'I'm separate from everything else.'

She told Maureen about it. Maureen was older. *The Twilight Zone* had just begun. "In a moment a child will try to cross that bridge which separates light and shadow," said the narrator, and that was when she told Maureen, "I jumped off the tree and woke up."

Everything was different after that—everything felt different. She couldn't say how.

Tsering

TSERING WAS PLAYING BY HIMSELF IN A COLD WIND. Behind the storehouse, near the road, sat a mound of yak hides. They were like things in a dream, real and unreal. The hair was still on them, including the long hair, the belly hair, the skirt.

Up the mound of hides Tsering went, fingers in their tangles. The top hide was frozen but not frozen solid. He could still smell its oil. Nearby, in the grass, yaks milled and grazed.

A gust came down the hill. The smell of the yaks came with it. One swiveled toward him, caught his eye, and snorted; steam streamed from its nostrils. 'It's thinking about me,' thought Tsering.

He realized something then. The hides he was sitting on were yak hides.

Tsering vaulted off. When his feet struck the ground, a jolt went through his chest. 'I'm alive,' he said to himself. 'I'm separate from everything else.'

That afternoon, from the crest of a hill, he noticed that all the people things were small—corrals, gates, tents, homes—compared to the size of the grasslands, the mountains, and the sky, and with that another jolt went through him, so that Tsering again thought, 'I'm alive, I'm separate from everything else.'

Evelyn

E VELYN HAD PERMISSION TO HOLD JIMMY, BUT FIRST she had to sit up straight and make her arms into a cradle. After that she had to sit still and support Jimmy's head.

She touched Jimmy's cheek. The cuckoo clock ticked. Sunlight made a bar on the floor because the drapes weren't closed all the way. The television was on but the sound was off. A fly was in the room—she could hear it but not see it. A bubble formed between Jimmy's lips, then disappeared.

Jimmy didn't have eyebrows or eyelashes. There was a dimple in his skull, plain because he hardly had hair. His eyes were closed, and one of his hands lay beside his head. It had perfect fingernails.

Jimmy's onesie had a carrot embroidered on it and a zipper. The pull was under a buttoned flap below his throat. The zipper ran down one leg and stopped above the footie. The onesie was from the Penney's downtown. They'd looked at The Baby Shop too, but the clothes were too expensive there.

The room was hot. Her mother got up and pulled the cord to close the drapes, and the bar of light on the floor disappeared. Other than the buzzing of the fly, the whir from the fan was the only noise.

"Here," her mother said, and took Jimmy from her.

Evelyn stood. She felt damp where Jimmy had been. She had bandages on her knees from Tag. Mosquitoes had gotten her just about everywhere. That morning she'd cut her bangs with desk scissors. They'd come out ragged, and in trying to fix them she'd made them worse. All day she'd felt ashamed of her bangs. Now they troubled her so much that, after holding Jimmy, she went into the bathroom to check on them in the mirror. Did they still look terrible? She stared at herself and then she knew: it didn't matter. Cutting her bangs right wouldn't have made any difference. She just didn't look good. Until now she hadn't understood that.

◆

THE HOUSE HAD TWO bedrooms. Evelyn and Maureen shared the smaller one. When Jimmy came, her parents moved the chifferobe out of their bedroom to make space for a crib. They didn't know where to put the chifferobe, so for now it stood at the foot of Evelyn's bed.

Something was in the chifferobe that could hear through wood, and this meant Evelyn couldn't make noise or move. If she made noise or moved, the thing would get her. She had to stay still until morning, because in the morning the thing wouldn't be there anymore. Her father would come to get his clothes, and when he opened the chifferobe there'd be nothing unusual. In fact, all day every day there was nothing unusual about the chifferobe, and even in the evening it didn't pose a problem. It only became a problem when the lights went out, and even then it was only a problem for her, not Maureen.

It also didn't matter what happened in her parents' bedroom. If Jimmy cried, or if her parents snored, the thing in the chifferobe didn't come out. It concerned itself only with her; it was after only her. This was so hard to keep to herself that one night she told her father about it. No, he said, he wouldn't move the chifferobe, and the reason was, there was nothing in it but clothes. And furthermore she was not allowed to watch *The Twilight Zone* anymore, and from now on she had to leave the living room when *Alfred Hitchcock* started.

◆

TO GET THERE YOU kept going past Arcadian Acres until you came to a ditch. It was steep but you could scramble out of it by hanging on to brush. After that you crossed the Traction Line. It had wires overhead and rails underfoot but no trains, just broken bottles and litter. Beyond the Traction Line were raggedy fields owned by a farmer who was never around. Finally after the fields were The Mounds.

A book said some people thought the Mound Builders were Egyptians and some thought they came from the lost continent of Atlantis, but no one knew which one it was. The book had drawings in it. One was of a guy called the Birdman who had rattles made from skulls. Another was of a guy who could turn into an arrow. The Mound Builders worshipped falcons, according to this book. They wore feathers on their heads and as few clothes as possible. Evelyn thought they had a good way to live, and that included Mound building. She could see being a Mound Builder. You'd work for a while, take a swim in the river, work more, eat, work, swim again, build a fire, watch the Birdman dance, watch the guy who could turn into an arrow do his trick, pray to the falcons, sleep on the ground, get up, build more Mounds. She wouldn't have a care in the world living like that. Everything would be perfect.

✦

THERE WAS A CHURCH nearby that wasn't their church. It was empty and looked dead. Behind it lay a field of weeds that smelled like mint. In the middle of the field was a pile of sticks and in a corner a heap of plywood scraps. If you laid the scraps out in the field evenly and jumped from one to the next, there were enough to get you to the pile of sticks. Between the stick pile and where houses started again were trillions of ants. They bit like the red ones if you riled them up, and they were shaped like the black ones, but they were bigger than the red ones, and brown, smooth, and glossy. These ants never messed around or wasted time. They lived in a mound with a hole on top and swarmed around it, all business. Evelyn felt tempted to jam a stick down the hole, but the string of thoughts she had about doing that always ended with her deciding not to. Sometimes, though, she maimed an ant by poking at it. A leg would get broken, or an antenna would get bent, or the ant's body would get dented. The injured ant would spin in place, or flop onto its side, or flail its legs, or all of that at once, but none of the other ants paid it any mind.

Something about ants justified blocking their paths with scraps of plywood. They'd pause just long enough to consider, then start figuring out the best way around. Evelyn blocked serially. She liked to turn the same ant every which way. Still, ants were worthy adversaries. They didn't succumb to frustration. Sometimes one got a notion and crawled up her leg or arm. If it bit her, she crushed it, but if not, she played with it until it was injured and then flicked it to the ground. After a long period of ant prodding and ant blocking, Evelyn could see that the field of ant activity was littered with corpses. That always prompted her to quit.

◆

EVELYN HAD TO GO to a school where the teachers were nuns. You had to wear a jumper at school, a bow tie, a beanie, a white blouse, and tall socks. At the beginning of the year they gave you a box with six pencils in it. Ethan Allen was on the box, and so was Fort Ticonderoga. The six pencils were supposed to last all year. What happened during school was that you read a book at your desk, then the teacher talked for a while and wrote things on the blackboard, and then you did a worksheet. You had to stay at your desk except that if your pencil got dull while you were doing a worksheet you could go to the pencil sharpener.

Evelyn liked the sharpener. She had to hurry when she used it, though, because after a few seconds the teacher would say, "That's enough, you'll end up with a stub, pencils don't grow on trees, get back to your seat." Actually, Evelyn thought when she heard this, pencils did grow on trees since they were made of wood, plus their erasers were made of rubber and rubber came from rubber trees, but there was no point in saying any of that because the teacher wouldn't care.

On the playground, somebody hit Evelyn in the back with a four square ball. She didn't think anything of it, but then it happened again a few seconds later. The second time, she ran down the ball, picked it up, and kicked it over the fence. For this she got in trouble, and her punishment was to put the blackboard erasers from all the classrooms in Hall B on a cart, wheel them to the boiler room, and run them through a machine called the Little Giant Eraser Cleaner. "Little Giant," the custodian said, after showing her how to run it. "Like you."

The boiler room was warm and the machine was fun to use. It had a bag attached to it, and when Evelyn ran an eraser over the brush, the chalk dust got sucked into the bag. Afterward she took the erasers back. In one classroom no one was around, so she stole pencils.

◆

"WHAT DO YOU WANT To Be When You Grow Up?" was her title because that's what the teacher wrote on the blackboard. The instructions were, have an introduction and a conclusion, have separate paragraphs with three to five sentences in each, spell everything right, explain.

A nun who lives in a convent in the sticks. The wall is a circle. Nobody is let in.

Sheep are there. We milk them. We take wool off. We make cheese. We make sweaters.

A truck comes to a hole in the wall. The back part comes through. We don't see a driver.

We open the truck back. We take out the food. We put in the cheese and the sweaters.

The truck drives away. We close up the hole. We eat the food.

We get to wear boots. We get to wear special hats. Secret hats.

My job is catching lambs and giving them a bottle. I sit on straw because of mud.

We sleep outside. We have a cave for Mass. The light is candles.

The convent is far away. There is a forest. The convent is in the middle.

We are the best nuns. No one talks. Only when we pray.

In conclusion, I want to be a nun when I grow up because of what I wrote.

◆

AT FIRST SHE HAD strap-ons, but then she got the type they wore on Roller Derby. Roller Derby was on television. Her father watched it first, and then Evelyn joined him. The best player was Joanie Weston, number 38 for the Bombers. Her father sent away for a Bombers game program, and in it were color pictures and player information. It turned out Joanie Weston was a California girl who hit eight home runs in a softball game once and jumped off a waterfall. Her teammates called her Wanda Bond after Ward Bond on *Wagon Train*, but otherwise she was called "The Roller Derby Queen." Joanie Weston also had a dog named Malia who traveled with her to games. In the program there was a close-up picture of Joanie—she had a big chin and a big nose, and wore her hair in bangs.

Joanie had an enemy named Ann Calvello, who they called Banana Nose. Ann Calvello spray-painted her hair before games to be intimidating, and screamed like a banshee. She took cheap shots at Joanie Weston's teammates, which made Joanie mad. Joanie would get to where she couldn't take it anymore, and then she'd go after Ann Calvello. Neither cared if what they did was legal. They laid into each other and broke all the rules. Sometimes Joanie would go down and not get up for a while. When she finally did get up she'd seem groggy, but before long she'd be skating again with steam coming out of her ears, determined to chase down Ann Calvello. They were both hard fighters, but there was a difference between them. When Joanie laid out Ann Calvello, she just went back to skating, but when it was the other way around, Ann Calvello celebrated. Evelyn liked Joanie better, but sometimes, skating, she pretended she was Ann Calvello. She would whip around a tetherball pole, and then, rolling, celebrate the Ann Calvello way, by clapping overhead while canted to the right, as if encouraging spectators to love her in spite of everything.

◆

TURNER POOL HAD A room where you put on your suit and another where you took a shower. The reason for the shower was because no one wanted your dirt in the water. You took the shower and then you went down a hallway to the pool. When you came back, you took another shower to get the chlorine off.

In the shower you could soak a towel and twist it into a whip. If you twisted it right, the towel snapped and echoed like a firecracker when you whipped it. What you did was, you stayed in the shower battling people for loudest whip. Sometimes someone tried to whip you hard enough to leave a welt, and you tried to whip them back. The fight could continue into the dressing room.

Evelyn was in the shower when two girls entered, blabbing. They were older and wore racing suits. She'd seen them in the deep end, diving for rings and doing cannonballs off the board. Now they were talking about food, and saying, in different ways, that they were starving to death. Evelyn said, "Wanna snap towels?"

They both shook their heads no. Then one said to Evelyn, "Ever been to the circus?" She had a sharp-boned face and long arms.

"Why?"

"There's freaks like you in it."

She and the other girl were smiling. Then the other girl started giggling.

Evelyn went out, got a towel, came back, soaked it, and started spinning up a whip. "Making a whip," she said.

The girls didn't answer. The one who'd giggled said to the other, "We're gonna be late," and they turned off their showers and left.

✦

HER FATHER WORKED AT George L. Mesker Steel, but she didn't
know what he did there. He left in the morning and came back
at suppertime. George L. Mesker was on First Street downtown.
Evelyn knew that because she'd gone there once, but not inside.
She'd waited on the sidewalk with Maureen while her mother took
something to her father. A row of columns was built into one side
of the George L. Mesker building. It had no windows and looked
like a fortress. It was mysterious, as was George L. Mesker. He'd
been magnanimous, though, her father said, which you could tell
because they'd named the zoo after him. That made Evelyn like
George L. Mesker.

George L. Mesker made it so they could join the Surf Club. In
twenty-five minutes you could ride your bike there. The Surf Club
had a swim team and Evelyn got on it. In the morning you swam
laps and did stroke clinic. In the afternoon you swam more laps.
The meets went so late they had to turn on lights. The Starter had a
pistol and it flashed in the dark. At the end of the race, a Timer with
a stopwatch would be kneeling where you touched the wall. You
hopped out and went to a podium, like in the Olympics, where they
gave you a ribbon. The announcer at the Surf Club pronounced her
name "Bit-nartz," and the parents in the bleachers clapped when
they heard it. There was a board you could look at if you wanted
to know the score. Your team stayed at one end and the other team
at the other.

They had a meet in Owensboro. On the starting block there,
Evelyn did what she always did—looked at the water until the
Starter said, "Take your mark." She took her mark like he said, but
then, instead of firing his gun, the Starter said, "Stand up."

There was a discussion. It turned out the Owensboro coach had
a problem. He said Evelyn couldn't be ten because she was too big
to be ten, so they disqualified her.

Coach Bob argued. He was Coach Bob, but her father called

him Bantam Rooster. Coach Bob had been on the diving team at the University of Indiana. He barked through a megaphone during laps, but mostly did pep talk. "Come on," he said to Evelyn, when he got done arguing.

They went back to where their team was. Coach Bob karate-kicked the ring attached to a lifeguard stand by the deep end. He was so good at it that the ring fell off. Next he kicked it into the air, and then he picked it up and threw it in the pool. Boos came from the parents in the bleachers. Coach Bob just looked at the parents and threw his arms wide like they were cheering for him instead of booing. He even waggled his fingers, egging them on. "You too," he said to Evelyn, so she did what he did. She stood beside Coach Bob for the booing with her arms wide, waggling her fingers. It felt good.

✦

WHEN THE WIND GOT strange, she knew it meant something. Just like the twister in *The Wizard of Oz* meant a door to another world.

First the leaves on the ground started rattling, then the trees stirred and the corn tassels flailed. It all stopped. Then it all started again. This time, the dry leaves rose clacking against each other and funneled skyward. Sunlight hit the leaves while they fluttered and twisted. Some exploded—leaves so brittle they couldn't hold together for the ride up. The priest had said, more than once, "What is seen is transitory, but what is unseen is eternal." And that you were not supposed to mourn without hope.

Toby was wrapped in his blanket. With a stick she'd carved clean sides to make a vault, so everything was set now. She put Toby in, and when she did, the wind came up so that leaves went in with him.

Dusk was in the corn when she started home. She felt bad in a way that usually only happened when she knew no one liked her. Toby had been the greatest dog of all time. He'd slept with her and licked her face at night. He could stand on his hind legs and walk across the yard to the fence. All she had to do was put one shoe on and Toby would know she was fixing to leave, which he didn't like. It wasn't that way with people. People never talked about anything that mattered. The priest came to class to give a moral teaching, and she raised her hand and said she didn't understand the Mass and could he explain it, and instead of explaining it he'd said, "I am not discussing the Mass now, young lady, I am talking about the cultivation of virtue and you are changing the subject and not listening." When the fact was, she listened better than anybody. She listened how an owl listens—like the owl on *Wild Kingdom* who could hear a mouse under snow.

✦

THE NEW PRIEST WAS younger. When he wasn't in church he wore a short-sleeved shirt. His face looked stuck in the smile position. Most people when they smiled their eyes did too, but not the new priest's. With him it was like the lower part of his face belonged to one person and the upper to another. He was a redhead, with freckles.

The new priest came to school and gave a talk. He was a neatnik the way he had his shirt tucked in and the way his hair was parted. The microphone was too loud at first and the priest said, "Oh my goodness, off to a bad start!" It got fixed and he began again, saying, "So let me tell you a little story and there's a reason why I'm telling it. Now, Satan can't do everything himself, so he trains up helpers. Satan, I'm sad to say, has apprentices. And, of course, after all of the training he does with them, he has to see if they're ready for the work of ruination. He has to give them a test. Three at a time his apprentices come before him where he sits with his pitchfork on his fiery throne, and he asks what they plan to do if they pass. Now, one day, in comes a trio of apprentices. They bow before him, and Satan asks his question. The first one answers, 'I plan to tell them no need to pray because there's no God.' 'You don't pass,' says Satan. 'Most of them won't believe you.' The second one answers, 'I plan to tell them there's no hell and they can do what they want.' 'You don't pass either,' says Satan. 'They know perfectly well there's a hell and you can't talk them out of it.' The third one answers, 'My plan is to tell them they have plenty of time to be good Catholics, so have all the fun you want right now and start when you get older.' 'Aha,' says Satan. 'You pass!'"

The priest let that sink in. Then he said, "Well, now, tonight is Halloween. And did you know that this holiday belongs to none other than the Catholic Church? Indeed it does, for Halloween was born as All Hallows' Eve, which is the vigil of All Saints Day, which is a Holy Day of Obligation and a feast day on our liturgical calendar, and the beginning as well of Allhallowtide, which for us is three days, called sometimes the Days of the Dead, during which we pray for the dead and for the souls in Purgatory. Thus are we reminded of Heaven and Hell, of the saved and the damned, of the demons and the angels, and of what awaits us, for we too shall one day pass away, and therefore we must live good and holy lives. But, of course, Halloween is not like that for corrupt society. In corrupt society, Halloween is for blood and gore and horror and sin and all the evils you can imagine or think of. This is not for us."

Someone asked if it was okay to go trick-or-treating. No. What about carving jack-o'-lanterns? No. What about eating candy? Ask your parents. What about *It's the Great Pumpkin, Charlie Brown*? Also ask your parents. What about scaring people? No.

Evelyn intercepted the priest while he was leaving. "Is it okay to listen for owls?" she asked.

"What?"

"Walk around listening for owls in the woods."

"Tonight?" asked the priest. "On Halloween? Goodness!" he exclaimed. "No!"

◆

SHE HAD TO PICK a book for a book report, so she picked *My Side of the Mountain* by Jean Craighead George. Except it couldn't be only about the book and what happened in it, you also had to say why it was good or bad, and you had to do research and tell about the author.

It turned out Jean Craighead George kept wild animals in her house and that her first pet was a turkey vulture. She kept a beaver except the beaver ate the furniture. One time when Jean was growing up she climbed a cliff to look at falcon chicks, then caught one and trained it. She built a lean-to and whittled fishhooks. Her real name was Jean Carolyn Craighead, but she married John Lothar George and they named their daughter Twig. Evelyn decided she would change her name from Evelyn to Twig and become a wrestler who goes to the Olympics and wins the final against a Russian, but when they put the gold medal around Twig's neck she doesn't care because the only thing she cares about is wrestling. She would live in the sticks and carry logs around and split firewood and drag a truck tire from a rope tied around her waist, all before six in the morning. Then she'd milk the cows, eat a loaf of bread with sugar and butter on it, drink a barrel of milk, and run five miles to school.

Really, though, she wanted to be like Sam Gribley in *My Side of the Mountain* and train a falcon and live in a treehouse with a weasel and eat smoked venison and wear deerskin. Was *My Side of the Mountain* good or bad? It was good because it had things in it like stealing a chick from a falcon nest, but it was bad because at the end Sam Gribley quits and goes back to his family.

❖

GRAM CAME ON SUNDAYS. She tied on an apron and got busy right away. She said, "Don't use so much milk in your potatoes, too much milk they get watered down." Other times she said gravy's better if you don't let it bubble, chicken stock's better if you strain it through cheesecloth, pie dough's better if you don't work it too much, put more bacon in with your green beans and you won't have to salt them so much.

Gram said her name was Della Whyler, and before that, Della

Crabtree. She was Della Whyler because she got married, otherwise her name would still be Della Crabtree. The reason it didn't look like she was married was because her husband died. The reason she lived in an apartment was money. The reason she didn't put her head in the pool was on account of something wrong with her ears. The reason she didn't care for hush puppies was they didn't settle in her stomach. The reason she didn't eat corn was dentures. The reason she walked how she did was her feet hurt. The reason she didn't have a dog was responsibility. The reason she kept canaries was less responsibility. The reason she carried a purse was it came in handy. The reason for her knobby fingers was arthritis. The reason pages were turned back in her *TV Guide* was those were show reminders. The reason she didn't use her china was she was saving it. The reason she never did anything was because she liked to stay home, and the reason she went to Florida was to visit her sister. The reason her closet was full was she had a hard time getting rid of stuff. The reason there was so much toilet paper in her bathroom was she bought it on sale. The reason she liked Red Skelton was he played so many characters. The reason she didn't pay attention to the news was she couldn't do anything about it. The reason she didn't go to church was she wasn't Catholic. She was a Disciple because all the Crabtrees were Disciples. Some of them were the strict kind who were against music in church, but she herself didn't object to music. There were Crabtrees near Maycross who made maple syrup, and about half were the type against music in church. Some of the young ones could clog, though.

◆

HER FATHER WANTED TO turn the garage into a den with its own bathroom, but her mother was against it. He said the main reason was there were shows he couldn't watch because of her shows and he didn't mean that as a criticism, he just liked different shows. She said it wouldn't be good for the cars. He said she was right and he planned to build a carport. She said that would cost too much. He said his commissions were getting better. In that case, her mother argued, we should put money in the bank. Putting it into the house is better than putting it in the bank, her father argued, because that makes the value of the house go up. That's true, said her mother, but then when you need the money you can't get it unless you sell your house.

He started in by jackhammering up concrete and digging a ditch for the toilet. When his remodel was done, he bought a television, a radio, and a record player in a cabinet. Then he said that as long as he had the construction bug he might as well go straight to the carport, and when that was done he built a greenhouse.

Her father knew a guy at George L. Mesker who pickled cukes, so he went to the guy's house to do it with him. He knew another guy who made beer at home, and since he wanted to do that too they made beer in the guy's kitchen. There was a third guy who had a cabin on a lake, so they fished there for walleye. They were all on a bowling team and had shirts that said "Mesker Steel" on the back.

In the refrigerator was a bottle her father used for martinis. "Am I putting together one or two tonight?" he always asked, in case her mother wanted one. He took his martini to the den with him to watch his shows, while her mother watched her shows in the front room.

In the *TV Guide* was a movie about a girl who becomes a pirate, only it didn't start until eleven-thirty. Evelyn snuck out of bed for it and went to the den, but her father was there. "What are you doing?" he asked.

"I can't sleep," answered Evelyn. "What are you doing?"

"I sleep here because your mother snores."

◆

MRS. LIND SAT NEXT to a kiddie pool in her front yard while Stevie splashed around nude. Every once in a while she scooped up water in her palm and washed it across his shoulders or smoothed his hair with it. Otherwise she kept a hand at the small of his back.

Mrs. Lind wanted to go inside for a minute, so Evelyn took over. She put her hand in the small of Stevie's back and moved his toys where he could reach them, and wound up his little plastic motor-boat and let it loose on the water, and then Mrs. Lind came back and gave Evelyn a quarter. "Real good," she said.

Evelyn's mother said Mrs. Lind came by asking on babysitting. It was fine with her if Evelyn started babysitting, but it was a big responsibility. "Evelyn," said her mother, "when you babysit don't make messes. Leave the house better than you found it. Don't snoop. Don't pull out drawers or eat food. Wash out the diapers and keep the baby clean. When the parents get home things should be neat and the baby should be asleep and you should be sitting in the front room waiting on the sofa. That's how you get a reputation."

She babysat Stevie. The best thing to do with him was to lie on the floor and watch him crawl around doing what he did from up close. Sometimes he put his nose against her nose so it looked like he had one eye in the middle of his forehead. Mostly he pushed his toys around or got absorbed in something like a car going by. When he heard a car he perked up and listened. He listened to the whole thing—the noise getting louder, peaking, fading—and even when it was over he stayed perked up awhile longer before going on to something else. Evelyn started standing in the window with Stevie on her hip so he could watch cars.

After babysitting Stevie twice, she knew when he was going to poop. He would stop what he was doing and sit there with this look on his face. He would do that a few times. Then his face got red, he held his breath, and he made little grunting noises. Evelyn always got him cleaned up perfectly and let him go naked for a while because he liked that. Easiest money in the world.

◆

THEY PUT A LIBRARY on Washington Avenue that she could bike to in five minutes, and they had a book there called *Living Off the Country*. On the cover was a drawing of a man kneeling by a fire holding a stick with chunks of meat skewered on it. One of his shirtsleeves was ragged, but other than that he looked pretty clean. He must have had tough hands, though, because the one hold- ing the stick was just about in the fire. Either that or the drawing wasn't accurate.

The teacher made the same assignment: read a book, say what it's about, say if it's good or bad, talk about the author—but this time you had to do it in front of the class, and this time the book had to be real and not a story. The directions were: bring the book and show it to the class; don't just stand there reading from a script; make eye contact, including at the sides and the back; enunciate; look confident; don't say "uh"; pause; and at the end say, "Are there questions?"

When it was Evelyn's turn, she went to the blackboard, propped up *Living Off the Country* in the chalk tray, got the pointer, and touched it against her book. "*Living Off the Country*," she said. "By Bradford Angier."

She put the pointer back. "Hey," she said. "Have you ever won- dered what you would do if it turned out you had to survive in the woods?"

No one answered. Evelyn looked left and right. In both direc- tions, people were smiling. "What would you do if you were out in the woods by yourself and you found a dead moose?" she asked. "What would you do if you got porky-pined? Did you know that if you drink four tablespoons of blood from an animal it's the same as eating ten eggs?"

She remembered to pause. She looked around again. More peo- ple were smiling. "Well," said Evelyn. "In *Living Off the Country* you'll learn how to get syrup from birch trees. You'll learn how to make fish traps. You'll learn how to do Morse code with flags. And what about wolves? What would you do if you met up with a wolf? Let's say you fell through ice into a lake. What would you do? Have you thought about that? Someday you might get lost in the woods. It can happen to anyone. Will you survive?"

No one answered. They all just went on smiling. "Okay," said Evelyn. "Is the book good or bad? It's good because everything in it is true. It actually tells you how to stay alive in the woods. This book is easy to find as well. I got it at the library."

She paused again. A couple people laughed out loud. "The author," said Evelyn. "The author is Bradford Angier. His last name is spelled *A-n-g-i-e-r*, like 'angrier' without the *r*, but I just say 'anger,' but it might not be 'anger.' Bradford Angier is alive at this time. He is married to Vena Angier. I never heard the name Vena before, but I found out it comes from Elvena, which means 'elf or magical friend.' "

People laughed again. "Quiet," said the teacher.

"Bradford and Vena Angier do not have kids," said Evelyn. "Vena draws the pictures and Bradford writes the books. Bradford got tired of making advertisements, so they moved to Hudson's Hope, British Columbia, Canada, where there is hardly anybody. Before that they lived in Boston, Massachusetts. For their dog they have an Irish wolfhound, one of the largest breeds on earth. I was not able to discover the name of their dog or any further information on Bradford and Vena Angier. Are there questions?"

No one had questions. "Okay," said Evelyn. "I hate you guys."

"Evelyn," said the teacher.

"Punks," said Evelyn.

"Enough," said the teacher. "Sit down immediately."

"Spoiled brats," said Evelyn.

◆

SHE LIKED TO MOW the lawn perfectly, but only if no one told her to mow. If she got told to mow, it wasn't the same. In fact, if she got told to mow, she was sloppy on purpose. If she got told to mow, she mowed as fast as she could, but when she wanted to do it, she was careful and used the edger. 'Don't tell me to mow the lawn,' she thought. 'Just leave me alone and don't say anything and it'll get done perfect.'

The nun who watched the playground saw her kick a four square ball over the fence again. The principal told her kicking a ball over the fence was illegal on account that balls didn't grow on trees and who did she think she was costing the school money? Evelyn said, "I went and got it," but the principal said it was against school rules to leave the playground, and anyway she shouldn't have kicked it over the fence in the first place because one, she didn't own it, and two, while it was gone over the fence nobody could use it. The first meant no respect for school property, and the second meant you thought kicking the ball over the fence was more important than other kids. The first meant no respect for money, and the second meant you were a selfish person lacking self-control who had now kicked a ball over the fence twice. "So be it," said the principal. "The punishment is cleaning all the blackboards in Hall A for a week. Lucky for you my rules are like in baseball—it takes three strikes to get you out."

"Out?"

"In my office after school five days a week for the rest of the semester."

The next day, Evelyn kicked another ball over the fence. What made it okay to sit in the principal's office for the rest of the semester was that it was like mowing the lawn perfect. You were Joan of Arc when you did that. No one could really burn you at the stake. All they could burn was your body.

◆

THEY WERE YELLING THEIR heads off at each other in the bedroom. There was no way to understand it because the things they yelled about were weird. Plus they had their door shut.

Maureen was gone, and Jimmy was in the closet with cotton balls in his ears, holding a flashlight and reading a comic book. "What?" he said, when Evelyn slid open the door.

"I need to get the vacuum."

Jimmy sat the way you would by a campfire—cross-legged in a

little pool of light. More comic books waited in his lap. "Come on," said Evelyn. "Get out."

"What for?"

"I need the vacuum."

"They're making you vacuum?"

"No."

"Then why are you doing it?"

"Noise."

✦

THERE WAS A SHED near the fire station where you picked up your papers, then folded them, put rubber bands around them, and loaded your bag. A guy in a van brought the papers to the shed, and he was the one who made the rules. The first was, papers had to land on doormats. If you threw one and it didn't land on a doormat, you had to walk to the door, pick it up, and put it there. "Guaranteed," said the guy, "you're not gonna wanna do that. You're gonna wanna keep making throws. Your paper's gonna miss and you're not gonna wanna pick it up. You're gonna wanna stay in your zone. Obviously if it lands in the bushes you're gonna pick it up, but if you only miss by a little you're gonna call it good. I know you think you're hearing me, but believe me, wait a month. You'll know so much more than me by then it's pitiful."

"I know what you mean about a zone," said Evelyn.

The guy liked to sit in the door of his van folding papers while he talked. Sometimes he rooted around in his beard. He always wore the same milkman jacket and the same overalls—weather didn't matter to him. "So you've been there," he said. "The zone."

"Yeah."

"Like unconscious. Like out of your gourd."

"Yeah."

"What sport?"

"Swimming."

"Hmm," said the guy. "Follow boxing?"

"No."

"What?"

"Roller Derby."

The guy laughed. "That's a good one," he said.

Evelyn hauled her bag up and poked her head through the straps. Now she was weighed down front and back. The guy said, "Okay, go on, get outa here, see ya. Know what? You're the only chick I know who's a paperboy."

◆

UNCLE BAXTER SAID SHE ought to take up shotput and that he'd holler when he needed muscle. He said Aunt Gail bought flimsy paper plates, so Evelyn should double- or triple-up before hitting the chow line. "Go to town," he told her.

In line she watched how Billy did things. He put three buns on his plate. He pried them open and, skipping the tongs, put a hot dog in each. He used every condiment—mayonnaise, mustard, ketchup, sweet relish. He slathered it all on. When he noticed Evelyn watching he said, "Technique," so she did the same to her hot dogs.

There was the girl area where they sat around talking about nothing and it was that or the parents because the boys all bolted. Evelyn went around to the front of the house, where Billy was shooting baskets with his shirt off. The garage door was open so he could listen to his speakers. Now that Billy's shirt was off, Evelyn noticed he had a hole in the middle of his chest.

They went into the garage so Billy could change records. He had long, double-jointed fingers that reminded her of a crab. Out of the sun, Evelyn could see that it wasn't actually a hole in his chest, it was more like a ball of it had been carved out with an ice-cream scoop. It made sense now that Billy always looked caved in on himself. Evelyn's father said he was like that because Uncle Baxter married hillbilly and hillbillies inbreed and some of them end up like Billy because of it and that was why Billy was so tall and skinny and had an overbite and a stoop.

Billy turned the volume down. Then he stepped out of the garage and did a trick where he flipped the basketball behind his back and caught it when it came down over his opposite shoulder. He said everyone always asked if he played basketball, but actually not only did he not play basketball, he didn't do anything except listen to records, sleep, watch TV, and draw cartoons.

Billy said Craig had enlisted in the Air Force, which he himself couldn't do because you had to be under six-six. He didn't know where Craig was, but he thought California. Most of the records were Craig's because Craig wanted to own a record shop someday, and if he did, Billy wanted to own it with him.

Billy said his family wasn't Catholic, and that was why he didn't go to Catholic school, and if he did they'd have to kick him out for insubordination. They'd say he was a warlock and drown him or something. About half the time his family didn't even go to any church at all because his parents got drunk on weekends, which was funny, since when they drank they said stuff. "Like what?" asked Evelyn.

"Bedroom stuff."

He stopped goofing around with his basketball and cradled it against his biceps muscle. "This is sorta weird," he said, "but . . . wanna make out?"

"No way."

"How come?"

"I don't make out," said Evelyn.

"Neither do I," said Billy.

◆

A MAN CAME TO class to show slides about The Mounds. He said that officially he was an archaeologist, meaning someone who found old stuff in the ground, but what he really was, was a boy in a man's body who couldn't stop feeling excited about The Mounds.

The slideshow started. There was a slide of the Sphinx, then one of archaeologists with pyramids behind them, scraping at dirt in a pit. Next came a slide of a Mound. "And here, now, we have a Mound," the man said. "Here we see depicted Mound A, central mound in our Angel Mounds Complex, which is located at the northwest intersection of South Green River Road and Covert Avenue, Knight Township, Vanderburgh County, the county in which Evansville is situated, the county where you and I are right now, and this is something we can rightly be proud of, because The Angel Mounds are a significant archaeological site and have been designated as a National Historic Landmark. They're named after Mathias Angel, or after the Angel family, settlers who came in search of farmland."

He clicked again. "Warrior of the Shawnee Tribe," he said.

He paused so they could look. "Actually it's Tecumseh," he said. "Tecumseh was one of the most famous Indians who ever lived. He didn't live here, though. He lived in Ohio. But, from this depiction of him, you get a general idea of the proud people who once lived in our vicinity."

He put up a fifth slide. It showed a Mound. "All right, now," he said. "No one can say who built The Mounds. Whoever they were, though, they're referred to by archaeologists as the people of the Mississippian civilization. It may be that the people of the Mississippian civilization were the ancestors of the Shawnee Tribe or of another tribe, or of a combination of tribes, but at any rate the Mississippians predated the tribes by many, many centuries. In fact, we believe this Mound to be about a thousand years old."

A sixth slide. It showed The Angel Mounds from a distance. "Tell me," the man said. "Have any of you ever been to The Angel Mounds?"

"Me," said Evelyn. "I have a question. Were the Mississippis from Atlantis?"

"Probably not."

"Egypt?"

"Doubtful."

"Did the Mississippis worship falcons?"

"Not that I know of."

"You ever hear about the Birdman they had?"

The teacher spoke up from the back of the room. "Evelyn," she said. "Stop."

❖

WHEN SHE CAME UP out of the ditch onto the Traction Line, a man was there with a shotgun. "Hold up," he said.

He pumped the shells out of his gun and put them in his pocket. A dog scrambled out of the ditch and started sidewinding their direction. When it got close, the man knelt and grabbed it by the collar. "Whoa," he said.

He tipped his hat at Evelyn, but just barely—tipped his hat and caught her eye and grinned. He looked handsome that way. He was one of those cowboy-looking men who got more handsome when they showed manners. "Which way you headed?" he asked her.

"Why?"

"Reason I ask is it's better you and me aren't headed the same direction."

He propped the shotgun against his leg so he could take his hat off. With his head uncovered and his eyes out of the hat brim shadow, she could see him better. "Why's that?" asked Evelyn.

The man laid his shotgun across his arms. "Don't want to pepper you with bird shot," he said.

Evelyn decided he wasn't the farmer. Anyway if he was the farmer he wouldn't be on foot. "You ought to have a horse," she told him.

"Hah," he answered.

He let his dog go. It trotted up the Line, sniffing bramble and snorting. "What's its name?" asked Evelyn.

"Lady," the man answered.

He rose up tall and put on his hat. "Which way you headed?" he asked again.

"Why?" asked Evelyn.

The man whistled. Lady came back on her own schedule. On the way, she stopped to sniff Evelyn's legs. "Hooky?" the man asked.

"No."

"So no school today."

"No."

"No school, then," said the man. "I'm headed south."

"Same," answered Evelyn. "Let's you and me go to Mexico."

The man settled his hat, still grinning. "If you say so," he said. "Go on, now."

◆

THE SCHOOL DIDN'T WANT her around anymore on account she kept kicking balls over the fence. The principal wrote that, after multiple incidents, and having already applied every in-building disciplinary measure at his disposal, he was skipping suspension and going to expulsion, his logic being that, expelled instead of suspended, Evelyn could get a fresh start in a more appropriate setting as opposed to spinning her wheels, falling behind, and returning to the same school with yet more challenges. He didn't like to give up on a student, or imply that a student was irredeemable or incorrigible, but in the end a transition seemed best to him for all concerned.

The new school wasn't better. People were the same. On her second day there, Evelyn told the office secretary that her old school was taking her back. Then, each morning, she left home like she was going to school, stowed her books in a ditch, and did what she wanted.

◆

"THE WAY YOU HANDLE liver and onions," said her father, "is you go to town on the meat with a sharp knife, dice it up small, and then you work the meat in with the onions and cover it with ketchup, and you salt and pepper that—go to town with the pepper—and mix it in and add hot sauce. That's how we did it freezing our keisters off at Camp Drum with the poor excuse for chow they slung up there, because necessity is the mother of invention, and when your back's against the wall you get creative."

"A hundred fifty-two," said Maureen.

"Huh?"

"A hundred and fifty-two times you've told us about liver and onions."

Her father pointed his knife at Maureen's plate. "Message didn't get through, though," he told her.

"Guess what?" said Evelyn. "The Comanches ate buffalo liver. Liver, tongue, hearts, kidneys, eyes, the guy balls—they wolfed it down like cake. Yesterday I found a dead rabbit and wanted to eat its liver, but then I remembered tularemia and how the Russians want to spray it on us so we barf before they kill us with atom bombs."

◆

THE PLAN WAS, THEY were going Tolo shopping because Maureen wanted to, but first they'd drop off Evelyn at the counselor place. Afterward, Evelyn would walk downtown and meet them in front of Penney's—Penney's even though Maureen knew there wouldn't be anything at Penney's because Penney's didn't have anything but Montgomery Ward did. And anyway Maureen had already been to Penney's with Jane Clung. At Montgomery Ward there was a dress Maureen wanted to try on again. It was pink chiffon with a back train and a waist tie and no sleeves, but there was this other one that was in second place right now and it was white chiffon with a waist-band. Jane Clung liked her in a yellow one with a lace ruffle skirt, said Maureen, but Jane wasn't the one who was going to wear it.

They dropped Evelyn at the curb. She used the stairs, not the elevator, then waited in the little room with the two chairs in it and the poster on the wall of a tree and stars with the words: "You are a child of the universe, no less than the trees and the stars; you have a right to be here. And whether or not it is clear to you, no doubt the universe is unfolding as it should."

The counselor liked books. They lined her office all the way to the ceiling. The counselor always wore the same thing—a pantsuit. Today she wore one with a turtleneck under it. She looked like she could be on television hosting one of those shows where people talk in front of an audience. She always sat at the far end of her office with a little round table nearby that had a notepad, a pen, and a box of Kleenex on it, while Evelyn sat at the other end in a chair like the ones in the Lincoln Hotel when you went there at Christmastime to gawk at decorations. What the counselor always said first was, "So what would you like to talk about?" This time she added, "Last time we talked about surviving in the woods."

"I guess the poster."

"Which poster?"

"The one out there."

"'Desiderata.'"

Evelyn said, "First, if spending all your time on clothes is normal, then I don't want to be normal, I want to be abnormal. So because of that, me, what I think about the poster is, it's a crock. My sister doesn't agree with this Jane Clung girl that a yellow dress is better than a pink dress and I don't get that either, but this is different. Jane Clung stayed over and they played Truth or Dare and talked about their zits. The dumbest. My sister doesn't think I have a right to be here. I can tell. She thinks I'm an idiot. I'm not an idiot. I like deep stuff, but only certain deep stuff. The poster says the universe is what it is. Like I told you, I'm super-logical, so I think 'What?' Nobody knows that. They make stuff up. The way it's set up is dumb. I know it's dumb. It's all stupid. Like the dresses but on another level. If the universe is going the way it has to, then why are there bombs? That level. Something's wrong and I know something's wrong. When I used to be a Catholic I wanted to be a nun because I thought, well, at least that isn't dumb. The one thing that isn't dumb."

Evelyn settled back in the plush chair. "And doing jobs," she said. "Doing them right and actually working."

HER FATHER WAS IN the den with his martini and his feet up and his show was *The Smothers Brothers*. "Evelyn," he called, "come in and sit down."

The room was dark except for the television. Evelyn said, "That's okay," but her father said, "I mean it, come in."

She went in. Her father put his martini on the coffee table and turned the volume down. "So," he said. "Evelyn. Do you know why your mother doesn't want anyone in the kitchen?"

"I didn't go in the kitchen."

"Do you know why she doesn't want anyone in the kitchen?"

"She's afraid we'll move something."

"That's right. And personally I think being afraid someone will move something is insane."

He bore into her with his eyes. "Basically," he said, "your mother has problems. Lots of problems. Really deep problems."

Her father sipped his martini. "Here's what's happening," he said. "It turns out Mesker is shutting down in Evansville. I took a job with U.S. Steel in Bloomington, so that's fine. Everything will be fine. Your mother can tell people Mesker shut down and I'm up in Bloomington. Which is true. That's where I'll be."

◆

SHE WENT UP TO Bloomington because they had a school there called Matrix that supposedly was better than normal school. Matrix had couches and chairs instead of desks and a woman named Kate who said not everyone learned well in a structured environment. Matrix had Rap Session. The subject was what people voted for. If you didn't say anything during Rap Session it caught up with you. To the non-talkers Kate said, "We're not hearing from you. This group needs your voices. Do any of you have something to contribute?" But they always just sat there, so Kate had to look at people and say, "Yes, you, Pete. I'm talking to you, Pete. Contribute."

Seven people were there because they got expelled from regular schools and four out of the five others you couldn't tell what was up with them. The one you could tell about was Kurt Johanson, because he talked during Rap Session, and the subjects he nominated were UFOs, Bigfoot, communicating with the dead, an instrument they used in horror movies called a theremin that made eerie sounds, a guy who robbed a bank and got away with it by jumping out of an airplane, and a huge fire in Siberia that got started by a meteorite—things like that.

Kurt Johanson was like her—lunky. People called him Herman after Herman Munster. When they called him that he said, "Thank you for recognizing that I am actually Herman Hesse, author of *Siddhartha* and author of *Steppenwolf, Steppenwolf* the novel, not Steppenwolf the band." If someone said, "Fuck you," to Kurt, he answered, "Are you saying you would like to engage in sexual intercourse with the individual known as Kurt Johanson, and if so, are you willing to use a condom?" One guy said to Kurt, "Shut the fuck up or I'll kick your ass," and Kurt sat on him for so long Kate had to get help.

Evelyn went to Kurt's house. He lived with his grandparents. His grandma had a broken arm; it was in a cast held up by a sling. She called Kurt's grandpa "Captain." "Captain" was sitting at the kitchen table listening to the police on a scanner. Kurt got a box of sugar wafers and they went to his bedroom. On the wall above his bed was a poster of a notice supposedly from the Office of Civilian Defense in Washington, D.C., that said in case of a nuclear bomb attack patrons on the premises should stay clear of windows, bend over, put their heads between their legs, and kiss their asses goodbye. Next to that was a poster of a hockey player with the words on it NUMBER FOUR BOBBY ORR.

Kurt's sister hung out. She was a stepsister, her name was Shari, and she was fourteen and wore a choker around her neck. She said no, she didn't want to do the Ouija board but they could do the *I Ching* sticks, but Kurt said he didn't want to do the *I Ching* sticks because he was off *I Ching* sticks, but they didn't have to do the Ouija board either, they could talk. Then he said his grandpa said when his first wife died he saw two angels who stayed up without wings. They put their hands on his wife where her heart was, and when they drew their hands up a white light rose out of his wife's body and went out the window with the angels.

Shari said Kurt already knew about this, but this girl named Connie committed suicide, and later this other girl saw Connie across a fence. Nobody believed her, but then it happened to someone else, and then it happened to Connie's sister—every time over a fence. So then people said maybe a fence was like a divide Connie's ghost had to stay on the other side of, and they started watching for her. They went outside at night and walked along fences hoping to see her. Shari said she drew the line there. Sorry, but she didn't want to mess with the occult. She'd been at this sleepover where they did the Ouija board and it creeped her out because it spelled CONNIE and FENCE.

Evelyn said she'd had a dream recently where she was in a building with all these levels, and a lot of rooms, doors, passageways, and stairs, until finally she got out. After that she was in a city, trying to find this street that went to a river with a boat on it. She kept walking down streets but nothing happened and she never got to the boat, and that was it, the dream ended. "I forgot one thing," she said. "There's a person looking at me, and whoever it is, they're pointing like that's where the boat is, go that way, go around that corner and don't go left or right, just keep going and you'll come to the boat."

◆

SINCE MOST PEOPLE AT Matrix wouldn't talk voluntarily, and said as little as possible when Kate tried to make them, Kate gave a normal school assignment: go home, choose a subject, learn as much as you can about it, write down a lot of things to say about it, come to class and be ready to talk about it for five minutes straight.

As far as a subject went, Kate said, it was up to you. Just take notes on what you want to say about it and come to class ready to talk for five minutes.

Evelyn's turn came. She set her notes down in front of her. You didn't have to stand up to talk at Matrix, you could just sit there like everyone else and say what you had to say. Evelyn said, "I found out, believe it or not from my dad, that the brother of the Dalai Lama lives in Bloomington. In case you didn't know this, the Dalai Lama is the leader of Tibet, so for his brother to live here means the brother of the leader of Tibet lives here. The brother of the Dalai Lama had to leave Tibet, so he got a job at Indiana University. When my dad told me that, I thought it was interesting, so the subject I chose was the brother of the Dalai Lama, but at the library there weren't any books about him, so I gave up and changed to the Dalai Lama, since they had a book on him called *Who Is the Dalai Lama?*"

"Perfect," said Kate.

"The Dalai Lama was born in a village on a hill," said Evelyn. "His parents grew barley, buckwheat, and potatoes. When he was born, one of his eyes didn't open, so his sister pried it open with her thumb. One time he pulled on his father's mustache, and for that he got beat up. He liked to play in a chicken coop. He would sit on the nests and make clucking noises. He liked to play a game where he would pack a bag and pretend he was going on a trip.

"Okay," said Evelyn. "So now I'm just going to read straight out of *Who Is the Dalai Lama?*, because it says things better than I can say them. So here I go. 'A search party was being readied to search for a successor to the thirteenth Dalai Lama, who'd been leader over all Tibet. They knew that after he'd passed away, during an after-death process called mummification, his head had swiveled from the south to the northeast, and this, they felt, was a sign about where to look. They also knew that a very high lama, while staring at the waters of a sacred lake, had seen there the Tibetan letters for A, K, and M, a three-story monastery with a turquoise and gold roof, a path connecting this monastery to a hill, and a small farmhouse with strange gutters.'

"Okay," said Evelyn, looking up from the book. "So the mummy turned its head and they knew where to look. So the searchers decided that 'A' meant Amdo Province, so off they went in that direction. When they got to Kumbum they told themselves that if 'A' meant Amdo, then 'K' meant Kumbum, and sure enough, they found the three-story monastery with the roof painted turquoise and gold. A path from this monastery led up a hill, and on the hill was a farmhouse with strange gutters, so it was just like the very high lama had predicted. And now I'm going to read again," said Evelyn. " 'Pretending to be poor travelers, the search party got permission to stay there overnight, and passed their evening in the presence of a boy who called their leader "Sera lama." This leader was a lama named Kewtsang Rinpoche, and indeed he lived at Sera Monastery. The members of the search party were encouraged to believe they'd located the right child when a rosary they'd brought along—one belonging to the thirteenth Dalai Lama—was claimed by the boy as his own. In the morning the search party said their goodbyes, with the boy clinging to Kewtsang Rinpoche and begging to be taken with them. A few days later, the search party returned, this time wearing their lama garb and announcing clearly their purpose and intention. Tests ensued. The boy's family watched in astonishment, as did many of the local farmers, while the boy selected, from between two ritual drums, the one that had been the thirteenth Dalai Lama's. Next the same thing happened with walking sticks—the boy, from between two, picked the right one. Now the search party knew the search was over. The four-year-old boy from the little farmhouse was the child they were looking for—His Holiness the fourteenth Dalai Lama.' "

Evelyn looked up from the book again. People actually didn't look bored. " 'Today,' " she said, reading again, " 'His Holiness is sometimes asked if indeed he believes he is the fourteenth Dalai Lama. He always answers that, when he considers his experience in life, what he's been trained to do and what he does, he has no difficulty accepting his connection to the Dalai Lamas who preceded him.'

"So that's my subject," Evelyn concluded. "Probably I didn't really talk for five minutes, but hey, it's pretty much a mind-blower."

◆

EVELYN GOT A JOB at an all-you-can-eat restaurant where fried chicken got served on platters. She stood over a drain in a stainless steel stall, wearing a rubber apron and heavy-duty gloves, and washed dishes, bowls, glasses, cups, platters, utensils, and ashtrays. The busers set loaded tubs on the ledge of her pass-through window; anything that rinsed clean she put in a tray; anything stubborn she scoured before moving it along. When a tray got full, she slid it on rollers into an industrial washer and dragged the door shut. Ninety seconds later, a buzzer went off—for no reason, because when the washer stopped, its racket stopped, too. It scalded everything and blistered your fingers.

The chef's name was Mickey. At the end of each night he tossed his towel over his shoulder so that it landed on the floor and with his back to everybody yelled, "Clean it up!" He had an office by the fire exit where he figured out what needed ordering and made calls. His phone cord was so long he could crane his head around the jamb with the receiver at his ear and his hand over the speaker and ream out anyone not working hard. Evelyn didn't blame him for that because no one, or almost no one, worked hard. They all hated to work, except for her and a cook named Lionel.

On Saturdays, after everyone else left, Evelyn and Lionel did "the weekly comprehensive cleaning." This meant everything stainless steel got wiped down, the mats got pulled up so the floor could be mopped, the ovens got hit with spray foam and the stovetops with degreaser, the walk-in freezer shelves got once-overed with cleaner and a rag, the blacktop near the dumpsters got swept and pressure-washed, the sinks got scoured, the employee restroom got spic 'n spanned, etc.

Lionel was albino. He kept his head tilted to the left, which he said he had to do because otherwise his eyes darted around so much he couldn't see and got a headache. Lionel had eyelashes and eyebrows but they were so pale you hardly noticed them. He had a sheath knife on his belt and a ball of keys on a retractable chain in one pocket and a jumbo pack of gum in the other. He was like Evelyn—just get it done, no messing around, no corner-cutting.

Lionel had a Gremlin he parked by the dumpster, and every Saturday he gave her a ride home in it. First, though, they sat in it without moving so he could toke. One night he told Evelyn that there were countries where they killed albinos. As soon as you were born they took one look and if you were albino, they threw you in the trash. Other places, he said, they let you live until you got to sixteen, at which point they slashed your throat and sold your body parts. "Brutal," said Evelyn.

"I see people giving you shit," answered Lionel. "You ever wanna stomp these motherfuckers toss shit at you, I'm in. I'll help you pound their heads into the ground."

◆

KURT JOHANSON LIKED TO drive around at night in his grandma's station wagon. He sang along to radio songs that were "so bad, they're good," and to advertising jingles. Out of his mouth, while he drove, came film lines: "I'm sorry, Dave, I'm afraid I can't do that"; "Bond. James Bond"; "What we've got here is a failure to communicate"; "Take your stinking paws off me, you damned, dirty ape!"

Kurt didn't go anywhere. He just drove. He said it was like in *American Graffiti*—nowhere to go, nothing to do. *American Graffiti,* he said, was a "horrendous" title; the movie had nothing to do with graffiti; there was no graffiti in it; actually it was a "basically embarrassing" movie; actually they just wanted the word "American" in the title; actually it was like the "American Pie" song. There was no pie in it, but so what.

In Evelyn's opinion, Kurt foamed at the mouth, but unlike other people, he didn't need dope for it. He said that if you went faster than the speed of light, it would be like on *Time Tunnel.* He didn't believe the story about Jim Morrison dying in a bathtub because "there's too many loopholes in it." He said life was meaningless, "but who cares." People were afraid to die, so they made up the Easter Bunny, Superman, God, and tons of other stuff.

Kurt liked Pringles and chocolate milk. He had a way of doing everything at once—driving, talking, eating, drinking, singing— that was like juggling. He favored farm roads where he could tool along at twenty, and if he needed free hands, he worked the steering wheel with a knee.

One night Kurt borrowed his grandpa's shortwave and they took it up on Weed Patch Hill. Stars were out. They sat on the car hood. Kurt set the shortwave on his lap and roamed. Stuff came in and would be clear but then fade. Something would well up as if broadcast from the next hill, but then, for no reason, trail off and end. They heard people on ships talking to each other. That ended and was replaced by a guy transmitting weather information for the Canadian North Atlantic. Kurt worked the dial and maneuvered the antenna. It could be from Guatemala or it could be from Venezuela. It could be Thai or it could be Laotian. One station, Kurt said, had to be from India. Definitely the music was Indian music. Kurt said that when the Beatles went to India, they got influenced. He said people in India had different ears and could pick up rhythms we couldn't hear. He turned up the shortwave, set it on the car hood, and leaned back against the windshield. "You know what?" said Evelyn. "You sort of look like Number Four, Bobby Orr."

"That's me. Nose smashed."

"It looks kind of cool," said Evelyn.

On went the Indian music. After a while Kurt said, "Heard of Gertrude Ederle?"

"No."

"You look like Gertrude Ederle."

"Yeah?"

"There's a hundred-greatest-sports-feats-of-all-time book and she's in it because she swam across the English Channel."

The next day, Evelyn found a picture of Gertrude Ederle. She was about to get in the water, greased up with lard and wearing motorcycle goggles. She looked like a robot built for heavy labor. Intimidating. On a mission. Look out, photographer, I'm gonna strangle you with my bare hands. No wonder Kurt Johanson hadn't wanted to kiss.

◆

EVELYN TOOK A JOB at a place where old people lived. One thing she did there was roll around a metal bucket with a built-in wringer and mop floors. When her water got dirty, she dumped it down a drain in a maintenance closet. A guy named Fred had the same job. His hair was ratty, so he had to snare it in a net. He didn't talk much, but after Evelyn had worked with him for a few days he started calling her Chief. "Hey, Chief, I gotta borrow your spritz bottle."

They had a talk once while mopping that started with Fred saying, "I need hazard pay, Chief."

"Why?"

"This place depresses the shit out of me to the point where it's a hazard."

There was a name on a placard between rails next to every old person's door. "Threads in and out," Fred said, pushing a placard left and right. "Easy to replace."

The number one rule on this job was: Be nice to the old people. Say hello, be respectful, be kind, explain: "I'm just going to mop and be out of your way," even if there was no chance you could be in their way.

A woman named Beverly was stuck in bed, but not quite. Next to her bed was a pole she could use to work herself into a wheelchair if it was parked in the right position with the brakes on. On the wall beside Beverly's bed, family pictures had been put up like on a refrigerator. At the foot of Beverly's bed was a shelf with baubles on it. "Go on and look," she urged Evelyn.

Evelyn looked. Among the baubles were two medallions made of green amber and painted with blooms. One said SMÅLAND and the other HOLLAND. "From overseas," explained Beverly.

The next time Evelyn was in her room mopping, Beverly—small beneath a quilt—croaked, "You scared a me?"

"No."

"When I was your age I was scared a old people."

"Why?"

"You know why."

Evelyn mopped.

"Sick folks, too," said Beverly.

Evelyn mopped on. After a while Beverly asked, "Ever see a dead body?"

"No."

"Well, put that in the hopper 'long with t'others."

"Okay."

"You got a surly attitude," Beverly croaked. "Ain't no future bein' a fool about facts."

＊

THERE WAS A GIRL at Matrix, Bert, who didn't wash her hair. People asked her about it but she never answered, except one time she blurted, "Just cuz 'mericans wash their hair doesn't mean I have to." Kate twisted her arm to talk about that at Rap, which Bert did looking out a window. She said washing your hair was one of five billion things people did cuz they were brainwashed by capitalism. There wasn't any point to it. And the way shampoo worked was, they wanted you addicted. "Who's they?" someone asked. Bert answered, "The military-industrial complex."

Evelyn would be on her way out of Matrix, and Bert would catch up to her saying, "Sorry to keep hassling you, but can I borrow some money?" Then they would hang out because you couldn't just borrow from someone and not hang out with them, was how it seemed to Evelyn, who didn't care.

Kate wanted a last-day party, so there was one. She brought a turntable and speakers and played the Alice Cooper song about school being out for summer. Other than that, the party mostly consisted of eating cake and potato chips. Afterward, Bert caught up to Evelyn on the street. "Gotcha a present," she said, and handed her an envelope.

Inside was what looked like a glob of gelatin. "Thanks," said Evelyn.

"That's same as a tab," Bert answered. "Just like a full tab."

"Hey, thanks," repeated Evelyn.

At the old people's home, Evelyn showed the glob of gelatin to Fred. "Right on," he said.

"What is it?"

"Window Pane."

Later she waited while Fred emptied his mop bucket. When he was done and it was her turn she asked, "What's Window Pane?"

"Acid," answered Fred. "LSD."

✦

SHE TOOK IT IN some woods near a golf course. One tree there was having a hard time growing because someone, years before, had cinched a cable around it. It was strangled and needed to be freed.

There were houses nearby. She sat against a tree beside a driveway. A man came out and said she was on private property and couldn't be there and had to leave. She got up and walked away without saying anything to him.

There were geese overhead. They were flying slowly. Their lives didn't seem short to them. In fact they lived a million years.

She went onto the golf course. A cart came along with three men in it, and when they stared at her she spread her arms as wide as she could and threw her head back so she was looking at the sky. Another cart came, and again men stared, and this time she showed them her palms and bowed her head, and wished them happiness and then sent them happiness which was not received, and because of that she felt pity and cried, and when they came close and said she had to leave she cried harder, and turned around and walked away.

Later, there was a come-down stage. She went into a tavern and in the back was a pool table. Three bikers circled it with cue sticks. One had a peg leg that made her wonder how he rode. She asked him about that. He said he'd figured it out. They split into teams and played eight-ball doubles. She'd never played pool before and told them so. They were transparent to her. They didn't mean her harm. It felt good. She could read their inner peace.

✦

HER FATHER GOT A Bronco with an after-market roll cage. He didn't buy it for the roll cage, he said—it was more that he could strip off the ragtop fast.

They convertibled down to Evansville. Her father wore mirrored sunglasses, and white sunblock on his nose and forehead. He stayed off the highway and drove back roads. Evelyn was supposed to hold the map, but her father kept taking it from her so he could read it while driving. "Twenty-five becomes East Sylvania and there's a left on 75. I went this way because we used to go to Koleen when I was a kid and me and my cousins spooked ourselves in the graveyard."

At the house, her father went in like there was no conflict. Jimmy came out of his room and said, "Hey, Mom's getting groceries and Maureen's at her classes."

"What classes?"

"Beauty school."

"Geez," said Evelyn's father. "You're looking pretty buff there, Jimmy."

They went in. Her father wandered around at first, then called for Jimmy. The two of them went to the den her father had built and her father shut the door.

Evelyn's mother got home and started putting away groceries.

Soon her father came and stood where she could see him. "Hey," he said to her. "Just sayin' hey is all!"

"Leave!" answered her mother.

He left. Evelyn stayed. It was summer now; there was no more school. There was no reason to be in Bloomington. Or in Evansville.

✦

AROUND SIX IN THE morning she started walking up the Traction Line. Someone had built a fire in the middle of it. Whoever it was had pulled brush out of the ditch for fuel and left behind a lot of beer cans.

Evelyn walked with the sun at her back. People had tossed their junk into the weeds—culverts, pallets, pipe, posts, fence wire, burlap, washing machines, refrigerators. At the Raccoon Ditch, a guy was fishing from a blow-up boat. A little while later came houses and yards. The Save-A-Lot was open early, so she went in and bought two apples and a bag of pork rinds. The gate was open at the cemetery, so she cut through. Most of the headstones lay flat on the ground. Some of the standing ones leaned toward the cropped grass. On one of the monuments was a skull and two crossbones; another had an urn on top. There were pillars, pyramids, angel statues, girls holding crosses, and girls holding pots. One man's face had been etched into stone. Another was buried beneath his own statue.

Beyond the cemetery were more houses and yards. Evelyn could have walked straight to the bus station, but instead she went down to the Waterworks Road and followed the Ohio upriver toward the center of Evansville. It didn't matter, really. She had time and more time. There were all kinds of buses at all hours, going everywhere. She had a map of the United States, a loaf of bread, and a jar of peanut butter.

It was late June. She could sleep outside. Nothing would be better or worse than the next thing. Everything would be equal. There'd be nothing to complain about. Whatever it was, it would be her own doing. All she wanted was to live the right way, if that wasn't asking too much from life.

Tsering

. . .

_____

..

H E FELL ON THE STEEP STONE STEPS TO THE MONAS-
tery while carrying an offering of mung beans. The bowl
clattered down ahead of him, but at the bottom of the steps he
caught up to it. The back of his head might have split open if it
hadn't hit the spinning mung bean bowl. His head had been saved
by that, but one of his elbows shattered against stone. When he
looked up to where he'd been before falling—following his mother
up the monastery steps—his mother was looking back at him. His
sister leaned against her leg. In his mother's hands was a bowl of rice
noodles. "Tsering," she said. "Get up."

He couldn't answer. It hurt too much. "Come up here," said his
mother. "Let me see what happened to you."

In the monastery they found a monk who was a doctor. "I'm
going to pull on your elbow," he warned, "but first you should put
this piece of wood between your teeth."

In the well of possibilities was this, he knew afterward. Pain of
such intensity that its existence seemed unfair.

❖

SHE TOOK HIM TO live with her uncle Samten, who was in
retreat not far from the monastery. To gain access to Samten's hut,
you climbed stairs to a terrace, then went down a ladder. There
was no way in or out but the ladder. There was a small window,
though, through which things could be passed, and through which
people consulted Samten. Samten grew flowers in large clay pots.

In the morning he put them out in the sun; in the evening he brought them in to keep them warm. He ate roasted barley meal wetted with tea, and meditated four times daily. When available for consultation, he rang a bell heard in the village. The people who came brought food for him. When he wasn't speaking with them, or meditating, Samten recited mantras.

Tsering's mother came to the window often, but his father rarely. The first time his father showed up he gave Samten a copper pail and a bronze ladle. For Tsering he brought soled leather boots, a wool cap, a coat, a prayer rug, and rock candy. One of his eyes was narrow and red. His nose and cheeks were bruised. In Kangding, he said, he'd been held up by illness. He was looking for horses now, young steppe horses, to take to Chengdu. "This is right for you," he said.

"What?"

"Living with Samten."

❖

SOMETIMES IN THE EVENING, Samten read aloud. All of the tales were about great masters. Their exploits, their travels, their abilities, their accomplishments. There were those who lived in solitude, never cutting their fingernails or hair, and those who journeyed to India or Bhutan. Some had visions of deities and rainbows. Some could fly, some visited other worlds, some knew how to interpret dreams, some knew the future. Some could melt snow by sitting on it and meditating. Some could levitate.

One night, late, while Samten slept, Tsering climbed the ladder to the terrace. There were no lights on in the village, but the moon lit everything. On the road below, a dog lapped water from a puddle, then raised its head in his direction. "*Tsss*," he whispered to it, and the dog relaxed a little. It lapped more water, rocked back, and sat, and the two of them faced the moon together. Even though the dog was far below, he sensed its befuddlement and sadness. He thought it might have words in its mind but, unable to speak, experienced frustration, and lived in protest against its condition. He pondered the dog more. It was a bull-necked runt with scant fur and a stubbed leg. "*Tsss*," he repeated.

The dog turned toward him again. Above its pug nose, its eyes glinted in the moonlight. It pawed the ground and whined, then turned circles and stepped into the puddle. "Speak," he said to it, but of course there was no answer. In fact, it seemed less interested in him than it had been before, as if he had faded into the background.

✦

SAMTEN PUT THE DAY'S food offerings on a plate. "Leave this on the terrace for hungry ghosts," he said.

"Aren't they in a different realm?"

"They are."

"Then why leave them food?"

Samten pushed the strips of meat together with the tip of a bone shard. "In case," he said.

"In case what?"

"In case they come here."

"Can they do that?"

"The food is always gone," said Samten, pushing the fruit away from the meat. "Here," he said, handing him the plate. "Take it up and leave it."

He took the plate up. It was dusk, nearly dark. The cold stung his face. On the terrace, hungry ghosts felt plausible. Their proximity, at least, couldn't be ruled out, nor could their ability to move between realms. He'd noticed, that morning, while looking in Samten's shaving mirror, that he was reversed there: his left was his right; his right, his left. He'd gone on looking at this for a long time, and then he'd felt afraid. Now, on the terrace, the same fear rose in him—the fear that things were not what they seemed. Samten had told him that hungry ghosts had mouths no bigger than the eye of a needle, gullets no thicker than a strand of hair, and swollen bellies that could never be satisfied. They had no home, no happiness, no life beyond yearning. "A person can be born a hungry ghost in their next life," he'd warned. "It can happen to a greedy person or one who is stingy."

Other bad things could happen, too. You could end up in one of the hells. What could be worse? Why was it like that? He set down the plate of fruit and meat and, after backing away from it, performed prostrations. Each time he pressed his forehead against a flagstone, he pleaded with the goddess of compassion to protect him from a bad rebirth.

◆

SAMTEN FELL ILL. HIS eyes yellowed, his tongue swelled, some of his fingernails grew fungus, some split. His gums bled when he ate. Sweat lit his skin. His robes looked damp, his hair looked greasy, and there were festering sores on his neck, throat, and scalp. Samten's chanting turned into a murmur. He stopped enunciating, droned, and trailed off. In front of the altar, slumped at the neck, he rocked side to side and worried his prayer beads. Finally Tsering told a villager who came to the window that Samten was sick and needed to see a doctor.

The next afternoon, a monk arrived with a bag of pork fat—for which, he said, Samten should break his vegetarian vows. He told Samten to pee into a vial, which Samten did. Then the monk put a cap on the vial, tucked it in his robe, and left.

The next day the monk brought two bags of medicine. He said Samten should take one ball from the larger bag three times daily, crush it in water, and drink the resulting decoction. From the smaller bag he should take one ball, crush it in water, and drink it with roasted barley meal each morning.

The monk crooked a finger at Tsering. They left Samten by the altar and climbed onto the terrace. The monk put his hands against his knees and bent until his forehead was close. "Does he eat?" he asked.

"No."

"Does he sleep?"

"Yes."

"What are you doing here?"

"Learning."

"Have you learned to read?"

"Yes."

"What about writing?"

"I know the block letters."

"You read and write."

"Yes."

The monk crouched and put a hand on his head. "How old are you?" he asked.

"Six," said Tsering.

The monk straightened. "Wait here," he said.

He went down the ladder. Tsering could hear him speaking with Samten, but he couldn't make out their words. When the monk returned, he handed him a book. "What's it called?" he asked.

"Names of the Buddha."

"Can you read from it?"

"Yes."

When Tsering was halfway through the first page, the monk raised his hand. "Which month were you born?"

"The first."

"Which day?"

"The third."

"Where?"

"The village."

"What color is your house?"

"Our house is yellow."

"Is it possible to see the river from your house?"

"Yes," Tsering said.

The monk crouched. "Tsering Lekpa," he said.

◆

A LAMA STARTED DOWN the ladder from Samten's terrace. At first he appeared only as stockings, sandals, and the skirt of a robe filling the cavity where the ladder was set. In that faceless way he offered muffled greetings before asking about the strength of the rungs. Samten answered that the ladder was old and that the right thing to do was to come down it slowly. The visitor's weight was not to settle heavily, and he should proceed only by a series of tests. Further, if a rung cracked underfoot, he should be sure to steady himself with his other foot and hands. When all of this had been elaborated, the visitor continued slowly down the ladder. Twice he halted in deference to a coughing fit. The third time he dropped his head to have a look. "Be careful," advised Samten.

The lama was so tall he had to duck through Samten's door-frame, and, once inside, tilt his chin toward his chest so that the top of his head wouldn't scrape the ceiling. Looming like that, he made the room feel smaller. His altitude was so great that he seemed removed; at the same time, he crowded things. "The last time I saw you," said Samten, "my ladder was stronger."

"That's right," said the lama. "It's not me, it's the ladder."

They touched foreheads. Then the lama, who was as old as Samten, turned toward Tsering. "You'll come with me," he said. "But first, for one week, visit your family."

◆

SAMTEN TIED A ROSARY around Tsering's waist. Then Tsering put on the coat his father had given him and, with his cap in his lap, said mantras by the window. After a while, three monks came down the road and gaped in at him. The one in the middle removed his cap, and then the others removed theirs, too. Tsering went outside, and the monks crouched a little. One asked him to pray for a journey free from bandits, wild animals, con men, and bad spirits.

He did, and then they beckoned him to lead. Tsering put on his cap and set out, and the three monks fell in behind.

They left the road and climbed a path. It was rocky in places, but as it rose, its grade eased. A stream ran beside it straight toward the river. Below and behind sat the monastery on its hill, with its wall of windowed residences in sunlight. Ahead, in the grass, uphill, yaks grazed. Only a few moved up or down. The rest hardly moved at all.

They contoured for a while, then crested a rise. Below were herders with sheep, goats, and cows. Beside the trail, bones lay scattered. Two packers came down the hill. Their loads, broad and high, were bigger than they were. They were headed toward the monastery, said one. The previous morning they'd passed a caravan. That same afternoon, two hunters had intercepted them. One carried a flintlock, the other a matchlock. They'd requested dried meat, which the packers had relinquished.

The monks and the packers talked for a while. Tsering mulled the clouds on the peaks. Samten had told him that the gods sometimes slid down golden ropes onto mountaintops but otherwise dwelt blissfully in their many heavens until, after eons, their merit ran out, at which point they dwindled, languished, and expired. Actually, said Samten, what looked like clouds boiling off mountains on certain mornings was smoke from incense bonfires lit by the gods.

They walked again. Soon he thought he knew where he was. Or about where he was. Around the swell of a few more hills they would cross a stream on three flat rocks, then follow the stream downhill to his home.

✦

HIS MOTHER'S BARLEY MEAL was coarser than Samten's, and darker too, and better tasting. She kept it in a carved wooden box on the kitchen table. Beside it was another box filled with butter. In the pantry were tea bricks wrapped in yak skin, a pot of soy sauce, and a pot of vinegar. There were dried noodles and grains on the pantry shelves, alongside sugar, salt, and rice. The kitchen, the pantry, the table, the boxes—they were all like things he'd seen in dreams.

The monks sat on cushions. His mother worked the bellows. Inside a warm covered pot she had bread. There was butter tea in another pot, and yogurt from the storehouse. Coal burned in the brazier, cats slept by the stove. His mother asked the monks about Samten. Were his robes clean, was his color good, were his eyes clear, was he eating enough, did he seem well now, was he strong again?

Outside, his mother gave each monk a pouch of rice. They bowed to her and Tsering, asked them to say prayers for their journey, and set off down the road.

In the storehouse his mother dug through crates. His father had been to Bhutan, she said, and had brought back silver tureens in large numbers. With the proceeds from their sale he'd purchased two summer tents, a pair of horses, a pair of ornamented saddles, and two sets of embroidered panniers. In the storehouse he'd laid up bolts of silk, rolls of wire, and crates of porcelain. He was now on his way to trade horses in Yunnan. "Here," said his mother, on finding what she was looking for, gifts his father had brought him from Bhutan—boots, a wool cap with earflaps, and a set of prayer beads made of sandalwood and turquoise.

Outside the storehouse his mother knelt, pulled Tsering's robe tight, and held him by the shoulders. He breathed her smell—the lambskin in her chuba, the bone marrow in her hair. "Tsering-la," she said.

✦

HE WENT TO THE altar room with his brother Sonam to empty the offering bowls and to fill the butter lamps. There were bits of hay in Sonam's hair, and his sleeves smelled of milk. Sonam told him that in the locked closet at the foot of the stairs was a cache of raisins, dried apricots, and dried plums. He'd pilfered some, and had raisins hidden away. He could leap from the hayloft, he said, and had a ram he fed and combed.

At school, said Sonam, it was always cold, but twice a day they had butter tea breaks, and if they did something well they were rewarded with treats, though this couldn't be counted on. For example, after reciting without error from *The Confession of Down-falls*, Sonam had gotten a chunk of rock candy, but after reciting a longer passage from the same book the next day, he'd gotten nothing. It was unpredictable.

They polished the offering bowls. Then they went to the river and threw stones. Sonam said he could ride a horse. Next he described the best way to milk a yak. First you brought the calf to nurse, next you tied it where the mother could lick it, next you milked, last you untied the calf and let it get what it could. He milked all the time, he said. He and Yangchen milked every day. Yangchen rode horses faster than he did. Small as she was, she could jump from the hayloft onto a horse and stand on its back while it trotted in a circle.

◆

HE FOUND YANGCHEN IN a pasture. She was leaning on a stick over one of the herd dogs. The wind had blown her hair around. Her belt was tightly knotted. "Duga," she said, "is lazy today." She rolled Duga's lip back and pressed her thumb into his gums. "Duga," she said, "wake up."

She let Duga go. He loped away and turned to look at them. "You're all right," called Yangchen.

Tsering asked her about a scar on her face. Yangchen said she'd been gored by a yak. She'd tried to give him hay to eat, but he'd shown no interest in it, and thinking what he needed was encouragement, she'd taken him by a horn and pulled his head down.

They'd heard about it at the monastery. The abbot sent word that, since this yak was characteristically docile, the goring was the responsibility of an unfriendly spirit. Nevertheless, the yak was to have its horn tips blunted, and then be led into the hills and freed. His fate, said the lama, would be left to the mountain gods.

Herders, Yangchen recounted, tied the yak to a post, pulled his head against it, and sawed off his horn tips. When he was calm again, she wove strips of cloth into his shoulder hair, and, with two nuns, led him into the hills.

Now, leaning on her stick, Yangchen plunged her hand inside her chuba and pulled out a cord strung with the yak's severed horn tips. The nuns had advised her to wear them for protection, and since then nothing bad had happened.

◆

WITH HIS BROTHER DORJE he lay beneath the stars. It was a windless night; the prayer flags didn't move. A mastiff barked, but then came silence. Dorje said he'd gone to Derge with their father, and that the Chinese in Derge lived near the river. Their shops were lean-tos but they were busy building huts. In Derge their father traded for tea and bolts of cloth, which he intended to carry only to Jyekundo. It was said there were bandits on the road to Jyekundo, so in Derge they joined with other traders and set out with carts, donkeys, yaks, and men on horseback front, rear, and sides. In Jyekundo there were more people than he'd ever seen in one place, most on a street that ran straight through the town, along which they had their shops set up. Which, said Dorje, brought him back to Tsering's question: he'd gotten his new chuba on the main street of Jyekundo in trade for a crate of cigarettes their father had from India, the chuba plus a belt, a needle, thread, a thimble, and a flint with which he could start a fire as long as the wood shavings he used were dry enough. He dried them in the pouch of his chuba. He put his hands in to loft them a little, got air moving through them until they were dry, so he could start a decent fire even in bad weather. What else? He'd seen people panning for gold dust in the Drichu River. He'd gone with their father to Gochen, in Dhoshul. The river there had boulders in it. Some kids in Gochen had sleds made of frozen dung.

On the way to Dhosul they'd seen a bear with yellow fur, and on the way back home they'd seen a skydancer. Their father had told Dorje not to make eye contact and then along came the skydancer with wild hair, wearing skins, and at that point Dorje had dropped his eyes and only saw the skydancer again when he was moving away from them in the direction of Dhosul.

It was cold on the roof. The stars were dense. Tsering told Dorje that the world wasn't flat. "How do you know?" asked Dorje.

"Great-Uncle Samten."

"What did he say?"

"He said they put pillars in the ground in two places. Pillars the same height. Then they measured the shadows the pillars made and one shadow was longer and that's how they know the world's not flat."

"That doesn't make sense," said Dorje.

Tsering fell asleep thinking about it. The next day the three monks who'd brought him there returned loaded down with medicines they'd ground. They all bowed to him again, and again they asked him to lead the way.

◆

THERE WAS A WING of the monastery for novice monks, but Tsering stayed instead in his teacher's quarters. His name was Khenpo Yeshi Wangchuk, and he taught with a stick. "Your mind's not in attendance," he would say. "Before lunch you were doing well, but since then your concentration has gone downhill. Constantly, since lunch, I've been having to prompt you. Now if, before lunch, you were memorizing adequately, then it follows that, after lunch, you're capable of that, too. Your mind didn't deteriorate in between. If anything, it got stronger! Due to more memorizing! A morning of work improved your mind! Don't say you're tired, because during lunch you had a break. That should mean your mind is refreshed! That should mean your mind is better! There's just one way to explain your performance—you've let your mind fall asleep again. This has become a pattern. I'm having to give this talk too often. What I ought to do instead is use my stick, and that's what I'm going to do the next time I see you're not putting in the right effort."

✦

HIS TEACHER WAS SLEEPING. It was quiet except for the hum of falling rain. Tsering sat in the light of butter lamps.

A fly landed on his book. Its glossy green back, its hind end, its eyes, and its wings all shone. It was facing his direction, and he wondered how it saw him through eyes with no pupils. So far it didn't seem to care that he was there, so maybe it was blind, thought Tsering.

He lifted his hand. The fly took off. Which meant it perceived motion and also grasped danger. But that couldn't be right because the fly soon returned and settled on his book again as if it were safe there—which could mean it had a short memory, or none at all, or that it had never understood danger in the first place. As long as he was still, the fly stayed on the page, but if he moved his hand, it left.

The next time the fly landed on his book, he kept his hands in his lap. It crawled around a little. It stopped and changed direction. Its wings hummed. It flexed its legs. Samten had told him that a fly lived for a week. A dog ten years. A yak fifteen years. A horse twenty years. A crane thirty years. The fly lifted up a little, then settled again. Did it live for a week from its own point of view? For there to be a week, there had to be days, and for there to be days, there had to be hours. Did the fly know about days and hours? If not, did time pass for a fly?

✦

"BUT AM I REALLY?" asked Tsering. "How do you know?"

"In your last life you lived in Amdo," said his teacher. "Your parents were nomads. They saw signs early. One was the way you were around animals. You didn't like it when animals were butchered.

You pleaded for their lives. You tried to put yourself between them and the knife. Your parents had to keep you in a tent when they butchered. They gave you a bow, but you didn't use it. Whereas your brothers liked hunting right away.

"Before that, in the life before—two lives ago—you were under the protection of a chieftain in Lithang, and at the end of your life, you gave him your hat, bowl, and mat, and asked him to keep them because you were coming back for them someday.

"Your parents—in your last life—knew this chieftain. And they told him what kind of child you were, and the chieftain told Polu Yongzin Rinpoche. Polu Yongzin Rinpoche made inquiries and discovered there'd been omens at your birth.

"In your last life you became a monk at twelve. Your name was Tsewang Rinchen. You went to Lhasa, and from there to Nalendra. Some lamas wanted you to teach at Nalendra, but they argued over how you spoke—your accent, your dialect. You spoke the way a nomad speaks, and they were Lhasa people.

"After leaving Nalendra, you went to Jyekundo. Over the years, you had hundreds of disciples. Also, maybe because of your nomadic roots, you traveled a lot. You even came here once. You gave teachings in our monastery. Before you died, you told three lamas, at different times, that you would be reborn near here, and that the house you were born in would be painted yellow and situated in sight of the river. When they found you—you in this life, you right now—they did divinations. Your birth date was auspicious. And someone in Thaklung remembered that, on the day of your birth, a jewel was found in the body of a sheep."

"But how do you know?" Tsering asked again.

"What matters," said his teacher, "is that you'll be our abbot. The sixth in your line, and abbot of Thaklung."

◆

THERE WERE FIVE TEMPLES on the monastery grounds. There were three chapels, an assembly hall, and four shrine rooms. Everything was built into the slope of a hill, including the stores, the reliquaries, the kitchens, the library, the new and old cells for the senior monks, the dormitories, the colleges, the meeting rooms, and the pharmacy. The flights of steps twisted, the paths turned beneath high walls. The main gates were red, the buildings white. In the morning a monk blew a conch horn from a roof. Sometimes the wind rattled loudly in the eaves. Sometimes it penetrated and made the lamps flicker. When it rained the assembly hall smelled of wet wool, and the mass of damp monks turned the atmosphere humid. The butter lamps emitted their odor of rancid grease and sent smoke into the hall's upper reaches. Smoke had blackened the paintings there. The lowest stones in the walls were crumbling and the stone pillars were dark with soot.

Tsering was in a cellar, and late for something. He snaked between pillars. A niche had been cut into a wall. Above the niche was a passageway. He climbed through it and into another chamber. Here there was a doorway with no door in it. Through that portal lay a larger chamber. He went up a narrow flight of stairs. The gaps in them were dark. There came a landing and a turn, then a room with a low ceiling. A boy was there, sitting on the floor. Tsering advised him to get up and leave. There was a pulpit in the room, and behind it, a curtain. Then he was on a ramp of cobbles. It was hard to make progress because the air felt thick. He couldn't be late. He had to keep moving. In a courtyard he saw the assembly chant master. There was space between his feet and the ground. I'm late for the assembly, Tsering told him, then went through a portico and into a temple. It was empty and silent. The butter lamps were out. No, it wasn't the assembly he was late for. Why had he said what he'd said to the chant master? He went down a passage and into a retreat cell, where a conch shell gleamed in a golden bowl. He picked up the shell and brought it to his lips. I'm dreaming, he thought, and awoke.

◆

HIS TUTOR IN MATTERS of scripture refused to look at him. When he spoke to Tsering, it was with his eyes averted, as if there were something of greater interest elsewhere. His disdain appeared total, and his rebukes were elaborate. At times he removed a slipper and thrashed Tsering with it. "You're worthless," he said one day. "You were born without the required intellect. There's really no point to further study. Why should I teach someone with a mind so dense? Someone who is, on top of that, lazy? If you had a natural intellectual gift, maybe I would be patient with you, but given the fact that you're devoid of that gift, my concerted efforts feel quite pointless. This is the way it always goes," said the scripture teacher, looking to his right while he spoke to Tsering. "Student after student wasting my time. How many have I seen who truly became learned? Three. In three decades. Three out of hundreds. Three who were determined. Three who weren't a disappointment to me. Look, suppose a rope is suspended over a canyon, and the only way to cross is to walk on the rope. That's what I'm talking about. That sort of concentration. You don't concentrate, you fall into the canyon. Now compare that to what you're doing when you study. Find some urgency! Every minute is a minute lost! A minute you'll never see again! A minute subtracted from the total of your life's minutes! And meanwhile, the charnel grounds wait for you, Tsering. Between now and then, what will you do?"

"Study!"

"A mere word."

❖

TSERING wrote to Samten:

> The monastery where I live now is very, very large. I believe there are a thousand monks on the premises. Things are well organized and carefully managed. A major endeavor is training for the printing house. Another wing is for the teaching of painting. There is a medical college that serves as a clinic. Here I wake at 3 AM. As you taught me to do, I contemplate first. Then I get out of bed and wash. Since The General

Union Of All That Is Rare And Sublime is central here, I perform the related phases of approach and accomplishment before making offerings. After that, I present gifts of water.

In the beginning here I studied in the scripture college. The initial text was A Commentary On A Praise To Manjushri. Next we read Jowo Je Atisha's commentary on the verse of refuge. Third was Words Of My Perfect Teacher. Fourth was Khenpo Kunpal's commentary on Shantideva. Soon we will take up commentary on Ascertaining the Three Vows. Then the root verses of The Light Of Wisdom.

Every monk here, no matter what, must perform the inner preliminary practices. This means 100,000 recitations of the refuge prayer, 100,000 hundred-syllable mantras, 100,000 mandalas, and 100,000 prostrations. My Sanskrit tutor has thoughts on this. In his opinion, the balance between ritual, meditative practice, and scholarship here tips in the direction of ritual. He's very smart, and kind to me, and complimentary, and encouraging. I don't think I have a gift for Sanskrit, so I'm glad for his approach, temperament, and demeanor. He reminds me of you.

I have permission to visit my family again. On the way I'll come to you with gifts.

◆

IT WAS SUMMER AND they were in the high country with the yaks. A number of churns, though, had been left behind, so Tsering's sister was going back for them. She had a donkey on a lead, but since the donkey was reluctant on account of her horse, Tsering, on foot, went along to lead the donkey.

They passed the tents of other herders. Whenever Yangchen's horse came close, the donkey stamped and brayed, for which Yangchen, from her saddle, reprimanded it. It was deaf to her entreaties, though, aloof and intractable. Tsering let it walk at its own pace, and though it glared at him with latent violence, he felt sure they had an understanding.

On the far side of a buttress the grass fell more steeply. Below them now were the pastures near the village. From a flat outcropping, two girls watched sheep. One was Dawa, Yangchen said, the other Ketu. "I have to go to them," she told Tsering. "I saw them on the way up and they said if I came back down, bring food."

She rode off and, when she reached the girls, made a running dismount. The horse, still loping, moved on without Yangchen, then came to a stop with a twist.

Tsering watched. One of the girls squatted, eating something. Another, after picking up a staff, headed off sheep. A dog ran to meet her. She laid her staff on the grass, bent over the dog, lifted its forelegs, and examined its paws. Then, fluidly, she took up her staff and returned to the other girls.

Tsering went on watching. After a while the girls started throwing knucklebones. One of them was animated about it. She whirled and the knucklebones fanned out before dropping. When she leaned over them to read their lay, he compared her to the girl who'd bent beside the dog. This one had a different way of bending. She tilted forward and craned her neck. The first girl's way had been more like folding.

Yangchen rode back to him. "They wanted to talk a lot," she said.

"About what?"

"Boys."

Tsering didn't answer. Yangchen said, "The whole time. Boys."

✦

HE WAS THROWING ROCKS into the river with his brother Sonam. Three vultures soared over them, wings wide, the wind bearing them aloft. The river was high, and the current so fast that a stick thrown into it was swallowed immediately. A tree traveled by, complete with its root ball. Sonam, leading it, lofted a rock and, when it bounced off bark, cheered.

Sonam's hair had grown long and thick, and since he didn't wash it much, it was matted. Now he swept it from his face and said, "I couldn't be like you."

"What do you mean?"

"Take vows. Be a monk. Study all the time. I couldn't take it."

They walked upriver, into the wind. The current here had undercut the bank. They came to a side stream where water fell sheetlike. "Yesterday," said Sonam, "there were two girls here. One washing her hair."

"What did you do?"

"I said hi."

"What did they say?"

"They said hi back."

Sonam drank. When he was done he wiped his lips with the back of his hand and said, "They live in Dronda."

He pushed his hair aside, then bit a fingernail. "She didn't mind me there," he said. "The one washing her hair."

He looked at his fingernails, then bit one again. "And they didn't tell me to leave," he said. "So I stayed."

The next morning Tsering said to Sonam, "I'm running away."

"How come?"

"I'm tired of the monastery. Tired of studying."

They went to the stables. "Which donkey is the oldest?" Tsering asked. "I'll take the oldest. When they ask, just say I'll replace it with a younger one. Eventually. When I return."

Evelyn

WHEN SHE OPENED HER EYES, A SHIRTLESS GUY WAS squatting on his haunches so close she could see he'd broken his nose a few times. Just his face and the dawn sky. Way too near and looking down on her, inspecting her. "I coulda murdered you," he said.

"Get," said Evelyn.

She rolled out of her blanket and got to her feet. The guy stayed low with his elbows on his knees. "Go on," said Evelyn. "Get."

He wore tall boots, and his pants were tucked into their cuffs. His shoulders were hairy, and his belt was a length of manila rope. "You should sleep in the woods," he said.

"Mind your business," answered Evelyn.

"Come on," said the guy. "Relax a little."

He seemed bland. There was no sense of conflict. It was matter-of-fact—like he was speaking from a higher place. Evelyn kicked dirt up so it flew toward his face. "Get," she said again.

The guy stood. "Come on," he repeated. "Relax."

Evelyn plucked her blanket off the ground and pulled her bag against her leg. "People like you don't last long," the guy said.

Evelyn kicked dirt again. "At some point, you gotta sleep," said the guy. "That's the problem."

"Get out of here."

"That's when they get you."

"Shut up," said Evelyn.

"Sleep on the sly. Get hid."

◆

AFTER MINNESOTA SHE DECIDED to put her thumb out. Near Grand Forks a guy picked her up. He drove a van and was out of washer fluid. His windshield was smeared with the remains of bugs. The back of his van was full of auto parts. He was a supplier, he explained. Garages ordered parts, he delivered them out of Grand Forks. The other thing he did was carry golf clubs. There were half a dozen courses in his territory, he said, and sometimes the timing of his day worked out perfect. If he had time for nine holes, he played nine holes, but mostly it was driving ranges. He also carried fishing gear. "I get walleye outta this one," he said, as they passed a lake.

She got a ride with a school secretary who wore her hair in a bouffant, teased up and sprayed, bangs to her eyebrows. She kept her hands at ten and two and lived in Minot. From Minot, she said, it was an hour fifteen to Knox, where she went twice a week, since her mother lived there. It worked out. She had errands anyway. Winter she'd rather not but did. Grew up with weather, drove in snow fine. Worst thing was drivers who didn't have a clue. Lot more of those than there used to be. Consideration was less. She held kids to standards. They came into the office they better be polite. If not she took the time to instruct them. I'm Mrs. Sprague, you don't just say hey. Say please, say thank you, say you're welcome, basic. Kids want that. They want it and are waiting for it.

Minneapolis was eight hours, Winnipeg five, Mrs. Sprague said. Winnipeg got overlooked but there was nothing wrong with Winnipeg. Bigger than Minneapolis. Even had a Chinatown. Hardly any Chinatown in Minneapolis. She and her husband went to Winnipeg for Jets games. "You oughta visit," she advised Evelyn. "You know who's from Winnipeg? Monty Hall—*Let's Make a Deal.*"

Evelyn got a ride with a guy who said he didn't pick up hitchhikers. He was a farm boy, immovable-force-like. "I'm Norman," he said. "They called me Stormin' Norman back when, but now they call me Norman the Foreman. Wanna smoke a joint?"

She didn't. He went ahead, then swooped in at a gas station. "Want anything?" he asked. He was going in, so if she wanted anything. He came back with a big bag of potato chips and a couple of tallboys, but by then Evelyn was out by the road. "What's up?" asked Norman.

"Nothing," said Evelyn.

"I insult you somehow?"

"You didn't insult me."

"Well, if I did," said Norman, "I'm genuinely sorry."

◆

THE OLD MAN BROKE ground with the leading edge of a tractor bucket. Eventually, though, he rumbled her way, shut down, leaned back into his throne, and said, "They're disinclined."

"Yeah."

"Don't take an interest."

"No."

"Leave you to your own devices."

He took off his hat and craned his neck. "One coming," he said. "Getcher thumb out."

A stock truck and trailer—they never stopped anyway. "It's okay," said Evelyn.

"Back's crooked," the old man answered. "Can't pick rock. Turning up a lot of rock. It's gotta be handpicked."

Three-fifty an hour, so she picked rock. He worked ahead scabbing ground while she piled. At intervals he stopped scabbing and did some collecting—sat up on his throne while she tossed rock in, after a while got down and braced against the bucket to sort of help, all the while talking. One subject being Hutterites. Hutterites being like Mennonites or Amish—maybe somewhere between. Big colony down the road, raised hogs and chickens, what they mostly believed in was keeping to theirselves, speaking their own language, and living the group way. Wore like the Amish—suspenders, the women kerchiefs. Drank bathtubs of hard stuff. Held their alcohol. People called them communist cuz nobody owns nothing. Fine with him. To each his own. They worked hard.

She went down there. They had a big mess of buildings. Their laundry was up, blowing in the wind. Before too long, dogs started in. They got up alongside her and did their harrying. They made forays, barking, and circled her, growling. Sure enough, first person she saw looked Amish. Big beard, suspenders. Hauling jerry cans, one on each side. When the dogs alerted him he set his cans down and came over. "What is it?" he asked.

"I got told about Hutterites."

"That's okay," said the Hutterite. "Who said what?"

People went about their business behind him, all done up the Hutterite way—girls in bonnets, boys in hats, women kerchiefed, men dead ringers for the Hutterite in front of her—and no one paying her any mind. "Just wanted to see," she said.

"That's okay," said the Hutterite. "See what?"

"See about joining."

"Acchh," said the Hutterite.

He turned around and called in his language. A woman veered off from whatever she was doing, came their way, and pulled up beside him. She had her hair covered. Actually everything about her was covered except her arms from the elbows down. She had that way where you curl your hands back at the waist and lodge your wrists in.

The man left. The woman sized her up. "You on foot?" she asked.

"Yep."

"What for?"

"I want to see about joining the Hutterites."

"Acchh," said the woman, and swiped her nose with her forearm. "You have any money?"

"Yep."

"How much?"

"Some."

"You want to give it to me?"

"No."

"Because no one keeps money here. You Christian?"

"No."

The woman set her wrists into her waist again. "What is it you want?" she asked.

"I thought to join up."

"You said that," the woman said. "What is it you want with us?"

"I don't really know."

"First thing," said the woman, "come to Jesus Christ."

"I tried that," said Evelyn. "It didn't work for me."

◆

THERE WAS MONEY IN picking apples. The upside was you got paid by the bin, so the more you worked, the more you made. The downside was that you had to get between branches, so if you were a big person you were at a disadvantage.

She found two shelter halves cast off into an orchard verge. She got them buttoned up and raised them on broken branch props. It was musty inside, but with fall, the weather was cold. The ground, now, was frosty in the morning. A piece of tarp helped. So did the stray dog she coaxed into sleeping with her. He was what he was— probably had collie in him. Kind of sleepy, a slow wanderer, a sitter. She didn't want to keep him, or get attached, or name him, but she named him anyway—Bear.

The apples were Goldens. Mostly yellow, but red where the sun got at them. The foreman assigned her a ladder with a warning. He said when someone was big like she was, they busted branches, and when they were tall like she was, they bottomed trees. Don't stroll around just picking in easy reach. One tree at a time, up and down—pick clean.

Evelyn met a Texan named Bill because when he went past one day he yelled, "Gettin' rich yet?"

"No!" yelled Evelyn from up on her ladder.

"Well," said Bill, "if you get too rich for what suits you, hand it off to me."

Bill swore by ladder sets. A good set, he said, solves half your problems. One day, after work, he drove Evelyn to a grocery store. Before they went in he said, "They drop the change into your hand cuz they don't want to touch you." Evelyn bought a cooking pot, a butane stove, saltines, and canned beans, and for Bear, canned dog food. She got toilet paper because the port-a-potty in the orchard was bring-your-own. She got Bill two candy bars and gave him gas money.

At the edge of the orchard she found an empty milk bottle and used it for water. She made a saucer out of a hubcap for Bear and fed him plenty, since otherwise she might not see him for a few days. Sometimes pickers sat in lawn chairs by a crate fire at night, and Bear would go over there because he had a mind of his own. She got his attention, though. She kissed his head at night. Scratched his belly and up behind his ears. She got to like his warm back too much, but in the end, she thought, it would probably be like on the album *Buddha and the Chocolate Box* Kurt Johanson used to play. She'd have to say goodbye to Bear one day, and that would make it a harder journey. Still.

◆

EVELYN WORKED UP A stake and bought a station wagon. It was easy because, after picking, the big thing in camp was trucks, cars, vans, motor homes, campers, and trailers. Some tried to fob off their beaters on suckers, but most just wanted out with no trouble so they could trade up and move on. Evelyn paid fifty dollars and got a half tank of gas and good plates along with the car for it, plus a set of snow chains and a spare tire and a jack. The ignition switch was gone, so you had to nut two wires together to start it.

When it was time to go she tried to be hard, but in the end she couldn't help herself and let Bear in on the passenger side.

THEY PUT A CHAIN up in winter so you couldn't use the campground, but she cut it with a bolt cutter and added a threaded link. It was deep woods, a little snow on the ground, a big river, and rain. No one bothered her for a while, but then someone came around from Natural Resources—actually two guys, replacing campfire rings.

She had her curtains drawn and could hear them out there wondering what was up with this station wagon, wondering what to do about it, if anything, one saying they weren't law enforcement and it wasn't up to them, the other saying they ought to check if any bathroom locks were busted. At which point Evelyn got out of her station wagon with Bear on a rope and said, "It's just me and I didn't touch anything except one chain link."

"Campground's closed," one of the guys answered.

"Not that we give a fuck," said the other.

She helped them with the firepits. The old concrete needed busting out. The new ones were steel with an enamel finish. It took four spikes to keep them in the ground. They got a few in but were short on daylight. The next day the two guys came back with beer. The day after that they brought more beer and built a campfire: "Gotta test our work," one said. Their names were Jones and Nelson. Jones had been married three times and had four kids between two women. Of those four kids, two would have nothing to do with him, which he didn't think was his fault, or not his alone—after all, it took two to tango, they just never took responsibility for their part in it and never would, which meant he had to move on from that situation, put it out of his mind, and go on with life.

Nelson said that in his opinion they should have put the fireboxes up on posts so people didn't have to lean over so much. Also, he said, last summer a cougar got out of line nearby and got shot out of a tree by a hunter who ran Plott hounds. The bears around here had figured out how to open dumpsters. For whatever reason, that tidbit led Jones to remember nearly choking to death on a fish bone, and then he and Nelson went back and forth with remembrances of painful episodes, from passing a kidney stone to dislocating a shoulder to pissing through gonorrhea. This led to horror stories. Jones had pulled a corpse out of a logjam upriver. Nelson had read about a dentist who'd died in his chair with his drawers dropped and his laughing gas on high—"I guess," said Nelson, "for kinky self-pleasure."

"Embarrassing way to go," said Jones. "My dad kicked the bucket when he was fifty-eight. I used to think that was old. Fifty-eight: that's twelve years from now. In twelve years I'm gonna be the same age my dad died."

"Don't think about it," said Nelson.

◆

SHE GOT A SALAL permit and located good thickets. Every twenty-five stems she bunched with a rubber band. Every twenty-five bunches she baled with twine. If she did it right she could fit three bales in her wagon. The guy at the packing shed who did the weighing and grading said she had the longest pigtails he'd ever seen.

His name was Dean Toomey—a lean, little guy in coveralls who smoked hand-rolleds. He said he would take off her hands all the salal she could pick right up through Valentine's Day at $7.50 a bale. He said she should watch her back out there because you never knew. He said the last time he saw pigtails like hers was on TV Injuns. He said last summer he went to a powwow and did the knife-throwing contest and would have won except his last throw was off. He said there was a Yakama called Injun John who brought salal in, and this Injun John guy picked fights with loggers. "Why am I telling you about John?" he said. "Oh yeah—your pigtails."

Dean said there were hippies down-valley who'd started a commune, and some of them picked salal, too. He'd never seen pickers worse than them—they just picked whatever, thinking they could fob it off on him spots and all. He didn't like them because they were a hassle and a headache, plus they bellyached, plus they stank, plus they didn't know shit.

Dean lived with his mother, who had cancer everywhere at this point. She'd gone to Tijuana for the apricot treatment, which turned out to be a scam, just like he'd warned her. Now she was home, he said. For good.

◆

DEAN'S MOTHER WAS NAMED Jean. She was listless and sweaty, weighed about seventy-five pounds, couldn't get out of bed by herself, and smoked Salems. A bald, gray lady with no eyelashes or eyebrows. Ashtray on her chest. Television on all the time, even at two in the morning when there were no programs and it was just the bull's-eye. Dean had snipped the TV speaker wires, nutted in extra, run it across the floor, and hooked up a toggle switch so Jean could mute from bed. "Saves me," he told Evelyn. "Otherwise I gotta do it."

The easiest thing for Evelyn was to get naked, strip Jean, pick her up, and walk into the shower, then step out and sit on the toilet with Jean on her lap like Jean was visiting Santa Claus, and soap her up. Get her back in the shower for a rinse, then carry her to her bed and set her down on a towel and dry her off, the whole time Jean making "oof" noises and maybe putting in a word or two, like, "Get the water warmer," or, "You don't gotta soap my feet."

The best way in the kitchen was to open a can of chicken broth, get it warm, and pour it into a baby bottle, but really it didn't matter because Jean didn't want to eat. Which there wasn't any point in talking to her about. Dean kept telling her, "You gotta eat, it's time to eat, come on, eat," but no, Jean wasn't hungry, in fact you could hardly get her to take a sip of water—she only took enough to get her pills down. Pills were what she wanted. Pills and cigarettes. Those were the good things. In bed with the television on, smoking. In the good feel of her painkillers, tranked so things didn't matter so much, deep down inside her narcotic daze, sometimes wanting to hear about Evelyn, like where she was from and who her people were. "I never been to Indiana." "My people are Idaho people." "Dean's bein' good but he's got his own problems." "Dean's got three half sisters in Wyoming." "Dean's losin' patience." "Change the channel." "Outa matches."

Dean got a hold of morphine. The injectable kind. Up by Fort Lewis. No, it wasn't legal. They didn't want it legal because the way the system worked was, they wanted you to die in a hospital. They wanted to bill you for kicking the bucket. They wanted to clean you out before you croaked. "I mean, come on," said Dean. "As if it's not bad enough without getting leeched off."

◆

THE HIPPIES HAD SET themselves up with yurts and an outdoor kitchen, but the best things they had going for them were a barn and a well house. One of them had rebuilt the well pump, and another had gotten lowered in to clean out silt. They had water. They had power to the barn. They tended a garden and kept goats. The garden was fenced, but everything else the goats had turned to mud. The barn roof leaked. Someone had scrambled up there to investigate, but for now the answer was strategically placed rain barrels.

There wasn't much money. Someone would go off, paint a building or dig a trench, and return with a little cash. One guy rebuilt wrecks that weren't totaled. Three women drove up to Seattle with handmade jewelry and sold it at street fairs. A half dozen people were picking salal. "My thing," a woman named Serena told Evelyn, "is I ask a tavern guy if he wants to get high, and then I take him out to my van for reefer, and then I say, 'I could use thirty bucks.' He's like, 'Yeah? What would you do if you had thirty bucks?' It's . . . barf. Gas, beer, reefer, mouthwash—those would be my tax deductions."

"Hmm," said Evelyn.

"Takes a toll on mental health," Serena said. "Don't do it."

They gave Evelyn dinner—whole wheat spaghetti. Someone

wanted to know if she'd been to the Indiana Bean Blossom Blue-grass Festival. Someone else said they had a friend named Mike who played guitar for a band from Fort Wayne. After dinner, the mood changed. The hippies spoke in hushed voices now, about people who didn't pull their weight, or were obnoxious, or a bad fit. About a grifter: what he took to the store in the form of cash and came back with in groceries didn't match. About a woman in their midst who might be a sociopath. About whether a guy named Josh was only there to get laid, and to what extent he was succeeding.

◆

EVELYN TOLD DEAN HE was maybe half right about the hippies. Yes, a lot of them bellyache, but they weren't stupider than other people. Okay. Did he know anyone in the veterinary trade? Something was wrong with Bear.

She went to Centralia. She had to carry Bear in because he couldn't walk. The vet said, "All right, before I do anything, you sure you want to spend on this?"

"No," said Evelyn.

"Let's call it ten bucks," said the vet. "To start. The problem is—and I see this all the time—one thing leads to another, and by the time you decide to have your animal put down, you've spent hundreds."

"Ten works," said Evelyn.

The vet took Bear in back. Evelyn looked at magazines. After five minutes the vet returned and asked, "Has he been bit by a raccoon lately?"

"Probably. Knowing him."

"Because I think what he has is coon hound paralysis. From raccoon saliva. He's paralyzed, except for his head. Good news," said the vet, "is dogs come back from it. Bad news is, it takes a while."

Evelyn didn't answer. "This is where putting him down makes sense," the vet went on. "Otherwise you're going to be hand-feeding him and syringing water down his throat. I can catheterize him, but there's nothing I can do about his, uh, defecating, so he'll be laying in it. Plus you'll be his physical therapist, because if you don't range his limbs, he isn't going to walk again. How old is he?"

"Old."

"Well, maybe he's had a good life and this is it and I take care of it. Otherwise I'll start him on medications and a drip IV and hold him until morning."

"Let me see him," said Evelyn.

Bear was on a stainless steel table. He'd shed hair there and looked pathetic. "Want to think about it?" the vet asked.

"No," said Evelyn, and picked up her dog. "Come on, Bear," she said. "Let's get out of here."

◆

DEAN WAS SUPPOSED TO sell the house so his three half sisters could get their pieces. "It's paid off," he told Evelyn. "I'm gonna stall."

He let her stay in Jean's old room—seeing as how she'd seen Jean through. Evelyn folded her shelter-halves to make a mat, cut up her tarp to lay over it for hygiene, and situated Bear. When it was time to feed him or get water down his throat, she lifted him bundled in the piece of tarp onto the bed. When he pissed, the tarp cleaned easy. When he shit, she slid him onto a fresh piece of tarp and scraped the shit off the old one into the toilet, then carried Bear into the shower, laid him over the drain, soaped him up, and rinsed him clean. Afterward, she wrapped him in a beach towel and let him splay out on the bed. As for the physical therapy, she got this baby bungee bouncer that could also work for a dog's four legs— just needed two more holes was all, one for Bear's head and one for his tail. She scissored out the holes for him. She clamped the thing overhead to the doorframe and got the height just right so Bear had to fight his weight while he bounced off the floor. That made his legs give. She'd give him a rest and dangle him again. Sometimes he shit or pissed himself at night and she had to get up to deal with it, but for the most part getting Bear through was easy. All she really had to do besides play nurse was lie around on Jean Toomey's bed reading books and watching television.

Dean had a partner named Patricia. She was craggy at the brow and had a cleft in her chin. Patricia liked to mill in the hall while Bear did his bungee routine. She wore her coat in the house, zipped tight, and kept her hands in its pockets. The left one was mangled.

They would be in the kitchen at the same time. Ten minutes for a bowl of cereal would turn into a half hour of yakking. For example, Patricia running down dogs she'd had, starting with the blue heeler–Jack Russell mix killed by toppled hay bales when she was a kid, all the way to her current animal, a bullmastiff with no clue, blind as a bat and deaf on top of it. Patricia kept him kenneled, because otherwise he'd get in trouble with the neighbors.

Patricia said in farm country, where she was from, people grew stuff, and that made them one way, but in logging country, like where they were now, people cut stuff down, and that made them different. She said the good thing about Dean was, Dean was like a farm guy, and didn't hang with drunks, and was even-keeled and harmless, and she wished he'd just go ahead and sell the house already so they could leave.

He sold the house. Evelyn took her station wagon back to the locked campground. Bear got up on his feet again there, but was permanently hamstrung and dragged his hind legs. One day he wasn't around anymore. She stood by the river, figuring he'd gone for a drink and drowned. From then on she searched for him a lot, thinking maybe he was hung up in the woods someplace—she called his name while she wandered in the forest, but nothing came of it, which she finally had to admit, at which point she gave up and cried.

◆

SHE GOT CONTACTED BY a lady named Lois Farrar who'd worked with Jean Toomey at the Fisher Flour Mill "back when

Seattle had saloons." Lois Farrar needed someone to do things for her, and in return whoever did it could have her extra bedroom plus food and ten dollars a day. She had a car but didn't drive it anymore. She was going blind, which made things hard.

Lois lived in Spanaway. Her house was mildewy, and her wall-to-wall carpets stank. Her car, an Oldsmobile with a dead battery, was entombed in a carport. About half the food in her refrigerator had gone bad one way or another. Evelyn could tell the oil furnace wasn't working right because, while the house was warm—too warm, actually—it smelled like fumes.

It wasn't bad. There was nothing wrong with the job. It took Evelyn a week or so to get things in line, and after that they sat on the sofa a lot, Lois with her feet up and laughing at herself for being the kind of old person who can't see the TV but watches it anyway. Lois was all in on the grandma-at-home look: sweatpants, sweater, those slipper-shoes you don't have to bend over to deal with, doubled-up socks, *TV Guide*, toothpicks, lemon drops, and—in her case—a thing that looked like a welder's shield but was actually a magnifier. With that thing in place she could see her *TV Guide*, but even so, she couldn't always tell what was coming on next, which didn't matter, because she wasn't picky. Same with food. She liked candy, but she'd eat anything you put in front of her. If it came in a bowl, so much the better, because that way she didn't have to get off the sofa. Still, she wasn't going to buy one of those chairs that shoots you into a standing position, because that would be pampering yourself. "I'm pampering myself with you, instead," admitted Lois.

It was a lot of this and that. Cut Lois's toenails. Help her into and out of her underwear. Walk around with her at the supermarket because she couldn't read labels. Change the ice packs for her herniated disk problem. Read the slips the bank teller put in front of her, read what it said on her little bottles of medicines, explain bills that came in the mail, run to the drugstore for milk of magnesia. Listen to Lois talk about stuff. For example, Lois had a son who made her sad for all sorts of reasons, but mainly because he didn't respect her and thought she was an idiot. She'd assumed that as a grown man he'd at the least be civil, but instead he spoke to her as if she were a child, so that gradually she'd had to distance herself from him and let him be what he was. She had a daughter who'd married a pipe fitter from Anchorage, and the daughter seemed, on the phone, fake—like to her Lois was just an obligation. Lois had no grandchildren—another thing she didn't like about how things had turned out. On went Lois. The kids' dad had left her, and the second guy she married died, which was unfortunate because they'd made plans, like traveling to Ireland, touring national parks, attending music festivals, maybe going to fairs in all fifty states. Instead he had a stroke and was touch-and-go for a long time recovering from it, even got better a little—enough to come home—but then he had another stroke. His name? Martin. Martin Lantz, from Spokane. A mason who did big jobs for a long time but then went solo. She should have married Martin first instead of the other guy, because Martin was her true love. "I mean, he was tender," said Lois, "and he woulda been here instead of you right now, doing what you do, if he'd made it. That's how I imagined it. Me and Martin, the kids nearby, grandkids, travel. Golden years."

◆

LOIS TOOK A FALL and ended up in a home where they took care of people who were bedridden. Evelyn got hired to take care of a man named Harold, who stayed hunkered in a chair like he'd drawn a curtain around himself. Goobered into a balled-up, yellowed handkerchief, coughed dry and breathed shallow, picked his scabs and chewed his cheeks. Evelyn pulled him up by his smashed blue hands and took him by the scruff and down the sidewalk for some exercise. A couple times he stopped to bring his fists up by his face and feint like a boxer. A couple times he craned his neck to look into the sun for longer than was good for him. At the corner, Evelyn tried to help him step down from the sidewalk into the street, but he balked the way mules balk—dug in his heels. Okay, they could just as well turn left and continue walking, which they did, but then when they came to another crossing he said, "Not doin' it," and a third time and a fourth, which meant they'd walked around the block.

Harold narrowed down the food he ate. At first she could give him all sorts of things, but gradually it got to where it was mac 'n' cheese, salted cashews, bacon, and spumoni ice cream. Anything else and he went on a hunger strike. You couldn't put a tomato or a potato in front of him. He stayed with his four food groups—mac 'n' cheese, cashews, bacon, spumoni—until he quit eating mac 'n' cheese. Next went cashews, and then spumoni.

Bacon went last. He started dropping it on the floor instead of eating it. He got so frail he ended up in a wheelchair. After that, Evelyn had to ease him onto his toilet and wipe his butt for him.

Harold started having panic attacks. The guy would get nervous about something like running out of spumoni even though he didn't eat it anymore, and that would spike his anxiety to where he had to go fetal and wail. It was hard to take—a grown man curled in on himself like a baby, and crying like one, too. Evelyn could hardly listen to it, and the idea went through her to shut his bedroom door and let him lie there bawling. What she actually did, though, was get up on the bed and put Harold's head in her lap. "Never you mind," she said to Harold. "It's all right. Hush, now." Things like that. Until he died.

◆

THE BUS WAS MOSTLY asleep or comatose. The woman across the aisle had a laundry bag full of stuff, though, and stayed busy with it. Every time she wanted something she had to loosen the drawstring and rummage around in it up to her armpit. She had a bed pillow lodged between herself and her window, and sat tilted against it with her legs folded sideways. She didn't look out her window much; it was half-blocked by her pillow anyway, and the way she'd set herself up it was like the world didn't mean a thing.

Evelyn watched dried-out fence posts go past that had to have been set before there were power augurs, and wondered how many people over how much time had dug the postholes and strung the wire and drove the staples and put in the buttressing and the gates. Maybe working from wagons full of beans, coffee, and rice. Maybe sleeping on the ground. Maybe it was the people in those black-and-white pictures looking stout and worn-out at the same time. *Maybe one day*, Evelyn thought, *I'll build a little house*, and after that she saw it in her head. Like where the windows would be and the kitchen sink and the woodstove and how the roof would slope and where the power and water would come in. Deer would want to wreak havoc in her garden, so she'd have to figure out what kind of fence was economical, maybe the kind where all you did was weave brambles together.

The woman across the aisle rifled through her laundry bag again. Went through it het up, turned everything around and over and reached down into the bottom of it, and finally, coming up empty, said to Evelyn, "Desperate for an aspirin."

"If I had one I'd give it to you," Evelyn said, "but I don't."

After another mile or two the woman said, "I should tell you about something."

"Okay."

"There's a place up here it's free room and board if you work some."

"What is it?"

"A Buddhist retreat center."

◆

THEY WERE BUILDING A trail with a series of huts. They were expanding their kitchen and putting up guesthouses. The way it worked was, they gave you a bunk and four shelves. If you pulled your weight, you could stay indefinitely, but if it turned out you were taking advantage, somebody was going to talk to you about that, and then you'd have to leave.

It was hot and dusty. They gave Evelyn work gloves and a tin drinking cup. She and three guys and another woman scraped paint off a building. The guy in charge wore a red T-shirt and orange shorts. They'd work until two, he said, and after that there would be optional activities—seated meditation, a class, a discussion, walking meditation. You didn't have to do anything after two if you didn't want to, but most people took advantage of the free opportunities.

After scraping paint, Evelyn lay on her bunk. There was an air conditioner in the room, but it made a racket and couldn't keep up. The only other person there was named Barb. No one else was around, Barb said, because the air-conditioning was better in the dining center.

People were sitting around in the dining center. Near Evelyn, on a table, was a brochure about The Stupa Project. On the front it said that a stupa is a shrine, and that the idea of The Stupa Project was to build one on Peace Mountain. There was a picture of one with its parts identified. It looked like a chess piece—like a Queen, but swollen. What they wanted to do on Peace Mountain was build one out of stone, but that was going to take money and effort.

On the back of the brochure was a list of benefits from helping to build a stupa. One was reaching nirvana more quickly. "Seen this?" Evelyn asked a woman nearby.

"What?"

"It says here if you help build a stupa, you reach nirvana faster."

"It does?"

"Yeah."

"Maybe they mean 2,999,999 lifetimes instead of 3 million," said the woman.

"Huh," said Evelyn. "So you get to skip one life for working on a stupa."

"Not literally," said the woman.

"Like seventy or eighty years or whatever off the total. That's part of Buddhism?"

◆

THEY HAD A TEACHER at Peace Mountain named Lama Lobsang. He talked about things that were hard to understand, but you could ask him questions. You could also sign up for a meeting between just you and him. Barb said if you did that he would ask you about yourself, figure out your obstacles, and help you overcome them.

Evelyn went to see Lama Lobsang. He was a grizzled-looking guy with bags under his eyes. He was gnarled in general and had a hard time moving. His plump, soft arms were dimpled at the elbows, and on his left shoulder was a vaccine scar. Lama Lobsang wore a maroon skirt, a yellow shirt with cap sleeves, black stockings, and clogs, and there were prayer beads wrapped around his wrist. Although he looked old-school his English was good. He made cutting motions with his hands a lot, as accompaniment to explanations. He had a lot of moles and skin tags, and there were tracts on his face he'd missed with his razor. His lower lip protruded. His head was probably supposed to be bald but instead had a shadow of hair on it, plus liver spots. All in all he looked stove-in. "What's your name?" he asked.

"Evelyn Bednarz. Bednarz's Polish."

"You were born in Poland?"

"No. Indiana. Evansville, Indiana."

No answer from Lama Lobsang.

"Yeah," said Evelyn. "Otherwise known as Nowheresville."

Still no answer.

"And as you can see, I look like Bigfoot."

"Do you feel sorry for yourself?"

"Not really."

"So what are you doing here?"

"Working on the stupa. Because they say that if you work on a stupa, you reach nirvana faster. Is that true?"

"I don't know," said Lama Lobsang. "How did you end up here?"

"I left home when I was eighteen and now I just wander doing whatever."

"So a great variety of things."

"Yeah. Like this."

"Like what?"

"Like checking out Peace Mountain."

"You have free time."

"Yeah. But I waste it."

Again no answer.

"So, Lama Lobsang. Barb said you could maybe figure out my obstacles. Barb. You know. Barb?"

"One obstacle."

"What?"

"Not enough freedom."

"Freedom from what?"

"Freedom from Evelyn Bednarz."

✦

ON THE WALLS OF the The Stupa Project office were project blueprints, an artist's rendering, a site map, a framed photo of Peace Mountain taken from an airplane, a framed black-and-white photograph of Chiracahua Apaches, a framed letter of endorsement from a lands commissioner, and an oil painting of juniper and pinyon trees on a slope overlooking grasslands. "What it is," said Maya, the project director, "the way to look at it, the way to see it, it's like— you know the pyramids? A stupa is a pyramid."

"Okay," said Evelyn.

"Not shaped like a pyramid," said Maya, "but—you know—a burial mound."

"Got it," said Evelyn. "Who gets buried in it?"

"Ours will be a reliquary," said Maya. "Ours is going to house sacred relics." She put a thumb up. "So you'd like to volunteer," she said.

"Definitely. I promise I'll work my butt off."

"Wonderful," said Maya. "Our thing right now is we're all about logistics. Would you be interested in helping with logistics?"

◆

SHE HAD TO MEET next with a guy named Joe, who was the volunteer coordinator for The Stupa Project. He took one look at her and said, "Perfect, great," and then they walked into the mesquite beneath Peace Mountain. On the way Joe asked a whole bunch of questions. He was from Wisconsin, where was she from? Until lately he'd worked in the compressed gas industry—what kind of work had she been up to? First aid and that stuff—did she know CPR? Working with people—did she like working with people? Was she good with her health—did she have health problems? Some people were better in the heat than others. What about her when it came to heat?

They came to a place where cut stone was piled. "This is the end of the line," said Joe. "This is where the trucks turn around."

He pointed up the mountain. "So up there," he said, "that's where the stupa goes."

"Okay."

"So that means we gotta get everything up there, starting with these stones here."

They looked at the summit. "See what I mean?" Joe asked.

He pointed at the stones. "Indiana limestone," he said. "This load's got gray in it, bluish gray, sometimes it's more silvery, sometimes it's brownish."

"Looks good," said Evelyn.

"So feature this," said Joe. "So this stupa is like a three-story house. And the whole thing's gonna be built out of limestone. And these guys here"—he pointed at the stones again—"they're forty-by-fifteen-by-fifteen and weigh sixty pounds each."

"Great," said Evelyn.

"That's right," said Joe. "And they gotta get up there. One thousand two hundred fifty feet."

"So like the Empire State Building," Evelyn said. "Because in school we went on this field trip where they gave the height of the Empire State Building."

"Really," said Joe.

"Yeah," said Evelyn. "We went to the quarry where they got the limestone for it."

✦

EVELYN WENT BACK TO Maya and said, "How 'bout we go with a one-year contract?"

"What do you mean, a one-year contract?"

"I don't want to work every day until two, and then take advantage of opportunities. I want to skip the opportunities and work on the stupa."

"Okay," said Maya. "That works for us."

"That way," said Evelyn, "I can accomplish my goal of packing a thousand stones to the top of Peace Mountain. But just one thing—I gotta have the right pack."

"Which is the right pack?"

"So that's what I mean by a contract," said Evelyn. "There's expenses up front, so you'll wanna hold me to it."

She got the pack. They had it in Albuquerque at a place called Surplus City. It was a mainframe with a scabbard and military-grade load buckles. Only a frame; it didn't have a bag. The main thing was, though, it had a good base. You could set a stone there and strap it in place. You could set it the long way and suck it in tight. It had the forty inches and the fifteen across and the long-enough straps and it cost $30. Plus, when she put it on, it felt right.

She ate in Albuquerque. One of those big double breakfasts you get for lunch, plus bought a box of cookies to scarf on the way back. After that she went to a library, where she learned that Sherpas put everyone to shame. They started out in Jiri because that's where the road ended and walked sixty miles to the base of Mount Everest with loads on their backs that weighed more than they did. How did they do it? Nobody knew. Some of them used tumplines, but that didn't explain it. The book in her lap said Sherpas were a mystery. It said what they did was superhuman. The author had gotten so curious about Sherpas he wore a pack on his back that weighed what he did on a mountain trail in Colorado and then had to laugh at how lame he felt. Well, thought Evelyn, I'm pretty sure I can do it. Carry my weight if it comes to that.

◆

THE PACK WORKED. JOE called it a "meat hauler." Hunters used them where he was from. When he came back from a trip to Wisconsin, Joe had his own meat hauler and a new pair of boots. "All right," he said, "I'm in."

They rested a lot. They sat in the mesquite on their way up the mountain. There wasn't much to see. It was all mesquite. Joe said genetically he sweated like a pig, which was good in some ways but bad in others. He said that in his twenties he'd gone to Mount Kailash but altitude sickness did a number on him there. He said in Tibet they had a thing called sky burial: someone died, they quartered him with knives, made it so they could lash his parts to a meat hauler, portered him up to the top of a mountain, and left him for buzzards to turn into bones. Seeing how they couldn't build a funeral pyre on account of a lack of firewood in their vicinity.

You put your head down. The footing was good. The dirt wasn't hard; it gave a little. After a while they'd made their own track. They followed their own rut and stopped at the same resting places. Some people came out who didn't want to carry stones and left jugs of water at intervals for them.

Joe got sick—something with his kidneys. He went to a doctor who said not to carry stones. It didn't matter. She went on by herself. She ate a big bean-and-rice burrito for lunch, and toast for breakfast with bananas and oatmeal, and spaghetti for dinner a lot of the time, but where the pack straps ran over the crests of her shoulders she felt sort of bruised now permanently. Other than that, no problems at first, seeing how the weather was on her side until it wasn't. In April it started to be kind of hot, and by the end of May it was way too hot, the answer being to haul at night with a head-lamp on like coal miners used and to crash in daytime when it was a hundred at noon, which the Sherpas, she thought, didn't have to put up with but probably could if they had to.

It hardly ever rained. It got windy sometimes. Sometimes in the morning there was fog over the mesquite. The moon seemed mas-sive on certain nights—whenever it was near the horizon. As far as the stars—according to Maya—the earth was in the Milky Way galaxy near one of its edges, and the Milky Way was shaped like a spiral, so that explained, Maya said, the band of white light you saw from Peace Mountain where there was zero light pollution. There were birds in the chaparral. There was a roadrunner once on top of Peace Mountain. There were snakes sometimes, including whip snakes. They didn't mind if you picked them up, just curled in your hand and stayed there.

From Peace Mountain you could see pretty far. Things looked big and it made you feel small. Evelyn lay down on the summit a lot. This mountain has the right name, she often thought.

◆

EMILY CHAPMAN FROM THE *Herald* had a camera slung from a strap around her neck, and a notepad and a pencil. "What brought you here?" she asked.

"I fell into it," answered Evelyn.

"The project you're working on—The Stupa Project. What is it?" "How far is it to the top of Peace Mountain?" "How long does a trip take?" "How many stones have you carried to date?" "Ever feel like giving up?" "What motivates you, Evelyn?" "How would you explain this to someone who asked about it?" "Why is it you decided to carry a thousand stones? A thousand stones—that's sort of unbelievable." "Yes, I've heard of the Sherpas in Nepal. Yes, they carry unbelievable loads."

On went Emily Chapman with questions. "So the school in Bloomington called Matrix, what was that like?" "Did you seriously think about joining the Hutterites?" "Never got married, never had kids?" "Okay, I agree—too many questions. So okay, sorry, let's get a photo, then. I think the light is on our side, yes? You and these stones on the ground here, yes? You and the stones would make a good picture. You and the stones at the base of Peace Mountain."

◆

WHEN EVELYN WAS DONE—when she'd got the thousand stones to the top of Peace Mountain—Maya gave her a ride to the bus station in Truth or Consequences. The depot was four high-back benches and a ceiling fan, plus a vending machine, pamphlets, and a cigarette ash bucket. Three other passengers waited there with Evelyn. One was slumped—legs out, feet crossed, head down, arms folded—and another chain-smoked. The third looked like Paul Bunyan if Paul Bunyan had just walked a hundred miles through Death Valley. He was one of those guys who goes around on a hot day in hardly any clothes, a bad perspirer with a monster backpack in jean cutoffs with the fringes left on, sandals, and a flimsy shirt unbuttoned to his belt buckle so that a lot of wet, dark hair showed. His calves and thighs were hairy too, and so was his head and his face because he didn't shave or get haircuts and had a big dark beard.

Evelyn tuned in to the Paul Bunyan guy. He got a water bottle out of his pack and drank half of it, then pulled out a bandanna and mopped himself. Dropped his head so he could reach the hairy back of his neck, slid the bandanna up inside his shirt to mop his armpits, all the while not self-conscious about it one bit. He didn't even look like 'if you think it's gross I'm wiping my pits in public that's your problem'; he looked more like it didn't occur to him one way or the other that someone might have an opinion about it. Just mopped away, then laid the bandanna over his pack to dry and plopped down still wet to gnaw at his fingernails. Fidgeted and scratched. Bounced a heel off the floor like his leg was a roto-hammer. After about two minutes of restlessness the guy looked her way and said, "Hey, wanna talk?"

"What subject?"

The guy had big white teeth, or maybe they only looked white because his beard was so dark. Anyway, he showed them— big teeth, meaty lips, beard coiling around his mouth—and said, "Wide open."

✦

HIS NAME WAS SCOTT WIDERA—Widera being Polish—and he was born in the Catholic Home for Unwed Mothers in Cincinnati, which his parents didn't hide from him or for that matter from anybody. In fact, they told him he was special, and read to him aloud from a book called *The Chosen Baby* that included lines Scott knew even now: "This is our Chosen Baby. We don't have to look any further."

His parents got divorced, said Scott. His mother was a doter but her doting wasn't good, especially when he got older and it turned out he wasn't as great as she thought, just someone good enough to get into Ohio State, which was what he did without thinking about it, and also where he threw shot put as a freshman and soph- omore and then quit because he tore his rotator cuff. On the plus side, he got interested in physiology and majored in it, and then studied Feldenkrais in Santa Fe. Feldenkrais was hard to explain, but basically if he finished eight hundred hours he could get himself certified as a Feldenkrais practitioner and go into business doing Functional Integrations, which meant he'd have a room with a mas- sage table in it where clients kept their clothes on while he did bodywork. Feldenkrais training, Scott said, was exorbitantly priced, so somebody like him, who worked at a transfer station, could only do it a little at a time. But anyway, that was all on hold now, because he'd gotten a ninety-day bus pass and was bopping.

"Okay," said Scott. "When you meet somebody, you're not supposed to talk about yourself, you're supposed to be interested in the other person," so she gave him a rundown, and then he went back to talking about himself. He was color-blind, he had a deviated septum, he was allergic to wasps, as a kid he'd had to wear a lazy-eye patch and had gone around pigeon-toed, when he was thirteen he'd read the *World Book Encyclopedia* straight through from *A* to *Z*. The way his mind worked was an issue because it meant he went down rabbit holes, which lately he'd been thinking might be a psychological problem. He couldn't think in a straight line, he said. Probably, he thought, it was from smoking too much dope.

◆

DOING IT WITH SCOTT was like crossing into paradise. Doing it with Scott was in its own category. She did it with Scott as often as possible. Crossed to the side where all but a single problem was solved—that it didn't last forever and there was always an afterward. You had to come back but didn't want to come back. What kind of universe was this where you had to come back?

The reason Scott's backpack was so big was that he had everything either in it or lashed to it, like a sleeping bag, an air mattress, a stove, tons of food, a transistor radio, and books. In other words, you could go into the woods with Scott for a week and do great, so she did that. Went down by this river where nobody was, made a bed of moss and ferns, stayed naked all day, swam, talked a lot. Scott told Evelyn that when Buddha got close to figuring out nirvana, a super-demon called The Lord of Death couldn't deal with it. "Wait," Scott interrupted himself, "I gotta take back 'figuring it out' because it doesn't happen in your head, you experience it."

"Experience what?" asked Evelyn.

But he couldn't explain it. And that wasn't the point, he said. The point was that when Buddha got close to nirvana, The Lord of Death made power plays. He tried to squelch Buddha with his power cards. Buddha was having none of it, so The Lord of Death had to pull out his Ace of Hearts: naked dancing girls. Which didn't work either.

Evelyn and Scott were sprawled naked on a slanting slab of river rock in the sun with white water around them. "Here's what I think," said Evelyn. "I think nirvana is like doing it, multiplied."

"What multiplier?"

"Infinity," said Evelyn.

◆

SHE GOT TO WHERE she knew that if you want to be happy in a relationship, it's sex first and everything else second. Sex or forget it. You're going to have problems with whoever it is, but if you've got sex you can move them down a bunch of levels. Because Scott wasn't perfect, but who cared. Riding the bus through a forever desert looking out the window while Scott explained *The Dancing Wu Li Masters*, by Gary Zukav: who cared. Or out in the heat wandering around and Scott drinks all the water: who cared. Or Scott folding up the tent like a total and complete idiot. Having to be in charge, having to be right, having to control everything, not listening, going overboard with opinions, not knowing when to shut up. Just not accepting how dumb it is to try to talk your way through everything. Playing the game where you pretend you're humble, where you say you get the other person's point of view, when really all you want is to manipulate them into something. Going way too far down the road in an argument, harping away on the same point like a maniac, responding to everything Evelyn said with, "You're not being logical." Getting pissed off about slights that weren't slights, saying, "Look, it's not like I need you to praise me all the time, but at the very least don't be critical," when all she'd done was point out something could be tweaked a little, for example a tent line. Mostly just talking too much, explaining things she never asked about, like how they got power from nuclear power plants. Okay, Scott had faults and shortcomings, but then she and Scott would do it, and after that he had no faults at all. Great guy, super-smart, super-interesting, super-good-looking, super-everything. Superman.

✦

THEY CAUGHT A FERRY to Alaska. On the top deck they crashed under heat lamps with people who passed books around and played card games. It was windy, but on the other hand, as far as the view went, it was the same as from a cruise ship. But really you couldn't look at trees and water the whole time, so a lot of people just got down inside their sleeping bags with nothing but their faces showing and read.

Scott learned to read hexagrams made out of *I Ching* sticks from an English guy named Roger. The first question Scott asked was, "What should I do with my life?," and the first answer he got was, "Be true to yourself so that the creative forces of the universe will remain at your disposal." Scott went on asking questions and getting answers: "Be open-minded—this is your time to follow"; "You're facing a period of potential growth and a fresh start, maybe with some initial difficulty"; "Examination of your actions and words for their sincerity will lead to stronger bonds with others"; "Do not anticipate the future or hold on to the past"; "A period is coming which requires a return to simplicity"; "Now is the time to begin a new undertaking"; "There is an obstacle here, possibly an incorrect attitude that needs to be dealt with."

It stayed light late into the night. Scott sat on his sleeping bag throwing sticks until one in the morning. "You wanna try this?" he asked Evelyn when she looked up.

"No, thanks," she answered.

Scott looked at her like she didn't make sense. "It sorta reminds me of a Ouija board," explained Evelyn.

✦

THE LAST STOP WAS Haines. They tented in a campground south of town. Scott said that if you wanted to know where you were, and

if you wanted to meet people and figure things out, the best option
was to hit bars.

In the bars all manner of subjects came up. Commercial fishing,
blueberries, cannery work, road building, drugs, bears. The pool
had showers for seventy-five cents. One guy had two years' worth
of moose meat in his freezer and was selling it cheap. Another guy
had a gold claim on Porcupine Creek.

The guy with the claim was named Tommy Fredricks. He bought
beers but didn't drink them. He told Scott and Evelyn he bought a
beer every half hour as rent on a barstool. No one gave Tommy a
hard time, or if they did it was mild, which was interesting because
he was probably the least rugged-looking guy in Haines—bald like
monks are bald, with a ring around a shiny crown, in a way that
made Scott think of the word "cranium," which was the nickname
he gave Tommy for when Tommy wasn't around, as in, "Hey, let's
go hang out with Cranium."

Tommy had worked gold claims on Porcupine Creek off and
on for a long time. At the moment he was staked to six hundred
mountain acres and two hundred creek. "I'm not really a miner,"
he said. "More like a prospector." Only once, he said, had he made
a real strike.

"Real strike?" wondered Scott.

"Hit gold," said Tommy. "Mass gold."

"Wow," said Scott. "You struck it rich?"

"No," said Tommy. "Sort of."

◆

THEY WENT TO WORK portering for Tommy. The way it
worked was that he pulled in at four-thirty in his monster truck and
they went up Porcupine Creek Road as far as they could, banging
through potholes. Not that it mattered, because banging through
potholes was easier than portering. For that, Tommy had made
backpacks out of thirty-two-gallon plastic garbage cans belted to
Trapper Nelson frames. They were so big you couldn't strap in

without help, and so heavy you had to walk bent over. You hauled your load up to Tommy's camp—literal bags of concrete, jerry cans of diesel, canned food, tools, tarps, generator parts—and walked out with an empty pack so you could use it the next day.

It was the same day at drop-off. Tommy pulled out a roll of hundreds and gave two to Scott and two to Evelyn. "Work like a dog but get paid like a lion," he said the first time he shelled out this way. "I don't know shit about economics but if that makes me a communist, I'm good with it."

Tommy was knotty and portered like a worker ant. He also wore an infantry belt with a sheath knife on one side and a revolver on the other. His camp was four miles upriver, steep. Grunt to get there—"death march," Tommy called it. The camp was bear-proof, meaning he'd cut poles on-site, placed them with a posthole digger, strung barbed wire between them, and fronted them with razor wire. Inside this perimeter were five canvas tents, plus a fire ring and tarps. Tommy cooked on an open fire, ate sitting on the ground, and, as far as mosquitoes went, burned incense. He fed chipmunks by hand and tossed bread for ravens. He said he didn't like to kill anything, but yes, he'd shot a bear once that didn't look like it would stop. He called his camp "the hooch," as in "when we get to the hooch," or "the hooch needs straightening." The first time he used that term, Scott said, "For a second there I thought you meant liquor."

"No," said Tommy. "I picked up 'hooch' in Vietnam."

Inside one of Tommy's tents was a locked trunk. Inside that were two twelve-gauge shotguns on slings, two boxes of slugs, and—the weird thing was—Buddha statues. Each day, as soon as they got to camp, Tommy retrieved a shotgun, put slugs in his pocket, and then placed the Buddha statues on perches around his camp. "So what are those about?" asked Evelyn.

They went around to each. Tommy made a little speech at every stop. "This one here is Shakyamuni Buddha crowned in the jewels of impartial awareness." "This is my protection Buddha, which some people call a blessing Buddha." "This is my medicine or medical Buddha, and that's a bowl of medicine in his hand." "That's a contemplation Buddha in case you feel like not being humble." "This one's doing the bhumisparsha mudra for overcoming evil." "That one's not a Buddha. That one there they call Green Tara, who is always ready to come to your rescue from the eight great terrors of the world."

◆

AN HOUR UP THE creek they sat in the dirt with their packs peeled off, drank water, peed, and swiped at mosquitoes. Tommy pried loose bark from a log with his knife until a creature crawled out he said was a newt and don't touch it because it's got a toxin that messes with your nervous system. In the Philippines, he said, the loris was toxic and bit a guy he knew and the shit got in his brain and fucked up his eyesight and his digestion and his sex drive. In South Africa was the boomslang, five feet long, one of these fuckers bites you you're fucked. And that's just the tip of the iceberg, said Tommy. Half the people in Europe died between 1346 and 1353 from plague. Wanna know why?

So, said Tommy, these Egyptian guys on camels find a jar in the ground. They break it open, inside's papyrus books. These guys are brothers. These guys give the books to their mother. These guys, their dad got killed in a feud, these are some murderous motherfuckers, they found the guy that did it and ate his heart, then they got nervous cops would see the books and fuck them over about it because you were supposed to turn in shit like that to the antiquities authorities. They gave the books to a priest and it turned out they were the Gnostic Gospels.

Okay, said Tommy, so in the Gnostic Gospels it's not God the Father it's God the Mother, she's called Sophia, she controls the universe, the other gods are minor gods doing minor things in localized solar systems, saying shit like, I'm the only God, it's just me—bullshitting people. Here on earth it's Jehovah, this little minor God Jehovah bored doing nothing all day, so he makes people out of mud and plays around with them like he's a kid, like moving them around and shit, like dolls or whatever, so God the Mother sees this and says, Okay, if that's the way you want it, Jehovah, you want these creatures for their entertainment value, I got an idea, give them each a piece of yourself, Jehovah, put a little spark in each, that way they'll be more fun for you, and move around on their own and be alive and shit. So Jehovah is a sucker, it's a bad move for him because this little spark of his he's giving us is a piece of him he can't get back and now he's weak. So this pisses him off, he's pissed off all the time, he fucks with us constantly, completely evil shit, seriously evil shit. We're fucked because he hates our guts and fucked because he put this spark in us so something isn't right and that's the fundamental problem and explains why there's the loris and the boomslang and the plague and all the shit that happened in Vietnam.

◆

THE WEATHER WAS GOOD. The mosquitoes were down. Tommy's camp was a lot better stocked. Every day it was the same with him—he portered a huge load, stowed and squared things away in camp, got out his shotgun, checked on his bear-proofing, and sussed out if anyone had messed with anything. Put out his Buddha statues. Lit incense. Built a fire. Opened a huge can of whatever it was—say, chili—heated it up, and ladled it out. Sat on the ground eating head down from his tin bowl. One day, after rinsing his bowl with boiled water, he said, "I'm gonna teach you guys tummo now."

The way it works, said Tommy, is you sit lotus or as close as you can get; belly-breathe five times nose in, mouth out; on the sixth breath hold for ten seconds; next, breathing in, lift your chin, and then, breathing out, press your chin against your chest; next, lock your breath up and squeeze your butt muscles. Now imagine you're an empty bottle and light a fire in your belly. Imagine two channels down your spine that come together at the fire in your belly and use your breath like a bellows to get that fire roaring. Finally, when the fire's roaring, imagine another channel coming straight up from your belly and let your breath explode out the top of your head.

They did tummo. When it was over Scott said, "The breath didn't explode out the top of my head."

"Keep at it," Tommy answered.

◆

TOMMY'S TRUCK THREW A rod on Porcupine Creek. His solution was to abandon it. "Karma," he said.

They walked out in rain and went to eat bar food. In the middle of their meal, Tommy stood and zipped his jacket. "Truck's a sign," he said, pulling out his wallet.

"Of what?" Scott asked.

Tommy counted bills, zipping them from top to bottom like playing cards at first, then gave up and put them on the table. "Whatever that is," he said. "That's what I have, so that has to cover it."

"Cover what?" Scott asked.

Tommy ignored him and spread the bills apart. All of them were hundreds. "Evelyn," said Tommy, "maybe see you in the next life. Scott, get your shit together—that's my parting advice."

He swiveled on his heels then and left.

Scott counted immediately: six thousand dollars. They split it down the middle in mutual disbelief. Scott put a bill on the bar and got shot glasses and whiskey. "To Cranium," he said. "Cranium the Magnificent."

Scott poured himself a second shot. "Once more to Cranium," he said. "He's like when the teacher says 'What is Buddha?' and the answer is 'Three pounds of flax.'"

After the third shot, Scott drew a breath through his teeth and quickly poured a fourth. "Take a leap!" he said and winced. "You got three thousand dollars!"

"Me?" asked Evelyn.

Scott tossed down his fourth shot with violence. Some of it ended up in his beard. "No, not you," he said. "Me!"

◆

SCOTT DIDN'T TAKE A leap; instead he bailed on her. First he said he wanted to be friends, then he stayed out overnight a lot, and then he said he was getting on a seiner to the Lower 48 and they should stay in touch and here was his address in Santa Fe on the back of this grocery store receipt, which she threw in a campfire.

Evelyn bought a new tent, a white-gas lantern, a better sleeping bag, and a folding camp stool. The tent came in a box she could prop on one shoulder and the other stuff fit in a big drawstring bag; she got it all out to the campground on foot—way easier than portering up Porcupine Creek for Tommy.

It was cold but sunny. She took down the old tent. Everything slow—one step at a time. Make tea. Sit on the new campstool. Eat a can of chili and a bag of crackers. Fill the water jugs at the tap. Throw the old tent in the dumpster. Do nothing for a while—keep your act together, look around, tighten your bootlaces, run a brush through your hair, don't pick at scabs, get busy with a toothpick between your teeth for once, stretch a little, make circles with your arms. Then it was time to put up the new tent and hang the lantern inside. Roll out the new bag on top of the old one, get in, try it out, not bad, fuck everything, it's getting dark already anyway, enough effort, crash.

When she woke up it was still dark, but on the other hand she had the lantern. Evelyn put a mantle in it and pumped it bright. Kind of a sterile light but so what. Maybe if she got candles things would feel better. Maybe incense. Hash and a hash pipe. Hand-warmers, a hat with built-in earmuffs, keep gum and mints around. There was only one book right now and it wasn't hers, it was Scott Widera's, another thing he didn't take cuz he left traveling light. *Chess Openings: Traps and Zaps.*

Another trip in. She bought a plastic tub. In the tub went

candy bars, boxes of crackers, boxes of cookies, a party-size bag of sour-cream-and-onion chips, a gallon jug of ginger ale, a radio, a book about the invasion of earth by extraterrestrials, and a book with a hunky guy on the cover. And a pregnancy test kit. The answer was yes.

Another day, another trip in. This time to the library. You could sit at a monitor with headphones on there and watch a movie. Evelyn watched *The Outlaw Josey Wales*. Why not? It had cowboys in it. Weird how the old Cherokee guy Lone Watie got in bed with Little Moonlight. She'd been taken captive in a raid and got violated, so Chief Black Kettle had a dirty nose sign cut into her nose because he didn't think she'd resisted enough. Sondra Locke was supposed to be Little Miss Innocent but got it on anyway with Clint Eastwood. Best character: Ten Bears. They had this super-huge bronze-skinned guy done up in blue face paint with red dots painted on his brow and red slashes painted on his forehead slanting into the bridge of his nose, hair down over his shoulders, fat eagle feathers sticking out of his head, sitting proud all naked from the waist up on his shaggy-maned white horse and carrying a long rifle. She looked him up afterward. Six-foot-seven, Muscogee from Oklahoma, rodeo cowboy, bronco buster, painted pictures, this was the best guy in the movie to sleep with. His name was Will Sampson.

She went back to her new tent, ate shit food, thought about Ten Bears, wished she had some hash, slept.

◆

THERE WERE MORE PEOPLE in the campground now. They'd come in to watch eagles. This guy in an army field jacket with a huge pair of military binoculars told her yeah, every year he came for this—for all the eagles that showed up on the Chilkat in November to feed off the chum run. Cuz the rivers here had upwelling under them so they didn't freeze 'til late. So this was easy pickings, the chum dead after spawning and now meaty carrion floating downstream.

She went. They were so busy feasting you could sit close and they ignored you. People had cameras set up with long-distance lenses on them. The eagles perched on snarls of driftwood, ruffling their neck feathers, opening their beaks to the sky, huge, ignoring each other, meanwhile in the shallows near shore the dying chum wriggled in their final death spasms, churning the water a little with their tails, their top fins exposed to the light and translucent. The eagles had this way of standing on their carrion, pincering it firmly in place with their talons so they could rip meat free, just like a butcher has to keep hold of meat with one hand while bringing in the knife with the other. They had it down. It was old hat to them. They just wrapped meat in their talons and leaned down over it and sunk in their beaks and ripped away. The beak of a bald eagle, the point on it, faced down, down and even inward a little, a little back toward the white head—perfect ripping tool, worked just right with the talons holding meat down, the two in sync, perfect phys-ics. There was so much meat they got sated and stood around a lot. They liked to turn toward the sky and open their maws. They shiv-ered sometimes. Or they walked in sand. Big old three-toed claw feet with the talons on top so they could put the toes down without dulling the talons. Walking wasn't their thing. They had to take it slow, lift a foot, put it down carefully, snow falling on their backs, one walked down to the edge of the water and with his beak pulled out a carcass, getting only one foot wet and just a little, hopped on, locked in, ripped away, this was twenty yards from Evelyn. What a lot of them did was soar low and glide in, at the last minute hover and stay there with a lot of flapping, drop their legs and ease in like paragliders, bob around a little, get their balance, get in close to another eagle eating and act intimidating until a fight broke out, a little skirmish—open maws, spread wings, jumping at each other, little bobs, little flairs, little attacks, bravado—but mostly it was oth-erwise because of easy feasting. Their legs when they were flying low and coming in went down like scary landing gear, like hands, and since the talons were on top they had to bend in a little to get them sunk into the salmon flesh. A few ravens hung around who had to be quick about it. Steam blew from the mouths of eagles. Snow fell on their cape-like closed wings. Whole trees had fallen in the river, gone downstream, and hung up in gravel, and the sated eagles perched on their branches preening and using their talons to scratch their chins. They turned their maws to the sky and let snow in before launching themselves toward another spinning carcass.

Scott Widera and his *I Ching* sticks. He'd left them behind too, plus the book that went with them. "Be true to yourself so that the creative forces of the universe will remain at your disposal"; "Be open-minded—this is your time to follow"; "You're facing a period of potential growth and a fresh start, maybe with some initial difficulty"; "Examination of your actions and words for their sincerity will lead to stronger bonds with others"; "Do not anticipate the future or hold on to the past"; "A period is coming which requires a return to simplicity"; "Now is the time to begin a new undertaking"; "There is an obstacle here, possibly an incorrect attitude that needs to be dealt with."

Screw all that, though. She stayed in her tent a lot. Snow fell on it and bled through as a drip. Kurt Johanson—she remembered his room and his stereo and his albums. They'd gotten high after Matrix and listened to *Buddha and the Chocolate Box*. Kurt said Cat Stevens was on an airplane with a Buddha statue in one hand and a box of chocolates in the other worrying about plane crashes, so that's where he got *Buddha and the Chocolate Box*. Which made sense. Buddha in one hand and chocolates in the other while worrying you're gonna die.

Tsering

BEYOND A PASS, HE CAME ACROSS TWO HERDERS. THEIR tent was up and they were eating dried meat. They had two mastiffs, and yaks in the hundreds. Tsering asked how far it was to Derge. "Two days," one answered—a man with few teeth.

The day was warm and windless. The man with few teeth poured tea. The other man, who was bowlegged and kept a dagger behind his sash, went into the tent and came out with a mat. "Use this," he said, setting it beside Tsering.

"You're muddy," said the other.

"That's because I lost my donkey in the river."

The donkey had lost its footing at a crossing. Tsering, running, had caught up to it. For a long time he'd trotted along the bank, encouraging the donkey, coaxing it, but the donkey was unable to change its circumstances, and he wasn't able to swim to where it was. Eventually it went under and disappeared. The mud on his robes was a result of all that.

The man with few teeth chewed his gums while Tsering spoke. Then he hawked spit and said, "Too bad."

He raised his chin toward the bowlegged man, who went to the tent, came back with a box of roasted barley meal, set it before Tsering, and said, "Eat."

The bowlegged man sat down on his shins. "I want to ask something," he said.

"Okay."

"I was in Derge," said the man. "I never go to Derge but I was in

Derge. It turned out that way on account of horses. I was in Derge and I was walking around and I heard a person say—not to me but to someone else—that the world isn't flat, it's round. That was a while ago, and since then we've wondered about it, because the person who said it was a lama."

"It's round," said Tsering. "The lama was correct."

"Thank you," said the man. "That settles it."

◆

THERE WERE HORSEMEN IN the west. At first their advance had the quality of a mirage, blurred out of focus by distance and sun. They rode in a phalanx, carrying flintlocks. There were twenty or more, at an unhurried pace. The grass was so tall that their stallions peeled through it by dint of chest girth before trampling it beneath their hooves. Scarves had been woven into their braided tails, and tassels had been hung from their throats. The chieftain wore a rifle on his back. He dismounted, folded his hands, nodded, and said, "As a man in robes, you're safe here."

He gave his name: Lozang Palden. There was a sheath knife at his waist, and an amulet box against his chest. His hair was tied in two loose topknots. He represented seven hundred families, he said, and led four clans and eighteen headmen. They, in turn, led eighty officials. His people were enjoying a season of good grass. They were at their leisure currently. In the neighboring district there was trouble with horse thieves, but for the moment he wasn't contending with that. He'd come, he said, to offer guidance to a traveler. His uncle, he said, was Shenga Rinpoche, who at first hadn't curried much favor in the monastic world, but was now so highly regarded that the ruler of Derge had ordered Shenga's commentaries carved into stone at Palpung.

Rugs were set out. All dismounted. Lozang Palden sat cross-legged for tea. "My uncle Shenga," he said, "was once like me. A man from a family of chieftains, not a monk. In fact, Uncle Shenga was a horse rustler. This is something we don't do anymore. I've forbidden it due to the trouble it causes, but in Uncle Shenga's time, raids were how it was, and Uncle Shenga participated. One time they rustled up horses and made their getaway, but a mare who was pregnant was slowing them down. Uncle Shenga got to where he'd had enough and slashed the mare's belly open. The foal fell out, and the mare started licking it. You know how they do that. Lick them into life. Lick them until they get on their feet. The mare and the foal died, which was too much for Uncle Shenga. He fell apart then and there and the Buddha grabbed him."

❖

THERE WERE NO TREES in the highlands. The nomads used an impenetrable dialect. The monastery—a large felt tent surrounded by smaller tents—was not much more than a weathered encampment. Its main tent had been divided in two. On one side the monks read aloud and debated, on the other they assembled for prayers and teachings. Their kitchen tent was full of smoke.

They were taking tea—Tsering and the abbot—in the abbot's tent. His bed was a mat and, because butter was scarce, he limited his use of lamps. "I sit in the dark," said the abbot. "We save our butter for the altar. We don't mix butter into our tea. We pour our tea and put butter on top. That way we can blow it aside before we drink. Eventually it arrives at the bottom of the cup. When we pour again, there's butter for another serving. We have the habits of scarcity here. Our monks are the kind who don't mind it that way. The ones who don't like it leave."

The abbot didn't have much of a beard. It was more like a crop of scraggly white strands, which he picked at and pulled on while he spoke.

"We have few visitors," he said. "The country, frankly, is beset by bandits. Not to mention that with snow in winter it's just about impossible to go anywhere."

The abbot massaged his eyes. "I'm as good as blind," he said. "Everything is blurry. But at least I don't see hairs anymore."

"Hairs?"

"A man like me, whose eyes are tricking him, will see hairs on a bowl, and try to pick them off. Another man, whose eyes are good, will wonder what the first man is doing. One sees hairs, the other doesn't. Those are the hairs I'm talking about."

The abbot sipped his tea. "My brother's a doctor," he said. "I told him I see hairs. He said no, they just look like hairs. What it was, what caused it, my eyeballs were changing. There were places in my eyeballs where fibers were growing. One part of my eye see-ing another part of my eye. But like I said, I don't see these fibers anymore, even though, according to my brother, they're still there. They didn't heal. They didn't disappear. I just don't see them."

"I don't see how that can be."

"The mind just decides to ignore them," said the abbot.

◆

HE'D WALKED ALL MORNING without seeing anyone, or any sign of anything human. He had seen, though, a flock of wild sheep, and a trio of gazelles. Now, at noon, he found an antelope in a leg trap. The hoof and lower shank of her right foreleg were underground. She was poised over it, weight forward. Maybe she'd been standing like that all morning, he thought, or overnight, or even longer, standing so that the points of the trap didn't pierce her flesh.

Tsering didn't move, and neither did the antelope. Instead she stared down her muzzle at him. Her ears were up, her head lowered. She had her forelegs pinned together, locked for balance, and her rear legs splayed. To make matters worse, she was pestered by flies, about which she could do nothing but toss her head. She did so in between staring at him.

In the middle of the afternoon, four hunters came on horseback. The antelope knew of their approach before he did. She turned her head but was otherwise motionless. The hunters dismounted at an ample distance. One walked toward Tsering with his palms pressed together, then stopped and ducked his head. "I'll come to you," called Tsering.

They sat down. "At first we thought you were a spirit," said the hunter. "But when we got closer, you started to look real. Are you?" he asked. "You seem like it."

"Yes."

The hunter smiled. "Hah," he said.

He turned and looked at the antelope. "How often do you check traps?" Tsering asked.

"This time of year whenever we get to it."

The hunter stood to get a better view of the antelope. Then he sat again and said, "A lot of snow this year. Our herds are down."

He pointed over his shoulder at the other hunters. "All of them over-slaughtered for winter," he said.

He looked Tsering in the eye. "They like to check traps," he said, "but we'd be better off if they stayed back and milked."

He had a pistol, he said. The problem, though, was a shortage of lead. Yes, he could dig out the bullet after shooting, but it would end up deformed and take effort to reuse. With that in mind, they'd gather rocks. Rocks were at hand and would work just fine. They could use small rocks until the antelope was down. Then, with large rocks, up close, they could smash in her head.

◆

THE BACK OF THE ferryman's coat was pocked with burn marks. His earflaps were down, and his collar was up. The ferry he operated—for the moment docked—had a wooden horse head mounted on its prow. It was fissured and cracked from years of freeze and thaw.

To the north the river made a bend between slopes. To the south it ran in ribbons and channels. A nearby gravel bar bore low, sturdy willows. Much closer, two donkeys stood motionless in a corral. At the moment the ferryman was nursing a fire. There was a clay pot beside his leg.

Tsering waited. It was soon apparent that the ferryman was drinking beer. "I was a monk, too," he said, "but I quit when I was twelve."

"Why?"

"I didn't like it."

His clay pot had a pebble beneath it and sat crooked. Noticing this, the ferryman lifted his pot and brushed the pebble aside. "I got beaten by my teachers," he said. "We all did, but I was a bad student, so it was worse."

"I see."

"I couldn't take it," explained the ferryman. "My mother said, Very well, then, if it's that bad, come home."

He drank from his pot. "I was lucky," he said. "She took me back."

With a stick he drew his fire together. He prodded at the coals and coaxed the flames higher. He pushed the end of his stick into embers, then took it out and poked the cold ground. "Have you been to Gyantse?" he asked.

"No."

"Lhasa?"

"No."

"Have you seen the rope that runs between them?"

"No."

"Well, it's there. Strung from poles."

"Why?"

"That's what I want to know," said the ferryman.

◆

IN MINYAK THE CHIEFTAIN insisted on protecting him from bandits. Tsering was to take along four horsemen, armed. Solo travel, said the chieftain, was ill-advised. It was true, he said, that he wasn't in a position to tell a traveler what to do, but nevertheless Tsering shouldn't be taken aback or surprised if four of the chieftain's men were in shouting distance until he passed from the chieftain's territory.

They rode on a ridgetop. On the second day, they came to a road, and coming along it was a party of nobles. Some held umbrellas over their heads. Some had attendants who held umbrellas for them. Two of the nobles rode in sedan chairs, well off the ground on four-man litters. The party included laden yaks and mules, driven along by handlers downwind, so that the dust they kicked up wouldn't land on the nobles. "They've been to the races," said one of the horsemen, "and now they're on their way to the hot springs."

The top part of this horseman's near ear was missing. It had a ragged edge, having healed roughly. He looked to be sixteen or so. Some of the threads in his sweater had come loose. "The two in the chairs," he said, "got married a few days ago. Afterward they had a party at the palace. His family's palace; she's from Shigatse. When the party was over they went to the races. Two days at the races, now on to the hot springs."

The nobles halted. The litter bearers set down the sedan chairs. The new bride and bridegroom stepped out with assistance. The groom brushed the dust from his clothes. Attendants removed the bride's headdress carefully. "You see," said the horseman, "they're away from the races. They're not going to see anyone who makes any difference. Not out here in the middle of nowhere. Because of that she's decided not to wear it. There's no one around, so she doesn't have to."

"The groom's brother is a lama," the horseman continued. "People came from all over for his enthronement. The line was so long it left the monastery grounds. That was two years ago. The last I heard, he was making the rounds, visiting people in Lhasa."

At this point the horseman must have thought better of talking so much. Flustered a little, he patted his mount. Then, lowering his head, he said to Tsering, "I thought you might like to know about them, to better understand the territory."

TSERING CAME ACROSS A pair of Europeans. They were a married couple with Nepalese porters. They had one tent for sleeping, one for eating, one for work on photographs, and one for offering medical treatment. As for their purpose, it wasn't specific. They were making an open-ended foray. They hoped to travel as far as Ladakh but had no itinerary, schedule, or mission. They had a table set out, and four chairs, and an interpreter. Both the man and the woman smoked tobacco continuously. The man sat sideways, one leg over the other. He had a dense, dark beard and dark hair on his arms. The woman, windburned, wore a broad-brimmed hat. Her lips were chapped. One of her arms, bandaged, was suspended in a sling. For three days now, they'd been camped, she said, collecting themselves and updating their notes, conducting interviews and making inquiries, taking advantage of sun, grass, and water, shooting photographs and gathering specimens. They were interested in plants. They'd plucked up dozens, roots and all, and were taking them home to add to a botanical collection.

On the table, beside their teapot, sat a bowl of dried apricots. Occasionally one of them would push the bowl toward Tsering, at which point the interpreter would encourage him to eat.

The interpreter now said, "I'm to tell you that, where they live, some people believe lamas can levitate."

"I've never seen that," said Tsering.

"They've heard that lamas can, by meditating, melt the snow underneath them."

"That I have seen," said Tsering.

"They've heard that lamas are clairvoyant, and that they can fly, walk on water, walk through walls, disappear—things like that."

"I haven't seen any of that."

"They've heard that some lamas are reincarnations of other lamas."

"Some people believe that to be true."

◆

FROM THE MONASTERY IN Minyak he sent a message home. The following month, his father came to see him. He had a stiff gait now, and walked as if his feet hurt. His back was crooked, his nose was bent. His hair had thinned, and he no longer wore a mustache. He'd been to Ladakh twice, he said, since the last time he'd seen Tsering. Both had been successful journeys. In Horkhok, though, he'd been beaten and robbed. They'd taken everything. There was nothing he could do about it. The weather was cold, and smallpox was rampant. For a month he was shunned wherever he went. In every village they'd demanded a wide berth. He'd been turned away with guns and swords. It was said that in Lhasa they were dying in droves. Other travelers delivered bad reports, always in loud voices from afar.

Crossing Sok Pass, he'd gone snow-blind. For a day and a half, he couldn't open his eyes. One good thing: he was more devout now. When he was younger he'd thought he would live forever; there was no reason to worry about aging and death. He could think about things like that in the future. Now, though, he knew what the Buddha meant. Why hadn't he given it deeper thought? Why had he lived as if the truth didn't matter? Here the truth was staring him in the face, yet he'd found a thousand ways to ignore it. Everything else had been more important. Everything else had gotten in the way. To fill the storehouse at home with goods, that had been the meaning of his life. Now here he was, old and worn out. He'd come to see Tsering carrying little, on foot. "Actually," he said, "I like traveling like this. Maybe in my next life I'll be a monk."

◆

TSERING LEFT MINYAK WITH a monk named Lobsang Khen-rab. On their third day, at midmorning, they came to a road. For as far as they could see in both directions, it ran across the plain unerringly. Wherever it was going, and wherever it had come from, this road had been laid without a waver or curve, without a turn or bend. Tire tracks had furrowed its dust. Dust frosted the grass beside it. In the breadth and silence, the road seemed out of place. It seemed like a gash. On the other hand, it was easy to walk on.

They took the road eastward. It dropped into a marsh. Its builders had inundated the marsh with rocks and laid the road on top of them. Farther on was a steel bridge. A stream passed beneath it on its way into the marsh. Herders had made camp there. They'd built fires. They'd left bones in the grass. The grass was matted where they'd staked out tents. Lobsang Khenrab found a spent rifle cartridge nearby. It had glinted, he said, because of the sun's angle—otherwise he wouldn't have seen it.

At midafternoon, Lobsang Khenrab pointed at a haze in the east. "I thought that might be a mirage," he said, "but now I think a lot of trucks are coming."

The haze grew larger. It became a billow, and then it became a wall. They left the road and watched. In the cab of each truck three men sat bunched. One opened a window and spit as he passed. Another tossed out an empty pack of cigarettes. All the trucks were the same color, green, with freight boxes covered by canvas over frames. Some of the men wore kerchiefs across their faces. Others had their windows down. One driver honked. One made a fist. Someone leaned out and yelled in Chinese.

The noise receded. The dust blew away. Lobsang Khenrab asked, "Do you want to know what that guy yelled?"

"What?"

"He said we should be intimate with a yak."

✦

TSERING TRAVELED WITH AN escort of Khampa horsemen. It snowed overnight, and was still snowing in the morning. The horses were led in single file in order to stamp out a path into the pass. On the far side there was less snow but the rocks were ice-rimed, and on top of the ice lay a dusting of frost.

They came to a place where prayer flags moldered. Some stopped up crevices. Some shuddered on their lines in gusts. Still others were heaped with rocks to hold them down. The majority of the prayer flags lay on the ground and were so far along in their disintegration as to be nearly unrecognizable.

In the afternoon they made camp and started fires. In the village nearby were Chinese soldiers. They were weaponless and gaunt, and kept their hands in their pockets and their collars turned up. Almost all were boys and, in manner, aimless. Some wandered in groups, talking among themselves. One was so windburned that his cheeks had cracked open, and because he'd scratched at them, they were purple and inflamed.

There was a shrine in the village. Snow had caved it in on one side; scaffolding had been erected and men were repairing it. Nearby, beneath a canopy, women worked churns. When the soldier with the cracked cheeks drew near, a woman came out and gave him a lump of butter. He didn't know what to do with it. He stood there with it cupped in his hands. He wore a greatcoat against the cold. It had red stars on its lapels, two on each side. It bunched at his armpits and hampered his movement. As thin as he was, it strained across his chest.

The woman pantomimed: rub your hands together and smear the butter on your face. Then she put a hand on his head and patted it, as if he was her child.

That night one of the horsemen said to Tsering, "Someone told me you were born in Thaklung. Which I only bring up because down there in the village I heard they're having trouble not far from Thaklung, in Jyekundo. Trouble with Chinese soldiers."

◆

HE WALKED FOR THE most part, but then he bought a donkey with a half-decent attitude, and rode it for the last three days of his journey, and when he came into the yard in front of the storehouse dismounted and said to his brother, Sonam, "It's like I told you. Here I am with a fresh donkey to replace the old one."

Sonam was married. He had three children. They were boys over thirteen but none yet twenty. One was a monk. Another had gone to Lhasa. The oldest one rode with rebels—they never saw him. Dorje was in Bhutan—like their father, a trader. Yangchen's husband had died, so she lived on the road now, herding horses for nobles.

The storehouse was empty but the herds were strong. Garlands of knucklebones hung in the kitchen. The stove had been outfitted with a fresh set of bellows. Tsering's mother leaned on a stick. She'd never cut her hair; it was pinned to her head. She still rode, but riding hurt her legs.

The river had run over the bank the year before. The year before that a sickness had come through and killed a number of children in the village. It was true, said Sonam, there were more Chinese soldiers. They'd fanned out. They were everywhere. They snooped. They had spies. You didn't want to say the wrong thing, said Sonam. You never knew who was listening.

Tsering was in the kitchen with his mother by the brazier. She spun wool there. The churn with the brass rings still hung on the wall. They were in the warmest place in the house. They were sitting between the stove and the brazier. "Tsering-la," said his mother. "They're waiting."

He didn't know what to say. She tapped him with her stick, abruptly. "Tsering-la," she said, "I call you Tsering-la and will always call you Tsering-la, but at the monastery they call you the sixth Norbu Rinpoche. I know you understand what I'm telling you, Tsering-la."

❖

THEY MADE HIM ABBOT. They called him Norbu Rinpoche now. Which he accepted.

Yet another boy was brought to see him. This one looked as nervous as the rest. He wore his new robe and belt and held a scarf across his hands. His hair had been cut, except for one strand. His parents had brought him, along with a gift of yak butter. "He can read, Abbot," said his mother. "He understands."

"Wait outside," answered Tsering.

When his parents left the room, the boy started fidgeting. He held the scarf stiffly, as if it were made of glass. "Do you want to be a monk?" Tsering asked.

"Yes, Abbot."

"I'll tell your parents we don't accept you. I won't say it's because of reservations you expressed."

No answer.

"Do you want to be a monk?"

"Yes, Abbot."

"I can't talk you out of it?"

"No, Abbot."

"Do you want to think about it?"

"No, Abbot."

"Is there something you want to talk about?"

"No, Abbot."

"Is there something you want to ask about?"

"No, Abbot."

"You want to be a monk?"

"Yes, Abbot."

"I never wanted to be a monk," said Tsering.

No answer.

"I ran away from here once. I was tired of studying."

No answer.

"It's hard," said Tsering. "Are you sure about this?"

"Yes, Abbot."

"All right, then," said Tsering. "I'll cut the last hair."

◆

A LAMA WITH A limp and a cane came to see him. His name was Dagpo Kyosang Rinpoche, and he perched on a bench, swaying as he spoke and gesturing dramatically. His attendant was content to stand by the door, blinking steadily as if dust were in his eyes, the keeper of his master's cane.

Dagpo Kyosang Rinpoche told Tsering that he'd passed his early years in Sakya. At seven he'd taken vows at a Sakya monastery. At twelve he'd moved to a monastery in Garje. Five years had passed there, and then he'd gone to Thaklung, where his education flagged. His efforts became sporadic. He couldn't hold the point of practice in mind. Feeling this way, he'd gone to see the abbot. He'd told the abbot that he'd lost motivation; the abbot had replied that once, he had too. When he said he regretted taking vows, the abbot had replied that a lot of monks did. Some broke rules. Some only acted devout. Some remained monastics mainly to eat, and some remained monastics out of habit and stasis. Many went through periods of low motivation. They had downturns of spirit and made progress in spurts. As far as returning to lay life, said the abbot, it wasn't really one or the other. Lay life had its own opportunities, and monastic life was wasted by many. A lot of monks, explained the abbot, were less disciplined than laypeople. "All of that," Dagpo Kyosang Rinpoche told Tsering, smiling, "was of invaluable help to me. You really were a great help to me."

"Me?"

"I was your disciple in your last life."

◆

HE HEARD FROM HIS sister Yangchen. She was currently in the employ of traveling nobles. Some of their horses had fallen ill and as a result the party was moving slowly. At the moment they were taking a hiatus in the high country three days north of the monastery.

Tsering went to see her. She didn't stand on ceremony with him. They walked among the horses, up into the hills. Eleven of the horses had gone ill from bad grass; a twelfth had gone ill because of bad water. Yangchen had been running this last horse hard for three days, with a view toward sweating out the infection, but so far this treatment had only left it listless.

Yangchen had a second husband. He'd gone ahead to make arrangements for the nobles. Her first husband had died of gangrene. Her new husband—he was not exactly her husband. Not in the formal sense. Not in the sense of family and household. He made offerings and said prayers. He prostrated daily. He could pluck a rock off the ground at full gallop. His way with horses was uncanny. He was direct in his approach to them and she never saw unkindness. He'd learned to speak Chinese fairly well by picking up phrases and seeking conversation. He coaxed Chinese soldiers to teach him enunciation. "My husband is a peaceful person," said Yangchen. "At night he likes to look at the stars and wonder about the universe. Aloud."

✦

FROM A DISTANCE THE persistent dropping in of vultures suggested a large animal, since that was what usually brought them in such numbers, but as it turned out they were feeding on human corpses. Each boy had been placed on his back with his head upslope and his arms spread. All were frozen, which didn't deter the vultures, who went about their feeding with cooperative efficiency, having arrayed themselves in rows alongside each corpse like guests at a table. They bobbed, paused, preened, and swallowed, contorting their necks and ruffling their feathers. Meanwhile, the dead boys—Chinese soldiers—wore no boots. Their coats were open. If they had once been associated with weapons, they weren't now. Nor was there kit of any kind—no packs, canteens, belts, knives. They'd been stripped of their equipment, laid out in a manner that made it easy to fleece their pockets, and left for the vultures.

Tsering went from corpse to corpse, which perturbed the vultures not in the least, angling himself to look into the faces of the dead. In all cases they looked stricken and astonished, as if they'd been in the midst of crying out at the moment time stopped for them.

✦

THE DISTRICT ADMINISTRATOR WORE a tunic buttoned at the throat, with the button showing between the points of his collar. He sat at a desk with a pen in his hand. His silver mustache was a narrow swath of bristles; otherwise his face looked polished. "Stay standing," he said, in Tibetan.

Tsering stayed standing.

"Abbot," the administrator said. "Your monastery is supporting reactionary bandits. Do you deny it?"

"Yes."

"You have associated yourself with enemies of the people. You have betrayed the unity of the Motherland. You support armed rebels and give them assistance. You spy on us and report to them. Do you deny this?"

"Yes."

"Buh," said the administrator. "Meanwhile, you live by exploiting the masses."

"I'm not aware of exploiting anyone."

"But you do," said the administrator. "Every morning you wake up to a full bowl of food. Where does it come from? What makes that possible? The same with your robe. Where does it come from? Who made it? Not you. You produce nothing. You are of no benefit to society. You spend your days chanting and banging cymbals and meditating, all of it on the backs of the Tibetan people, who've been duped into working on your behalf."

"That is one way of viewing it," said Tsering.

The administrator leaned toward him. "We know what's in your storerooms," he said. "Your lamps with jewels in them, your bowls lined with silver, your silver cups, your statues made of gold. Do you know where all of that comes from?" the administrator asked. "It comes from the sweat and tears of the people, who have nothing and are as poor as dirt. What has been normal for Tibetans for many centuries is to starve to death while lamas chant. That's over. The people have awakened to their exploitation. There's no future for lamas here. The people see you for what you are—a wolf in sheep's clothing."

◆

THERE WERE HUNDREDS OF people urgent to cross the river, but the three coracles on hand each carried only ten—ten plus the man who paddled against the current. He'd brought the coracles on the back of a dzo, he told Tsering, because at this time of year the river was in flood and no one should attempt to cross without a boat. He'd become a ferryman, he said, along with his sons; they'd been there for three days now, making constant crossings, and if and when the time came that no one needed ferrying, he and his sons would fight the Chinese. They were willing to fight to the death, he said, but on the other hand he didn't think they'd have to, because they wore protective amulets. As proof, the ferryman pulled a pendant through the neck of his chuba—a mani necklace that had rusted a little. "Please," he said. "Say prayers for us."

◆

THE WOMAN WHOSE DAUGHTER had died from a fever put a lump of frozen barley meal in her mouth, shut her eyes, and pulled her scarf against her ears. The girl had stopped breathing during the night and her corpse had stiffened in the cold. She lay to the woman's right with a shawl over her face; to the left the woman's other children lay wrapped in a yak skin. This early in the morning all was in silhouette. Beyond the woman, two men perched in the tent door; another stood next to them, pointing up the pass. The wind was trying to bring the tent down. The poles creaked and the canvas flapped. The tent was full of tired people. Some had come in during the night. Some were snow-blind and had rags over their eyes. Some were soldiers who'd retreated from Ralung. Their horses were outside, stamping against the cold.

Now the woman whose daughter had died took the barley meal from her mouth and divided it into portions. These she held in one hand while, with the other, she pulled back a corner of the yak skin under which her children were balled up like creatures in a burrow. She said something, and then she slipped three portions of barley meal under the flap of the yak skin one at a time. She held the flap for a while and, leaning, peered under it. After a while she let go and put the remaining barley meal in her mouth. Then, leaning the opposite direction, she made an adjustment to the shawl over her dead daughter's face. She smoothed a wrinkle from it and lined up its tassels. While she was doing this a soldier called out that he was familiar with the deities here and that, in his opinion, a fire should be built so that a tea offering might be made before they started up the pass. He would keep it going with butter if someone else could produce a flame. With the butter he was carrying he would build up the fire, then boil the tea and deliver supplications.

It had snowed overnight. The tent, having frozen, was difficult to pack. In full light now, two women broke up a tent pole and got a fire started in the lee of a boulder. Snow was melted over it. Tea was steeped. The soldier familiar with the local deities flung the tea in the four directions—flicked it off his fingertips—while pleading for protection. Then everything was packed except the corpse. "I can't carry her," called out the mother of the dead girl, with one child in her arms and two others by her legs. "I want to get her to Sekhar Gutok. A long way—a day and a half. I'm asking someone to take her on horseback. Anyone, if Sekhar Gutok is too far, I can leave my daughter near Druptso Pemaling. It's just that at Sekhar Gutok there are monks, and the monks will take care of my daughter the right way, in the best manner for her next life."

✦

TSERING AND A LAMA named Tsoknyi Rinpoche were sitting on boulders. Tsoknyi Rinpoche had one good eye; the other had rotated back into his head so that only the white showed. The white was no longer white, though; it had turned red, and resembled a bursting star. Tsoknyi Rinpoche had lost so much weight that his cheeks had caved in. Most of his teeth were gone, and the remaining ones were nubs. Chewing was a challenge for Tsoknyi Rinpoche; at the moment he was sipping from a bowl of nettle soup a monk had set before him. This monk, said Tsoknyi Rinpoche, had been helping him for months. He'd even carried him on his back like a porter. Without him Tsoknyi Rinpoche wouldn't have made it to the border. Frostbite had ruined Tsokyni Rinpoche's feet, and a lack of food had weakened him.

On the muddy ground nearby a horse was splayed, having foraged on rhododendrons. Two of its hooves were turned toward the sun. Flies buzzed around its muzzle. An observer might have thought it dead, until it snuffled. Beyond the horse stood a mildewed tent. Beside it a musk deer hung from poles, and beside the musk deer stood a Bhutanese soldier, berating the Tibetan man who'd killed it. The man didn't cower, though. Instead he urged his papers on the soldier, who took them angrily and crumpled them in his fist. "First you put up a tent," he said, "then you let your horse run loose, then you poach a deer." He threw the crumpled papers on the ground. "Wipe your ass with them," he said.

The man picked up his papers and began to smooth them. "Don't be here tomorrow," warned the soldier. "I'll throw you in jail."

At this point Tsoknyi Rinpoche sipped his soup so loudly that the soldier turned and glared at him. "What are you looking at?" he asked.

"You," said Tsoknyi Rinpoche. "Also, the horse. Is there anything you can do for that horse?"

✦

IN BUMTHANG, TSERING SPRAINED his ankle in a bamboo forest. Unable to walk, he sat and waited. The next day a trio of monks came along. One went ahead and came back with a horse, but Tsering's foot swelled up in the stirrup. "I know a doctor," said the monk who'd brought the horse. "We have to get to Jakar to see him, though. The rest of today, and all day tomorrow."

In Jakar they waited in the doctor's anteroom. It was evening and a lamp glowed yellow against the ceiling. "The way it works," the monk explained, "is that electricity goes to that switch on the wall, and from the switch, when it's on, from there to the lamp."

He got up, went to the switch, turned off the lamp, and then turned it on again. "Electricity travels to it in a wire from outside," he said. "Another wire goes from the switch to the lamp. That doesn't really explain it, though, not in the way you're asking about it."

"The lamp looks like glass."

"It is glass. But inside there's a wire."

The doctor spoke Dzongkha. The monk interpreted. The doctor could do nothing in the medical sense, but he could, and did, suggest a course of action. Tsering could put his right foot in the stirrup as he normally would, but put his left foot across the front of the saddle. The resulting instability would be mitigated by the monk, who would walk alongside him supporting his knee. In this manner, said the doctor, Tsering could ride while the swelling subsided. If Rinpoche could ride in the advised posture, then in Thimphu he would come across pain medicine. On the other hand, he could stay and rest in Jakar. He could stay in the home of the doctor's aunt and wait for his ankle to get better.

The doctor's aunt fed him buckwheat noodles. He sat on a chair in her kitchen with his foot resting on a stool padded with wool. "Your family, Rinpoche," she said. "What happened? Where are they?"

"I don't know," said Tsering. "I had to leave quickly."

✦

Tsering was in a jeep with three monks. The four of them were jammed into the rear seat together. In the front was a driver who wore a turban, and an Indian soldier with a shiny head. The jeep bumped through holes as it careened downhill. The road kept twisting; in each curve, Tsering leaned. There was a truck in front of them, and in the back of it a throng of people braced through every turn. They fell against each other, clutching at whoever was near. The truck spewed fumes and raised dust off the road. The jeep driver laid on his horn incessantly, but the truck stayed in front of them until they came down onto a plain, at which point the jeep driver passed it immediately. To no purpose, it seemed, because there were always more trucks.

They stopped where there were a lot of soldiers. The driver went for cans of gas. There was a stream nearby but it was slow, warm, and muddy. The plain stretched out in all directions, flat. Tsering and the others waited in the nearest shade. Now that there was no jeep noise, they talked. One monk had taught at Sera in the sutra college; the other two were Ganden monks. All three had abandoned their robes, trading them for thin white clothing. The Sera teacher had done so just that morning after seeing a doctor at the border crossing. He had heat rash, so no robes anymore, just the white clothes, he said matter-of-factly. Then there was the powder the doctor dusted him with—white too, and coating his face. He hadn't wanted to wear that either, but he had to admit that, since morning, he felt better in the physical sense. He couldn't see himself, of course, but he knew how he felt inwardly. Somehow he'd become a hungry ghost.

✦

In the office a fan spun noiselessly overhead. The Englishman spoke Tibetan fluently. He said he'd encountered it while stationed at Spiti, and thereafter had studied it in France. He was interested, now, in the structure of Tibetan Buddhism. As tragic as recent events were, he said, they were fortuitous for academics like him, joined as he was to a university in England. It had made it possible to seek answers to questions among figures in the diaspora community; it had broadened the scope and depth of his field. With a view toward advancing the knowledge base further, he'd been interviewing lamas from the major sects and monasteries, primarily in Dharamsala, where he'd learned Tsering was in Assam. And as for that, he said, he was sorry to find conditions in this refugee camp so appalling. Earlier, while tracking Tsering down, he'd poked his head into a number of tents, and had seen people suffering from heat prostration and what looked to him like malaria and dengue. This might have shocked him, he said, if he hadn't himself endured similar conditions in a camp for war prisoners.

The Englishman had two water bottles on his belt. He gave one to Tsering—"Keep it," he said. Next he took from his case a bag of peanuts and a bag of dates. "Keep those too," he added.

He set the bags on the table. Tsering asked him what he meant by the structure of Tibetan Buddhism. "This," said the Englishman. "There's an edifice of knowledge that fits together for you. Schools of thought that relate to each other. We haven't sorted that yet. We haven't put it together, so currently we have an incomplete picture and don't know how to organize it for study. You know," he said, "I've met a number of extraordinary lamas who don't have a grasp of global geography. Which I hope doesn't sound disrespectful to you. It's just that more than one has been surprised to learn that Europe and America aren't connected, for example— that they're separated by thousands of miles. An entire ocean lies between them. I'm sure you see what I'm getting at here. It's not their fault—they just don't have the picture. They can't see continents and countries in their heads. This is what I mean about us when it comes to the structure of Tibetan Buddhism. We're just like that. Lost."

◆

A GERMAN CAME, AND then a Belgian, another Englishman, and finally two Americans, Professor White and Professor Emerson. Professor White spoke Tibetan like an aristocrat, having learned it from a Swiss man who'd lived in Lhasa. Professor Emerson's parents had been missionaries in Amdo. For many years, he'd wandered in Tibet. Now he was a Buddhist who'd taken lay vows. For his current research, he'd based himself in Kalimpong. "Call me Jim," he said.

Professor White smiled. His own life was not as interesting, he confessed. There was not much to say about it, other than that, while attending college, he'd discovered he had an interest in Tibet. He too was based in Kalimpong, but for purposes of his research traveled a lot—to Sikkim, to Nepal, to other places in India. "Which brings me to my point," he said. "Jim holds down my home in Kalimpong. He has the first floor. When I come to Kalimpong I use the third. That, Rinpoche, leaves the second, which would certainly be more comfortable than here."

◆

NEAR KALIMPONG THERE WERE flowers on the hillsides. The air was clean. There were mountains to the north. Tsering watched Jim go about his days. He was a scholar and spent a lot of time reading. In the morning he ate fruit and yogurt, and in the late afternoon, vegetables with brown rice. For long stretches of time he was preoccupied and silent, with the look of someone lost in thought. He read in the kitchen while he waited for water to boil. He read while tea steeped. He had a wicker chair on his veranda, beside it a table piled with journals. He paced a lot with a book in his hands. He put markers in his books and wrote in their margins. He left books open, face down, on his couch. He took them out of bookcases and didn't put them back. He made stacks out of books on side tables and shelves. He had a lamp made especially for reading. He could raise or lower it. It swiveled.

Jim had a desk with a typewriter on it. Nearby was a photo of his wife and daughter. He kept a ledger on his desk, files, a notebook, a dish of anise seeds, and an incense burner. He had chairs in his living room for interviews, and a tape recorder on an adjacent table. For conversation with friends and colleagues, Jim used the veranda, with its view of far hills.

"Rinpoche," Jim said one day, "if it can be arranged, if I can arrange it, would you come to the United States?"

"No," answered Tsering. "I have no money."

"I'll start over," said Jim. "What I meant to say was, would you consider taking a position in the Department of Far Eastern Studies at my university in the United States?"

"No," said Tsering. "I don't speak English."

"I'm at the University of Washington in the city of Seattle," said Jim, "where we've recently acquired a lot of new Tibetan manuscripts. My department is in the process of translating them, but, having run into difficulties, sent me here to find help."

"I see," said Tsering.

"Yes," said Jim. "We want good translations. Bad ones do more harm than good."

◆

ON THE AIRPLANE TSERING asked how flying was possible. Most people thought it was because airplane wings are curved, answered Jim, but as far as he was concerned, that didn't make sense. For one, there were airplanes with flat wings, and for two, airplanes could fly upside down. As for the sun, it was setting at a very slow pace because they were flying toward it. Finally, that they didn't appear to be flying at the announced speed of 850 kilometers every hour, but instead more slowly, was an illusion that had to do with distance, in this case the distance from the airplane to the ground. Not something Jim understood.

Time was different in different places. The earth had been divided into zones. There was a phenomenon called jet lag which they would probably experience: groggy during the day, awake at night, headaches out of nowhere. Entirely normal. What would not be normal was everything else. When people saw a lama in robes they were going to stare. Few would know what to make of him.

There were hardly any Buddhists in America, said Jim. Ninety-nine out of a hundred people weren't Buddhists. When Jim told Americans he was a Buddhist, most thought it strange. Sometimes they brought up reincarnation, which almost no one believed in. Most of the religious people believed in an afterlife instead. You lived, you died, and then you went on to an eternal afterlife. Basically, if you were a good person you went on to a good afterlife, but otherwise your afterlife was bad. Jim used to wonder: why did people see that as more plausible than reincarnation? But then he'd come to realize they didn't. Plausibility didn't matter.

Not everyone was like this, Jim explained. A sizable number of people didn't believe in an afterlife any more than they believed in reincarnation. Many dismissed both as fantasies and illusions. In one regard these people were like Buddhists, because for them there was no such thing as a soul either.

"No evidence for the existence of a soul has been found," said Tsering. "But that doesn't mean the soul doesn't exist."

Jim didn't answer.

"The same can be said of reincarnation," said Tsering. "There's no evidence for it, but that doesn't mean it doesn't happen."

Time passed. Then Jim said that some people in the West believe their bodies, interred in the earth, will reemerge one day and be reanimated. They also believe that, after they die, their souls will dwell in heaven, but that eventually angels will bring their souls back to earth and place them inside their resurrected bodies, which will then be immortal. Not exactly reincarnation, said Jim, but close.

"Rinpoche," said Jim. "Speaking of evidence. Some lamas claim to remember past lives, or elements of past lives. I wonder if you do."

"No," said Tsering.

◆

AN AMERICAN BOTANIST, WHILE situated in Choni, had amassed a collection of block prints and manuscripts. Some of his manuscripts had been acquired by the University of Washington, and were stored, Jim said, in the basement of the building they were in, which otherwise was constituted primarily of classrooms. The paper, ink, and blocks used at Choni were of good quality, but on the other hand the manuscripts had sat unopened for three decades, and as a result their pages had stuck together. Through a process undertaken by the university, however, everything had now been successfully microfilmed. The originals were now in atmosphere-controlled storage, and the microfilm awaited scrutiny and analysis. The significance of the Choni collection had not yet been assessed because until now there was no one qualified to do that. "That," said Jim, "is one reason you're here."

They went into the basement. Jim unlocked a door and turned on a light. They were now in a room full of cabinets in rows. In each, said Jim, were texts acquired by the Department of Far Eastern Studies. He opened one, removed a manuscript, and for Tsering's benefit displayed one of its leaves. "From our collection of the Peking edition of the *Kanjur* and *Tanjur*. They're reprints acquired from Otani University in Japan, where a set of originals are held."

◆

TSERING LIVED WITH STEVE and Dan near the university. On the ground floor of their house was a front room, a dining room, a kitchen, a bedroom, and a bathroom with a tub in it. Upstairs were two more bedrooms and a bathroom with a shower stall. Steve and Dan slept in the upstairs bedrooms, but during the day one or the other was always on the ground floor.

They came and went. When one went, though, the other stayed. The one who stayed studied at the dining room table. Sometimes, in the evening, other students came. They sat at the table reading Tibetan aloud. They were serious about it, but when not studying, not serious. At the beginning, coming through the door, taking their coats off, sitting down, they were easy about things, and then again at the end, packing up their books, speaking in English, they were easy and light, but in between they didn't laugh or speak off-subject. Plus, Tsering knew, they were aware of his presence, aware of him in the front room, aware of him in hearing distance, though none of them peeked in at him, only Steve or Dan did that. Steve or Dan brought tea even though he didn't ask for it. Steve or Dan came into the front room regularly but didn't sit down, just brought the cup of tea on a tray and set it down where he could reach it and backed away until they were out of the room and could return to the others studying together at the dining room table in soft voices but intensely.

One night Steve brought with him into the front room a big person with a full beard and thick-lensed glasses. "Pardon me, Rinpoche," he said. "I would like to introduce my good friend Wynn. He's fluent in Tibetan. He's one of those people who learns languages easily. If you need an interpreter, Wynn can do it."

"Jim interprets," answered Tsering.

"Rinpoche," said Wynn. "If ever Jim—Professor Emerson—is unavailable, I can fill in for him. Just tell Steve. Steve or Dan. Tell them and I'll make myself available."

◆

JIM CAME EVERY WEEKDAY morning. He and Tsering drank tea and ate breakfast. After that they walked to Thomson Hall. The street that led to campus had trees down the middle of it, and on campus the paths wound around the buildings, passing through squares along the way.

In Jim's office, Tsering examined manuscripts. Jim asked questions and wrote in a notebook. In a nearby room was a microfilm machine. Jim ran it from the side while Tsering sat in front of its screen. At midmorning they drank tea again and at noon they ate lunch.

Outside Thomson Hall was a square called The Quad. Its paths were geometrical. The buildings around it mirrored each other. "That one," said Jim, "used to be a law school, so those figures on it represent jurists. Why are there figures like that on buildings? Those are what we call in English 'gargoyles.' People or animals or imaginary animals or magical figures we put on buildings. The practical reason is to move water away, but also, I guess, to thwart evil spirits. They put them on churches. On the ledges and the rooftops. These buildings here have them, and they were built in this century. Gargoyles," said Jim. "Wrathful guardians."

◆

THE WEATHER CHANGED. IT didn't rain all the time now. With Wynn, Tsering took a walk through a park. On its far side were streets full of shops. One sold shoes. Nothing but shoes. Wynn stopped in front of it to look in the window, then said, "Rinpoche, let's go inside."

They went in. For a while Wynn looked at shoes. Then a tradesman measured Tsering's feet, went away, and returned with a box. He put new shoes on Tsering's feet, tightened their laces, pressed their toes, squeezed their heels. "He wants you to walk around in them," said Wynn. Tsering did. "Are they comfortable?" Wynn asked.

The tradesman put Tsering's sandals in the box and put the box in a bag. Wynn carried it. They went into the park and sat on a bench. Nearby some people played catch with a flying disk. It flew their way; Wynn stood and threw it back. The next time it came, a girl ran toward them for it. The closer she got, the slower she ran. When the gap was ten steps, she stopped and pointed at the disk. When the gap was five steps, she bent at the waist. She was young and wore a cap and a sweater. Tsering pulled his new shoes back, and the girl, stretching her arm as far as she could, retrieved the disk.

He watched her go. She backed away, still looking at the ground, then turned and threw the disk, hard.

A pang hit Tsering. He remembered Yangchen in the pasture, leaning over the herd dog, Duga, with the wind blowing her hair around, her belt tightly knotted, and a scar on her face from having been gored by a yak.

◆

HE KNEW HIS WAY now. He could walk without Wynn. One day he walked through the park and past the shoe shop. Soon there were no more shops, just houses. It was hot out and his knees hurt, so he sat on someone's lawn. I'm a lama, he thought. Maybe the owner will see me as an insult to his religious beliefs, or as a vagrant or a madman. He could be looking out the little peephole in his door right now feeling concerned about me. I don't own this lawn but I'm sitting on it anyway. It wouldn't be wrong for him to come out here and say, Excuse me, I'm sorry, you have to leave, this is my property, and also, it's bad for our grass for you to be sitting on it. It wouldn't be wrong, but maybe he would hesitate to do it because of the impression it might make, not on me but on him, on himself; maybe he sees himself as someone who doesn't object to a stranger on his lawn and wants to keep that self-image intact. Maybe he honors the tradition of kindness to strangers and has heard tales of strangers who turned out to be deities; maybe he would like his request that I leave to sound, in his own ears, not mean, not angry. Maybe he thinks it better just to wait for me to leave—maybe that's his solution.

Tsering stood to leave and at the same moment the front door of the house opened about halfway so that he could see, assessing him in a guarded way, a boy maybe ten years of age. I shouldn't brush the grass off my robe, he thought. That might be rude.

Another boy appeared in the door now, this one bigger. He pushed it open all the way and the two boys stepped onto the porch enthusiastically. "Hey!" said the bigger one. "Kung fu!"

The smaller one crouched and displayed his fists. "Hah!" he said. "Ah so! Chop suey!"

✦

HE LIVED NOW WITH Wynn in an apartment building. Wynn taught him English names for things. He learned to make oatmeal. He made pancakes by mixing powder with water and pouring it on heated oil. He ate the pancakes with peanut butter. He used the rice steamer, the electric fryer, the toaster, the oven, the stove-top, the washing machine, the dryer, and the vacuum cleaner. He turned the heat up or down, the fan on or off in the bathroom and in the stove hood, he scrubbed the shower stall, he scrubbed the toilet and the sinks. He dusted. He swept. He cleaned the windows, which was easy because the apartment had few windows, just two plus a glass sliding door. Beyond the sliding door were a rough lawn, shrubs, trees, squirrels, birds, and a little place to sit on an aluminum chair—he had to be careful about the chair; he was heavy—tucked up under an eave, which was the same for everyone who lived in a first-floor apartment here, everyone had an eave to sit under where they could look out over the same lawn, trees, and shrubs. Which was also where they kept things they didn't want to keep indoors, under the eave because it rained so much, not hard, just steadily, a lot of times all night, sometimes all day and all night without stopping. It was damp all the time, everything felt damp, the wood buildings rotted, the eaves rotted, the moss grew, not very many people wanted to sit outside under eaves but some did, a few, some of the time. Someone would sit under an eave to smoke a cigarette or to watch their pet dog sniff out a place to lift its leg. Sometimes someone sat there drinking something or reading a book. Sometimes people tended flowers in pots—one person grew tomatoes in a barrel—which reminded Tsering of bringing Samten's flowers in at dusk every night.

✦

THERE WAS AN ARTICLE about Tsering in the campus newspaper that said he was "a notable presence on campus," with a picture of him beside a tree in The Quad. It had made for interest, said Jim, and had left students curious. Jim asked Tsering if he would meet with them, which he did now every Wednesday at three-thirty in a lounge. The ones who spoke Tibetan asked questions in Tibetan, but if they didn't Wynn interpreted.

A pregnant woman attended diligently. One afternoon she said in Tibetan that she did not want Rinpoche to think she was being disrespectful but she had to get up and leave.

She struggled to rise from where she sat on a sofa. Another woman rose and pulled her up. The other woman slipped into her jacket, picked up her book bag and the pregnant woman's book bag, then spoke to Wynn in English. "She's going to accompany her," Wynn explained. "She's leaving too."

"Excuse me, Rinpoche," said the pregnant woman. "It's very clear to me right now that this little girl wants out, so I have to leave—sorry."

When the question-and-answer hour was over, Tsering asked Wynn, "How does she know it's a girl?"

"Sound waves," said Wynn. "They send sound waves through someone's body to get a picture of what's inside."

❖

A PRIEST CAME TO see him. He wore a belted frock, a clerical collar, and shoes meant for running. He spoke Tibetan, having learned it while teaching at St. Joseph's College in Darjeeling. He was a philologist specializing in classical Buddhist languages, and a translator of canonical texts.

The priest said he was thirty-seven and in his fifth year of priesthood. He was a Jesuit, which he felt might be wrong for him. Lately he felt he was meant to be a Trappist—a monastic monk, given to silence. He saw a psychiatrist regularly, he said, which he knew to be unusual for a priest. The reason was, he suffered from depression.

Every morning he awoke without enthusiasm. Sometimes it was so bad he stayed in bed. He put a pillow over his head to block out the light and prayed he'd fall asleep again.

Why was he divulging this? Because he needed direction. In Darjeeling he'd known Westerners who, instead of going to a psychiatrist or a priest, had gone to a lama to discuss their lives, so now he was doing that too.

His psychiatrist's supposition, explained the priest, was that his depression resulted from engaging in a charade: he was posing as an avatar of sanctity, above reproach and free of vicissitudes. The psychiatrist believed that left him with two options: become more honest in how he presented himself or leave the priesthood. The former posed problems, though, since it meant that, in presenting himself honestly, he might end up at odds with what was needed from a priest; the latter posed problems too, because it meant changing his path in life. But all of that was really neither here nor there, said the priest, because he didn't share his psychiatrist's supposition or analysis. From inside his own being—from inside his depression—it seemed to the priest that the source of his despair was the reality of his death.

"It's supposed to be that, for me," he said, "there's absolute certainty death is not the end—that death is the gateway to eternal life in Christ. I'm meant to be an exemplar of that certainty. My role, as a priest, is to affirm and embody it. But in fact death frightens me and makes me sad."

"So," said Tsering, "you would have to know one hundred percent that there's such a thing as eternal life to be at peace with death?"

"Yes."

"If you had this certainty and were at peace with death, would that end your depression?"

"It seems like that in my head, yes."

"But at the moment such certainty isn't possible for you."

"No."

"So this could be temporary. This could be a phase in which your faith has become lesser."

"No," said the priest. "I've always had doubt. Doubting isn't new for me. It's depression that's new. I think it's because I'm thirty-seven and my life's half over. Or almost half over."

"Maybe," said Tsering,

"Personally I think even the Pope has doubts."

"The Pope doubts and believes at the same time?"

"Yes."

"But is not depressed."

"There are no reports of it," said the priest.

"So it's possible to be like that."

"It appears so, yes. But I'm not the Pope."

"It's possible," said Tsering, "for him but not for you."

"To doubt and believe both and not be depressed?" asked the priest. "That doesn't seem possible for me right now, no."

"So what will you do?"

"I don't know. That's why I'm talking to people."

"What can I say that will help you solve this problem?" Tsering asked. "I can't say death doesn't occur. I can't say that, after death, eternal life occurs. I also can't say that, after death, eternal life doesn't occur. That death occurs is a fact. That eternal life occurs is a belief. By definition, all beliefs imply doubt. If there was no doubt, there would be no belief. This is because if there's no doubt, fact has been established. What was once a belief has now become a fact. Only facts abolish doubt, so if you must believe, you must accept doubt. Certainly you must accept death, just as you must accept any other fact.

"If your belief in eternal life doesn't bring you peace about death, that doesn't mean dispense with the belief. It doesn't even mean you should work to make it stronger. It means accept death without conditions. Don't say death is only acceptable if it is followed by eternal life. Let belief be belief. Accept death with no conditions."

◆

A TIBETAN NAMED JIGME SANGAY wrote a letter to Tsering. Like Tsering, he was attached to an American university. Like Tsering, he'd come to America on a grant. Recently he'd been asked to write a history of Tibet. Jigme Sangay had contacts in India who were assisting him with this, but mail was slow, phone connections were unreliable, and the telegraph was only good for brief messages. For these reasons he'd decided to travel to India, and could arrange matters such that he flew through Seattle if Tsering would grant him an audience.

It was summer. Jigme Sangay wore a short-sleeved shirt. He was a layperson from Garje. At first, in India, he was in a camp at Samari; after that he was transferred to Bhalukpong. He knew Hindi, and had worked as a translator for the government-in-exile, and while living in Dharamsala acquired English, and rose in the ranks of the Department of Religion and Culture. It was through his contacts in the international Tibetology community that Jigme Sangay had come to Massachusetts, and it was in Massachusetts that he'd been asked to write a Tibetan history. Other than writing, he did a lot of teaching. He was a professor, he said. His students read enough Sanskrit to engage texts at a rudimentary level, but beyond that he parsed things for them. In fact, he spent most of his time as a language teacher. Even so, often he couldn't find the right word. "Take 'sunyata,'" he said, "which is an obvious one. The English correlate, as it stands, is 'emptiness,' but if I use 'emptiness' they think 'nothingness.' Like an empty glass—a glass holding nothing. An empty suitcase or an empty cupboard. The result is that I don't want to use the word 'emptiness,' but when I reach for another word, it isn't there." Jigme Sangay shrugged. "How long have you been here?" he asked.

"A long time now."

"Sometimes," said Jigme Sangay, "I feel like I'm dreaming."

"Me too," said Tsering.

◆

JIM SAID THERE WERE two people interested in meeting Tsering, each a religious leader. One was a priest, the other a rabbi.

Jim's idea was for the three of them to talk. The priest and the rabbi would ask Tsering questions; if Tsering wanted, he could ask questions back. All of this would happen in a room on campus where students could listen. Jim would translate.

They convened. Jim made an opening statement. He said that the religions represented by the priest and the rabbi had certain things in common. For both, there was a God, and for both there was a soul, and for both the soul and God were central. In Buddhism, Jim said, there might be a God and there might be a soul, but these weren't considered the most important questions. The important questions were—well, Jim couldn't say.

The priest said it was hard for him to understand how God and the soul could not be important questions. The rabbi said he had respect for Buddhism's investigation into the nature of reality. He said that the Buddhist emphasis on happiness made sense, too. He wondered if it wasn't possible, though, to pursue a clear view of reality, and to pursue happiness, and at the same time believe in God and in a soul.

Tsering said, "Yes. There is no contradiction between the aspirations of Buddhism and belief in God and soul. Those beliefs can be held while one pursues a Buddhist practice."

On they went. After some time the question came up: What about Buddhism and reincarnation? "I am supposedly the sixth in a line of reincarnated lamas," said Tsering. "I am supposedly the sixth Norbu Rinpoche. I say 'supposedly,' because, one, nobody really knows what is meant by 'reincarnation,' and two, even if we did know what it meant we could not say anything conclusive about it. Reincarnation, I think, is like 'God' and 'soul.' None of them are matters definitively settled. If a Buddhist wishes to believe there is such a thing as reincarnation, a Buddhist is welcome to do exactly that. But Buddhism is not a religion with a belief system. Beliefs are a separate matter."

◆

TSERING WENT TO ANSWER questions at a dharma center in a forest. They had a chair for him at the front of the room, and one for Wynn, but Wynn stood. Wynn wore a suit and tie, and had groomed his beard for the occasion. Facing the audience, he took the first question. "What is the Buddhist concept of 'No Self'?" he said to Tsering. Then he waited with his head canted, concentrating.

"That's hard," said Tsering. "First, we have bodies.

"Second, we have thoughts.

"Third, we have awareness. For example, awareness of our bodies or awareness of our thoughts.

"Fourth, we have sensations. We touch things, taste things.

"One kind of sensation is inward sensation. Pain, pleasure. Also, emotions. Emotions are sensations inside the body.

"Body, thought, awareness, sensation, perceptions—is there anything beyond these things that make a self?

"Is the self just one of these things?

"Is the self a gathering of these things?

"Can there be sensation but no body?

"Can there be perception but no awareness?

"If my thoughts are taken away, do I have a self?

"Imagine you become disembodied. You have thoughts, you have awareness of thoughts, but you have no body, and therefore no sensations or perceptions.

"Imagine you perceive nothing. You have thoughts, and awareness of thoughts, a body, sensations, but perceive nothing external to you.

"'Self' appears to be a gathering of body, thoughts, perceptions, awareness, and sensations, yet we experience ourselves as something else.

"We experience ourselves as the one who thinks, the one who has a body, the one who is aware, the one who senses and perceives.

"As if there is a little person in our heads who possesses the thoughts, the body, the awareness, the sensations, and the perceptions.

"There may be a little person in our heads who is the possessor of our thoughts, awareness, sensations, perceptions, and body, but this person has not been found. Furthermore, the existence of such a person would pose a problem, for if such a person exists, this person must have another, even smaller person in his head, and so on, with no end.

"We experience a self, but the experience is an illusion. And yet, if indeed there is no self, who, then, experiences this illusion?

"The problem, it seems to me, is language. Language, I think, is insufficient to reality."

◆

A LETTER CAME, WRITTEN in close script on handmade paper, front and back—three sheets. It was from Khenpo Dudjom Lingpa, former head of the scripture college at Thaklung Monastery, explaining that after fleeing to India he'd made his way to Sikkim, and from Sikkim to Nepal, and that he was now living in Nepal but as well in Taiwan, where a number of people had taken up Tibetan Buddhism. Nine months out of the year he was in Nepal, and three in Taiwan, those three months given over to teaching, empowerments, initiations, transmissions, and—frankly—fundraising. Nor was he the only one about such business, since other former Thaklung monks and lamas had also gotten out of Tibet, and had found one another eventually, so that the Thaklung community was reconstituting itself in exile and had established a budding monastery in Kathmandu. They had support from Taiwanese followers, and from followers in Singapore, but, of course, not enough. They couldn't house or feed new monks properly, or give them enough education. They lacked the funds to purchase surrounding properties and therefore establish a larger footprint for the monastery. Which was what he wanted to do. He wanted to resurrect Thaklung more expansively, and he wanted Norbu Rinpoche to again be its abbot.

"In Tibet," Tsering wrote back, "they put me on a throne. They blew trumpets when I came or went. There were elaborate processions. People told me I was special. I inherited land. I received gifts and offerings. Things made of jade and things made of gold. It was important that, when I came and went, hundreds of people dropped their heads and fell silent. If another lama had a bigger procession, I was supposed to feel it was a problem. Or if another lama got a higher seat, I was supposed to feel something was wrong. That's over. Now I teach whoever shows up—whoever tells me they want to learn something. I don't want to live in a monastery again and be an abbot on a throne who owns silver cups and can't go anywhere without people putting their foreheads on the floor. Besides, my knees are so bad I can hardly walk anymore, and on top of that, I'm always tired."

◆

THERE WAS A SCHEDULE and itinerary. In airplanes and cars, they would travel to eight places. At each, Tsering would answer questions in a dharma center. Tsering told Jim he planned to start each session by saying, "If I make a speech, you might have to listen to things that don't interest you. Therefore I think it's better for me to try to answer questions." Jim assured him this was fine. "But of course you don't have to do any of it," he'd added. "None of this is in your job description."

Wynn went with him. He pushed Tsering's bag and his own bag on an airport cart. He carried the plane tickets, the itinerary, and the schedule in a briefcase. On the plane he said travel mantras and worked his mala beads. In Chicago, Wynn procured a small rental car. "Rinpoche," he said, "the big roads here are faster, but the small ones more pleasant. I think you might like the small ones better. Driving on smaller ones, we'll see more of the country. Also, we have time to get where we're going. We're not in a hurry, fortunately."

They took the smaller roads. They passed through farmland. Sometimes through forests, sometimes through towns. "This part of the country is called the Midwest," said Wynn. "I grew up here, Rinpoche, in a place like this."

"In that case," said Tsering, "what's growing there?"

"Soybeans."

Wynn had answers. "A harrow—they use it to plow." "Drilling a well." "A stockyard." "That's a silo." "That's a water tank." "That's a courthouse." "A small church—also called a chapel." "Horse stables." "They crush rock into gravel there." "That's for loading train cars." "An old cemetery." "A slaughterhouse."

Wynn veered off the road near a cornfield. "This is what's called a historical marker," he said. "It explains what happened here."

"What happened?" asked Tsering.

"A boy was killed while defending his home against members of the Kickapoo Tribe, and his sister was kidnapped."

They stopped at more historical markers. "A stagecoach stopped here." "In memory of soldiers and sailors from this county." "In memory of people who settled here—brothers." "A school that only functioned in the winter because the rest of the time kids worked on farms." "This is to honor a famous nurse." "Rinpoche, this one says that the way the land rises here is because it's the site of a burial mound built between 500 and 1000 AD."

"AD?" said Tsering.

"Meaning the number of years that have passed since Jesus Christ was born."

✦

THEY STOPPED AT A library. Shade trees rose in front of it. The grass between them had withered in the sun. The library, built out of stone, had a roof of slate. It looked heavy and stout—a big building on a hill.

There was no one inside except a librarian behind a counter. She looked at them when they came through the door. She didn't try to hide that she was looking at them. She looked directly, without compunction, and as to what that meant it could have meant a lot of things, but one thing it probably meant was that he was in robes. Or maybe she always did this when the library was empty and someone finally walked in—looked up, watched. She was far off, you could turn left or right down rows of bookshelves without confronting her, the library was not arranged as if the counter were a station you had to pass through to go in or out, which meant no one was concerned you would take books and leave. There was a table with a globe on it—a globe of the earth—of the type that rotated. The windows were tall—like the windows in churches. It was midafternoon, light came through the panes at an angle, dust motes moved in it roiled by the fan above the wooden chairs and tables, the wood floors, the shelves, and the counter behind which the librarian sat looking at them. The wood shone, the books were neatly on their shelves. Someone had come along and pushed and pulled at every spine to line them up.

Wynn didn't turn left or right. They walked to the counter where the librarian sat. She stood as they approached. There was a pencil between her fingers. After she and Wynn had spoken, Wynn said, "Rinpoche, they indeed have a restroom, and you're welcome to use it. She adds that we're welcome to stay and browse among the books, that she's here to help or answer questions, that it's a hot day outside and on a day like this the library is cooler than out-of-doors, a place to get out of the heat for a bit. She says while this is a small town public library, they do their best to present a strong collection, so maybe we'll find something of interest on the shelves."

Later, in the car, Wynn said yes, almost every town had a library, and if it didn't there was a bus or van that went to towns bringing books to people. Mobile libraries, they were called.

◆

IN INDIANA THEY DROVE on a dirt road through tall grass toward the cabin Wynn's great-grandfather had built a long time ago. "The feeling I have here is nostalgia," Wynn revealed. "I had a high school teacher who talked about nostalgia. She wasn't that old but she still felt nostalgia and she said you didn't have to be old to feel nostalgia and that before long we'd feel it too.

And she was right, because I started to feel nostalgia when I was thirty, and places like this, I started seeing them in my head, the old places like this I knew from childhood, so this is nice for me, to be back here after all this time and see how this place has changed but stayed the same. Whereas for you, Rinpoche, there's no going back, is there, you can't go back to the places of your childhood, the places I've heard you talk some about, like the house near Thaklung."

The cabin had a brick chimney and a stone foundation. The field of tall grass ran right to its door. The field looked sun-burnished. The cabin's windows had been set in thick casements. The door was thick, too, and didn't want to open. Wynn struggled to turn the key in its lock.

Next to the door, a crabapple tree rose. Its light pink blossoms had loosened and dropped, and lay strewn on the ground in front of the house. The very moment Wynn finally pushed open the door, a gust picked up the nearest stray petals and blew them twirling into the house.

The floor planks had separated. Someone had filled the gaps between them with caulk. The walls were long, rough boards with knots. The windowpanes were hard to see through—they made everything out-of-doors look a little out of focus. At the back of the cabin was a porch with deep chairs on it. There were willow trees nearby, and a pond closed in by cattails, and on the cattails birds sat, or jumped now and then, fluttering their wings before settling again. "Red-winged blackbirds," Wynn said.

That evening the sky glowed. Between branches, above the pond, and against the dark sky, Tsering saw specks of light in the air. "Fireflies," said Wynn. "Flying insects."

Outside, they sat in the deep chairs. There was a constant sound now, hard to describe—a loud noise, as if the fields and pond were singing. "Crickets," Wynn said. "Also, frogs."

In the morning Tsering gave Wynn a piece of paper. "I had a dream and wrote it down," he said.

A monastery. I walk under a stone lintel, and up narrow stairs.
I go through a curtain and into an assembly hall. In the hall is
my teacher, but he doesn't see me. He pays no attention to me. I
want to speak but don't. He's facing an altar where butter lamps
are lit. Then I'm outside and can see a great distance. The sky is
cloudless. I am looking to the south. In front of me, children play
in a street.

I look out over a stone parapet. Below is a slow river stretch-
ing away in curves. On the near bank are smooth, round hills.
Between the monastery and these hills is a footpath. It makes a
straight line, like railroad tracks.

I hear frogs and crickets, and then I wake up, and outside the
noise is from more frogs and crickets.

❖

ANOTHER DHARMA CENTER. THIS one in Atlanta. "The center," said a man, "has described you to us as a reincarnated lama,
sixth in your line. Can you tell me what that means?"

"The word 'reincarnation,'" said Tsering. "Should I understand
it to mean 'born again in a new body'?"

"Yes," said the man.

"In my case six times."

"Yes."

"Would it mean that my consciousness is the consciousness of the
prior Norbu Rinpoche, et cetera, going back, from me, five times?"

"Yes."

"I asked my teachers this question often. One of them told me
that when a butter lamp burns low, it still has a flame, so another can
be lit from it. I told him I thought that was a bad analogy because
a lamp burning low is not like a dead person, in the sense that we
think of death as an extinguished flame, not a low one. My teacher
agreed his analogy was bad. He said I was right—that after death
we aren't like a small, waning lamp with enough flame left to light
a new lamp. He said, 'Let me try another analogy. Say I light lamps

and put them on the altar. One goes out but the others keep burning. The altar keeper comes along and sees a lamp's out. He gets another, lights it from one still burning, puts it on the altar, picks up whatever is left of the dead lamp, takes it away, and that's that. That's reincarnation.'

"I told my teacher I still didn't understand. He said it was difficult to find the right analogy but that a lot depended on the altar keeper."

◆

THE CARDIOLOGIST MOVED HIS chair to make a triangle. Wynn, Tsering, the cardiologist—a triangle.

"You have aortic stenosis," said the cardiologist.

Wynn translated.

"Aortic stenosis means a valve in your heart leaks," the cardiologist said.

Again Wynn translated.

"I'm going to go slowly," the cardiologist said. "I think it's important to go through this slowly because I want to make sure everything is understood.

"First," said the cardiologist, "you have a valve in your heart that isn't shutting the way it should. It's supposed to close off a chamber of your heart so that chamber fills with blood, but since it doesn't close all the way, the chamber doesn't get enough pressure built up in it. When it tries to pump blood, there's not enough pressure.

"Since the blood doesn't get pumped out to your body," said the cardiologist, "it backs up in your heart. You can think of it as flooding your heart. What does your heart do? Your heart pumps faster to try to make the blood move. That's what you've been feeling. Your heart beating fast.

"It can't keep up, though," the cardiologist said, "so the blood backs up from your heart into your lungs. That's why your breathing is worse when you lie down. Gravity isn't helping drain blood when you lie down. On the other hand, when you stand up or sit, the blood in your legs has to fight gravity to get back to your heart.

It's a hard battle, so it stays in your feet. That's why you have the swelling in your feet."

The cardiologist summarized. "Swollen feet," he said, "difficulty breathing in a prone position, fatigue, rapid heartbeat, shortness of breath—they all begin with a leaky heart valve."

He stopped talking for a moment. "Letting you digest," said Wynn.

The cardiologist continued. "You have two options," he said. "The first is surgery. We could replace your leaky aortic valve with a mechanical or a porcine valve. The mechanical one lasts longer, but the porcine is more reliable. With younger patients, I recommend mechanical, but for an older patient, porcine makes more sense."

Wynn translated. Then the cardiologist said, "You're of an age where, if you were to elect surgery, I would recommend a porcine valve, but that said, also given your age, I'm not sure I'd recommend surgery, the reason being that just seventy percent of people your age and in your condition survive it, and for those, the risk of an unsatisfactory recovery is fifty percent. By 'unsatisfactory recovery' I mean you might be permanently limited in your abilities and activities."

Again the cardiologist went silent for a moment. Then, bringing his hands together, he said, "As an alternative to surgery, we could manage your symptoms. Management means doing what we can to ameliorate. Management means not treating your condition in ways meant to cure it. Management means minimizing, to the extent we can, pain you might experience. Do you understand what I mean?"

After Wynn translated, Tsering said, "I understand," in English.

◆

TSERING THANKED WYNN FOR the gift: a cane. Its handle was curved, and it had a rubber tip on its foot.

Hot weather came. In the park they walked from bench to bench. Wynn brought a shade umbrella and bottles of water. When they sat he held the umbrella for Tsering while Tsering leaned on the cane.

There were a lot of people in the park. Some sat in the shade. Some doused themselves in a fountain. Some wore bathing suits and nothing else—no sandals or shoes.

Wynn opened one of the water bottles and handed it to Tsering. "Have a drink," he said.

They sat for a long time. Tsering dozed. When he woke, Wynn said he thought they should go to a store that had air-conditioning. From there he would call a taxi.

They walked along a street of small houses. The lawns were small too, the grass in them yellow. People were outside taking care of things—a man painted a wall, a woman washed a window, a teen-ager had the hood of a car open and a box of tools beside his feet.

Farther along, a lot of people had gathered. They'd filled a pool with water for children to play in. They sat on chairs with plates on their laps. There was a table with food on it, and an ice chest for drinks. The boundary between one house and the next had disap-peared. The party was spread over three yards.

"Please," Wynn called to a woman, "could you bring a chair?"

The woman brought one. Wynn settled Tsering in it. The woman said, "Let me get you cold drinks."

She brought iced tea. She gave a glass to Wynn, and then she knelt with the other beside Tsering and said, "Better drink all of it." Next she put the glass to his lips and coaxed him by swirling it. "Drink up," she said. "Come on—let me help you."

Tsering parted his lips for the tea, which tasted sweet.

The woman tilted the glass back down. She was big and broad-shouldered. She said that on a hot day she stayed in the shade. She said her children didn't like to wear sunscreen but she made them anyway. She said she was from Kentucky, where it got so hot you could fry an egg on the hood of a truck in the summertime at midafternoon.

A little white truck came down the street slowly. There was a speaker on top of it, and from the speaker tinkled music. The driver wore a white shirt and a bow tie. He plodded along with the music tinkling. "Popsicle Joe," observed the woman. "Hey, Joe!" she yelled. "Whoa!"

Popsicle Joe stopped. He stepped out in his white shirt and bow tie and went to the back of his truck. There was a metal box there, and when he opened it, smoke billowed out. "What'll it be?" he asked.

"Dozen Rainbow Pops," the woman called.

She turned to Wynn and Tsering. "Kids love Popsicles," she said.

"Wynn," said Tsering, when the woman went to get the Popsicles. "This has happened before."

"Really?" said Wynn.

"I must have dreamed this," said Tsering. "A long time ago, in Tibet."

Wynn didn't answer. Tsering shut his eyes. The heat, the shade, the tinkling music, the woman who'd knelt alongside him with the iced tea—it all faded into white mist. Tsering saw streaks of light against a dark background. From somewhere overhead, far away, came the noise of an airplane.

Cliff

· · ·
———————
· ·

E VELYN'S MOTHER CALLED IT A TUPELO. THAT AND thorn trees were all they left behind, she said, other than dirt, when they cleared for Arcadian Acres. The tupelo spread over the backyard and at the moment had a little orange in its leaves. Close to it was a sugar maple stump. The two trees, the tupelo and the sugar maple, had crowded each other until Evelyn's father had the sugar maple taken down by a guy he knew who could rope up and climb.

Cliff was on the sugar maple stump. Stick in hand, he poked at something. Cliff had never had his hair cut other than at the bangs, which made him look, said Evelyn's mother, like the Dutch boy on the paint can—especially when they got him in overalls and boots and rolled his sleeves over his elbows. Except right now, she said, with that stick in his hand, he looked like what's-his-name from the comic strips. What's-his-name with the Singing Sword. What's-his-name, Prince Valiant, with the pageboy. Except shouldn't Cliff have a big-boy haircut? Wasn't it time for shorter hair? She could do it with the electric razor if Evelyn wanted, or they could take him to Bill the barber where Jimmy used to go. If they went to Bill's they could go by Schnucks for t.p.

Cliff threw his stick into the bushes and leapt off the stump. "Mommy!" he called.

"What?" said Evelyn.

"Gra-mah!"

"What?"

"Watch!" said Cliff.

He balled his fists, ran in an arc, kicked a ball up out of the lawn, stopped, turned, put his hands on his hips, and looked at the two of them, waiting. "Good one," said Evelyn.

"Best boy in the universe!" called her mother.

Cliff kicked the ball more. Evelyn's mother talked about her health. The biggest problem with her bile ducts, she said, was being tired all the time, and sick to her stomach, and not doing anything. Second was dealing with insurance on bills and third was wasting time on doctors. Dragging herself to see a doctor who every time said wait and see. Plus it took the whole day and cost a lot. Plus she had the jitters. Plus she was constipated.

None of this was new. Nor was the way it ended. With Evelyn's mom saying she didn't want to talk about depressing things anymore. With Evelyn's mom saying life was too short for depressing things. "I want to talk about happy things," she said. "Happy things, like my honeybunch, Cliffy."

✦

THERE WERE THREE LAMAS at the door. Behind them stood a man in street clothes, and behind him, parked, was a blue Econoline van. "Hey," said Evelyn.

The lama in the middle said, "Are you Evelyn Bed, Bed—"

"Bednarz," said Evelyn.

They were decked out in the same outfit Lama Lobsang wore, one arm naked to the shoulder, and whatever it was they wore instead of a coat wrapped like a sash with the extra draped over the other arm, the whole thing red except for the shirt underneath, which was sleeveless and yellow. Since Evelyn didn't know what else to say, she said, "So what can I do you for?"

The lama looked past her into the front room, where Cliff was on the floor messing around with wooden train tracks. Cliff wasn't paying anyone any mind right now because his big concern was getting tracks hooked together, and for him, at the moment, there wasn't anything else. He was all drawn in on himself down low with his back turned, absorbed in getting the little round knob on one length of track fitted into the opening in the next, and he had about three-quarters of a course laid out, which Evelyn could tell wasn't going to link up before he ran out of pieces. He'd keep going into a dead end and then take everything apart and start over and the best way with him was not to say or do anything, just let him stay there wrapped up in his world of fitting tracks together even when it didn't work.

"My name is Lama Gendun," said the middle lama.

"I met a lama once," answered Evelyn.

"You met Lama Lobsang at Peace Mountain approximately five years ago."

"Huh," said Evelyn. "You guys must all know each other."

◆

THE DRIVER STAYED OUTSIDE with the van. Evelyn moved pillows out of the way so the three lamas could sit on the sofa, and while she was doing that Cliff scooted around onto his butt and got cross-legged and gawked at them. Evelyn's mother, who'd been in the bathroom, came in and gawked, too. "They were at the door, so I let them in," explained Evelyn.

"Well, I don't know anything about this," said her mother.

She sat down in an armchair. "Honeybunch," she said. "Come here."

Cliff did. He had on the bottom part of his Halloween outfit— the Batman cape and the gray leggings with the footies and the black underpants and the belt, but not the mask and not the shirt with the bat on it; instead his shirt was his pajama top. One legging knee was ripped. There was a milk stain over his lip from breakfast. He brought two train tracks to his grandmother, and after setting them on the arm of her chair went to work again at fitting them together. Evelyn's mother said, "Honeybunch, get up here now," and right away he got up in her lap, slumped there all relaxed, and went back to fussing around with train tracks. When he was settled like that, Evelyn's mother said what she'd said before: "I don't know anything about this, Evelyn."

"Well, they're lamas."

"Well, all right, but I don't know anything about lamas."

"Well, I don't blame you," said Evelyn.

"Excuse us," Evelyn's mother said to Lama Gendun. "Excuse me, I ought to say I've seen you before, in the airport in Chicago."

"No," said Evelyn. "Those were Hare Krishnas."

❖

THERE WAS SOMETHING CALLED a tulku, Lama Gendun explained. It meant a lama reincarnated from another lama. The Dalai Lama was a tulku; before him there were thirteen other Dalai Lamas. A lama died, and then, a little while later, his tulku was born, but no one, at first, knew who it was. There wasn't anything clear that said "tulku." This meant that other lamas had to find the right child. Maybe the prior tulku gave hints, or maybe someone had a dream or a vision, or experienced coincidences, or got a chill down their spine, or came out of mist into a crystal-clear valley, or crossed a pass on the other side of which there was a rainbow. Things like that—signs, omens. That's why they'd knocked on Evelyn's door. They'd knocked because they'd looked at signs, and those signs had told them that Cliff was the tulku of a lama named Norbu Rinpoche.

Cliff got down off his grandmother's lap and sat on the floor again surrounded by his train tracks and by the other pieces of his train set—the cars and engines with their magnetic couplers, the little crossing gates and the depot and the station, the trestle bridge and the grazing cows and the three people with suitcases beside them on the platform. Everything fit neatly in a box, in a prescribed way that was the only way; you only had to get one thing wrong, put one piece in at an angle or backward, to stop the lid from closing as it should. Cliff went at it in his half-Batman suit, absorbed, pulling at his lip.

Lama Gendun said that, to begin his search for Norbu Rin-poche's tulku, he'd made contact with people who'd known Norbu Rinpoche, and had heard in reply from a man named Wynn Kent. Wynn Kent had been Norbu Rinpoche's interpreter; the two of them had shared the same living quarters in Seattle. "From Wynn Kent, two clues emerged," said Lama Gendun. "One was a dream Norbu Rinpoche had, and the other was an episode of déjà vu in the hours before he passed away."

"I get déjà vu, too," said Evelyn.

"He had the dream," he said, "not far from here. He and Wynn were traveling together because Norbu Rinpoche had been invited to dharma centers. In his dream, Norbu Rinpoche heard frogs and crickets, and then, when he woke up, he heard them again, this time right outside his window. That, to me," said Lama Gendun, "was possibly significant, because it suggested a bridge between worlds."

"Huh," said Evelyn.

"The other thing Wynn communicated," Lama Gendun said, "was something that happened near their apartment in Seattle. The two of them went for a walk in hot weather. Norbu Rinpoche began to suffer from the heat, so they stopped to sit in shade on a lawn. A woman saw them and brought Norbu Rinpoche a chair, and then went back and brought him a cold drink. She knelt beside him and held the drink to his lips. She was a big, strong woman who explained to them that she was used to hot weather, having grown up in the Midwest. Shortly after that, Norbu Rinpoche reported to Wynn that he felt as if all of this had happened before."

Cliff gave up on getting all the train set pieces in the box. "Gra-mah?" he said.

"What, honeybunch?"

"Can I please have ee-ver fee jelly beans or fiiiive Soo-gur Babies?"

"In a few minutes," said Evelyn's mother.

For a while, Lama Gendun said, his search sat at a standstill, which he didn't consider concerning or unusual, as searches like this one often took time, proceeded in fits and starts, and depended on fresh occurrences. That being the case, a number of months passed before he came across an article about a woman carrying stones up a mountain in service to the construction of a stupa on its summit. Beside the article was a photograph of the woman, who was big, strong, and from the Midwest. "And then I did some research," Lama Gendun said, "and discovered that your son was born ten months after Norbu Rinpoche died."

"Wow," said Evelyn.

"Subsequently I spoke with the director of Peace Mountain, who told me that you achieved your goal of getting one thousand stones to the site of their stupa project. I also spoke with Lama Lobsang, who told me you'd come to see him about an obstacle."

On the dining room table was a plastic jack-o'-lantern. For the past few days, since Halloween, Evelyn and her mother had been parceling out the candy in it to Cliff. What he liked to do was pour it on the floor and lie down beside it, then line up the chocolate bars, make categories, put things to the side he didn't care for, twist open wrappers to see what was under them, move loads of candy in sweeps with his forearm, mound up candy in heaps, give some to his mother and his grandmother, and eat it.

Evelyn's mother put Cliff's jack-o'-lantern on the floor. "There you go," she said. "Have at it!"

Cliff reached in and clawed through his candy. "Choose two," said Evelyn's mother. "If you want to eat the jelly beans and the Sugar Babies both, go ahead and eat the jelly beans and Sugar Babies, but then that's all until dessert."

She straightened up and addressed Lama Gendun. "If it was up to him, he'd eat himself sick," she said.

"May I ask," Lama Gendun answered, "who Cliff's father is?"

"A guy named Scott Widera," said Evelyn.

"Are you certain?"

"Yes," said Evelyn.

"Does the father acknowledge Cliff as his son?"

"The father never even knew I got pregnant."

"Evelyn," said her mother, "you're making it sound sordid. Excuse me," she said to Lama Gendun. "My daughter's giving you the wrong impression. Evelyn was raised with Catholic values. She wasn't taught to go around and, you know. She got involved with the father but it isn't like she's, you know. Don't listen to her when she makes it sound like, you know. Evelyn's Catholic."

"No, I'm not," said Evelyn.

"Yes, you are," said her mother.

"Anyway," said Evelyn. "What was that lama's name?"

"Norbu Rinpoche," said Lama Gendun.

"So with him it's like what you said about fourteen Dalai Lamas."

"Yes. Except that, in Norbu Rinpoche's lineage, there have so far been six."

"Six Norbu Rinpoches."

"Yes."

"Lamas."

"Yes."

"So live in a monastery."

"Live in a monastery."

"Okay," said Evelyn. "What about the tests?"

"Tests," said Lama Gendun.

"Like they did with the Dalai Lama," said Evelyn. "Pick the right walking stick and things like that."

"Going back two generations," said Lama Gendun, "going back to the fifth Norbu Rinpoche—he was located without tests. Going back one generation, the last Norbu Rinpoche—he was also located without tests. Just dreams, visions, premonitions, hints."

"Honeybabe," said Evelyn's mother. "Come on over here, you're starting to look tired."

Cliff went to her. He got up in her lap, melted in, and started living in his head on the way to slumberland. Which Evelyn knew because she slept beside him every night and watched the course of it—how he went from here to there until he was all the way inside sleep, snuffling with his mouth open and his hair smelling good, his cheeks flushed, his breath warm, kicking around and changing position, butting her some, sighing his high treble note, someone who hadn't come to that moment yet like when Evelyn had checked on her bangs in the mirror and realized, *Uh-oh, I don't look good.* He wasn't Cliff Bednarz, no father in his life, mother a giant, lives in Arcadian Acres, ninety-fifth percentile height and weight, slobbery, hard on clothes, good eye-hand coordination, good mechanical ability, good attention span, good focus, knows the alphabet, likes crayons, wallows in a bathtub like a slick little whale, likes his stuffed alligator, likes Care Bears and Smurfs, likes forts made out of blankets and chairs, likes sitting on a floor register in winter. Just a little guy with needs, naturally and of course doing his thing, living in his dream world, not yet worrying about who he is, not yet worrying about what he does, not yet wanting this to happen or that not to happen. "He's gonna fall asleep," said Evelyn. "Watch."

Lama Gendun held a *be quiet* finger to his lips while Evelyn's mother got up and tiptoed down the hall. "Where were we?" Evelyn asked him.

"I am a representative of the Tibetan government-in-exile," said Lama Gendun. "The reincarnation of certain lamas is a political matter. A successor in the lineage of Norbu Rinpoche must be approved. In this case, approval has been granted. Cliff is the seventh Norbu Rinpoche."

"Huh," said Evelyn.

"Nothing need be done at the moment," Lama Gendun said. "Just go on living as you're living now. What lies before your son, what shape his life will take, where he will go and what he will do—no one is going to decide that but you. Please take all the time you need."

"Okay," said Evelyn.

"Ultimately," said Lama Gendun, "if you conclude that your son should live as the seventh Norbu Rinpoche, with everything such a life entails, you and he will come to Nepal, where both of you will make a transition. Eventually he will live full-time in a monastery. He will eat, sleep, and live in a monastery."

"Understood," said Evelyn.

"The monastery he will live in is called Thaklung. Your son's education there will be steady and rigorous. In late adolescence, or in early adulthood, he'll leave for a larger monastic college. It's uncertain which college he will attend at that point, but whichever it is, after a number of years there, he'll return to Thaklung Monastery and be ordained as its abbot. And after that he will be considered the custodian of a body of knowledge that has been passed down for hundreds of years."

◆

THIS "LORD GUMHEAD," EVELYN'S father said on the phone, was obviously a wacko. If he thought Cliff was whatever it was, or the second coming of whatever it was, so what—what difference did it make? It would be like if somebody came to your door and said guess what, Cliff's the King of England—what you'd do is shut the door in their face. Had Evelyn done that? Shut the door in their face?

"He's not Lord Gumhead," said Evelyn. "He's Lama Gendun."

"Evelyn," said Evelyn's father. "That's not the point."

"You called him Lord Gumhead. I mean—come on."

"His name is not the point."

"Lama Gendun—it's not that hard."

"Evelyn."

"What?"

"Did you shut the door in his face?"

"No."

"If he comes around again, shut the door in his face."

"Got it."

"Another thing," said Evelyn's father. "Last time we talked you didn't have a job."

"True."

"So did you get a job?"

"I did," said Evelyn.

"That's great," said her father. "What are you doing?"

"I clean people's houses."

"You clean people's houses."

"Yep," said Evelyn. "That's what I do."

❖

EVELYN CLEANED HOUSE FOR a man named Larry and a woman named Annette who wanted to move stuff to a storage unit. They were, as they put it, "a medical couple," recently retired and making a transition. Their plan was to move stuff little by little, then sell their house and move it all again, this time from the storage unit to a new house.

Annette and Larry didn't care about time. When Evelyn showed up, they put her on the clock, then made coffee and sat around talking. For example, one day Larry said, "Just finished reading on the treatment of 'phantom limb,' which is the illusion suffered by an amputee that their lost limb remains painfully intact. One patient felt like his missing arm was twisted. How are you going to treat that?" Larry asked. "Pain in a nonexistent limb?"

"How?" said Evelyn.

"You can do it at home with a box and a mirror," said Larry. "Just take the top off the box so you can look down into it. Cut two holes in one side. Put the mirror down the middle as a partition. Stick your arms in the holes—or, I guess, one arm and one stump. Now you're sitting there," said Larry, "looking down into this open box with the stump of your left arm plunged through a hole on the left and your right arm plunged through a hole on the right, with each arm in its own compartment because of the partition mirror.

"The key to this whole thing," said Larry, "is the mirror. You know how, in a mirror, left is right and right is left? That means that if you look at the reflection of your right arm in the partition mirror, you're sending an image to your brain of your left arm restored. All you have to do is move your right arm around until your brain becomes convinced that your left arm's no longer stuck in a painful position and it'll stop sending pain signals. Then no more actual pain in a nonexistent limb! Explain that, Evelyn!"

They went to work in the basement. There was a family room down there with a fireplace in it, and a ping-pong table swamped by books, some to go to the storage unit, others to be donated to the Friends of the Library. "Everything on this side of the table is for Friends of the Library," said Annette, "so if you see any books here you want, Evelyn, take them."

Evelyn took home craft books, recipe books, gardening books, travel guides, mystery novels, detective novels, books on health and diet, books on World War II, a book on how to build gazebos and arbors, James Bond books, westerns, atlases, and a book called *The Third Eye*. "I took this one," she said, showing *The Third Eye* to her mother, "because it's by a lama."

"Every time you say 'lama,'" her mother answered, "I think of camels in South America."

◆

THE THIRD EYE TOLD the story of a lama's life in Tibet. As a child he goes to live in a monastery, where other lamas drill a hole in his head—which they call a third eye—to make him clairvoyant and in other ways magical, and to turn him into a Master of the Occult with powers of telepathy, astral projection, crystal gazing, psychometry, aura reading, invisibility, and levitation. Later he undergoes the Ceremony of the Little Death, which involves traveling down stairs and along passageways before coming face-to-face with three old men who glow in a dark cavern and tell him he will soon see the past and know the future. For three days he has visions, and when he wakes up he's a Master of the Occult.

When she was finished with it Evelyn put *The Third Eye* back in its box and decided not to tell her mother about it because the idea of drilling a third eye in a little monk's head would freak her out more than she was already freaked out. The next day Evelyn took the box to Book Barn, where the clerk pulled off its lid, glanced inside, and told her, "Five bucks for everything."

Evelyn pried out *The Third Eye* and showed it to him. "Read this?" she asked.

"Ho," he answered. "That's by a con man."

"No, it's not. It's by a Tibetan lama."

"No," said the clerk, "it's by an English con man."

She followed him down an aisle. He pulled out a book and showed it to her. On the cover was a flying monk, followed by a migrating Canada goose. "Same author," said the clerk, "but after he got caught. Naturally, he's a con man; he writes another book. 'Oh yeah, I forgot to tell you something in the first book, actually what happened was, I was a Tibetan lama, but then I entered the body of this English guy. You got it, that's right, an English guy, I decided to be an English guy, basically for no reason but anyway it's true, and I'm gonna keep writing books so go ahead and don't believe me, I don't care, just buy my books.' Wait," said the clerk, "look at this one, too." He pulled another book from his shelf. On its cover, a cat sat on a lama's head. "*Living with The Lama*," the clerk said. "This one is dictated to the con man by his cat."

◆

MAUREEN CAME DOWN FROM Louisville with her kids but not her husband because Bud didn't do anything on Sundays he didn't want to do. Maureen lived in a house with a remodeled kitchen and one of those pools in back where you climbed a ladder to get in, which Cliff liked, and where he splashed around with his cousins and Evelyn in hot weather, the cousins being two boys and a girl who never got bored in a swimming pool. The bunch of them had come down to Evansville in June for the Shriners Parade, and to go to the zoo and to the war museum to ride the tank, and Evelyn had taken Cliff up to Louisville so they could go to Kentucky King-dom. Between that and birthdays and holidays and hanging out at Little League games, they had a thing going that was nice for Cliff because his cousins got a kick out of him and treated him special. They goofed around with him a lot and thought his hair was cool and had nicknames for him—Shaggy, Burly Boy, Thumper. Plus, they liked to get Cliff's toys out and go crazy with them in the front room until you couldn't walk around in there anymore and were better off watching from the dining room and putting in a word now and then to keep them from damaging the walls, or because Evelyn and Maureen's mother could only take so much. Which on this Sunday was the case. "Keep an eye on things," she said. "I gotta lie down."

When it was just the two of them at the table, Maureen said, "So Mom told me about the swamis. Saw them one time at the airport in Chicago."

"That's not them," answered Evelyn.

"Who was it, then?"

"Tibetan lamas."

"Okay," said Maureen. "So what did they want?"

"They said Cliff's a reincarnation."

"Reincarnation."

"Uh-huh."

"Like you die but then you come back again."

"Uh-huh."

"That's total b.s."

"Okay," said Evelyn

Maureen made the big head nod she'd started making in high school—the one meaning something was suddenly clear to her. "I know what they want," she said. "They want money, Evelyn."

❖

GRAM STILL LIVED IN the same apartment, still wore orthopedic shoes, still turned back pages in her *TV Guide* as show reminders, and still got around some, but now she had to take a walker along and wear splints on her hands because of carpal tunnel. As far as visitors went, there couldn't be any before noon because she needed time to get presentable, but on the other hand she was ready when Cliff and Evelyn showed up. The first time she saw Cliff she'd said, "That's a Crabtree!" When he started walking early she said, "That's Crabtree genes!" When he drew a half-decent picture of three children standing side by side she said, "Most kids couldn't do that until they're a lot bigger." She was in love with Cliff and thought he was perfect.

Gram had little white-bread bologna sandwiches with the crusts cut off ready, and Cliff's orange soda. "All this 'bout reincarnation," she said to Evelyn, "reminds me this boy grew up where I did said in his last life he was a girl and had red hair and wore girl clothes and his name was Lee Ann. People didn't discount him because in that place in those days we didn't discount out of hand. We had healers, we had plant medicine, we had water witchers, we had people knew what weather was coming, so we didn't discount.

"I saw a real good show," said Gram, "where the people in Tibet have their old way of doing things. One of their priests came over here, and when they asked him what did he like about America, he said *Lawrence Welk*. Isn't that interesting? *Lawrence Welk*? Who would have thought he'd like *Lawrence Welk*?"

✦

CLIFF LIKED AIRPLANES. IF you went to a store with him and milled around the toy aisle, he looked at airplanes. If a plane went overhead while he was playing, he stopped and watched. If it was a big plane up high, he watched in silence, but if it was a small plane flying low, he got animated and pointed at it. Cliff liked contrails. He liked balsa-wood gliders. He liked to draw airplanes with crayons, and he liked to make paper airplanes. His grandmother bought him a toy airplane with a propeller on it turned by a rubber band. At the library she checked out cartoon videos called *Plane Crazy*, *Plane Dippy*, and *The Flying Jalopy*. At the video store she rented *The Last Flight of Noah's Ark* because it had a B-52 in it, and kids and animals. Cliff loved *The Last Flight of Noah's Ark*. He also loved the kiddie ride plane that cost a nickel in the mall so much that if you put him on it you better have a lot of nickels handy.

Cliff liked to sit on the sofa wrapped in a blanket and watch cartoons. There was one called *He-Man and the Masters of the Universe* he couldn't look away from, not for a second, so much so that if he was eating candy he had to poke around in the package without looking at it and get pieces in his mouth in the most undistracted way possible, which meant his fingers got sticky and there were stains on the sofa, stains Evelyn's mother never would have tolerated when Evelyn was growing up but that she tolerated now, and about which she said, "Evelyn, it's just a sofa." When Evelyn answered, "When I was growing up, you woulda gone through the roof," her mother said, "Heard of Lois Wyse? Lois Wyse is one smart cookie. Lois Wyse writes books. Lois Wyse has a column in *Good Housekeeping*. And Lois Wyse says if she knew grandchildren would be so much fun, she would have had them first! So that's your answer!"

◆

CLIFF WAS IN THE bathtub making successive attempts to keep his face in the water. Each time he reared out he gasped with his eyes shut and acted panicky for a towel, which Evelyn had ready, and which Cliff pushed into. Once his eyes were good, he plunged his face in again, and blew bubbles while his hair floated on the surface and his feet thrashed and his butt shone, and there was something in all of this that made Evelyn think of Scott Widera. Which you sort of had to ask yourself, how did that happen? The answer people gave was genes, just like they said a television works because waves travel to it through the air, but those kinds of answers just moved the questions over. A lot of things were unexplainable and seemed like miracles, which Evelyn told Scott once, and his answer had been, well, yes, but things have to be some way, and this is how they are, so nothing technically speaking is a miracle, "miraculous" actually just being just a way of looking at things, and as far as that went, things only have the characteristics you assign them, or something like that, she hadn't really followed. Maybe, she thought, Cliff will be like that too, one of those people who thinks deep thoughts and has a brain that's going like a motor all the time.

Cliff resurfaced. Evelyn got his towel in place. While he had the towel pressed to his eyes and was busy drying his face, she kissed the top of his head, twice.

✦

MRS. LIND—STEVIE'S MOM—bolted out of her house one day while Evelyn was walking by with Cliff on her shoulders. First she said, to Cliff, that he was lucky to ride way up there, then she said Cliff looked to be the same age Stevie was when Evelyn was his babysitter, then she asked what was up with Maureen and Jimmy. She said Stevie was in his junior year at Purdue, majoring in chemistry. She said Evelyn had been a great babysitter. Finally she said she'd heard about the swamis coming to the door saying Cliff was reincarnated. "You heard about that?" asked Evelyn.

Mrs. Lind said her husband had gone through a period of being fascinated by things like Uri Geller bending spoons, telepathy, hypnosis, and near-death experiences, and as a result they had books in their house on subjects like that, including *The Search for Bridey Murphy*, which was about reincarnation. "Everyone likes to poo-poo reincarnation," said Mrs. Lind, "even though there's people who can remember their names, their jobs, their homes, their family members, all kinds of things from past lives."

"So you believe in reincarnation," said Evelyn.

"Not really," said Mrs. Lind.

✦

SHE WENT IN, PULLED the curtain shut, and waited. After a while the window slid open. "Hello," the priest said.

"Someone told me this is confession hour."

"This is the hour for confession, yes."

"That's good because I want to bring something up."

"What?" asked the priest.

"Reincarnation."

"You want to bring up reincarnation."

"I remember from being Catholic that priests are against it."

"From being Catholic?"

"I used to be Catholic."

"What happened?"

"I decided it was wrong for me."

"I see," said the priest.

"Yeah," said Evelyn. "But nothing against Catholics."

"Well, it's interesting," said the priest, "that you've come to confess."

"I didn't come to confess," said Evelyn. "I just looked in to see if anyone was around, and since there wasn't anyone, I thought maybe it could be more like an office hour."

"Let's do that," said the priest.

"So the way I remember it from Catholic school is, there's no reincarnation."

"Correct. We have but one earthly life."

"What about people who remember past lives?"

"I haven't looked into that," said the priest. "I admit I haven't taken that seriously. Is it all right if I ask questions?"

"Okay."

"A person lives, and then they die, and then they come back again and live on earth. Does this cycle ever end?"

"Good question."

"A person lives, and then they die, and then they come back again and live on earth. Are there any other mechanisms by which people end up here?"

"'Nother good question."

"When I was little," the priest said, "there were about two billion people on the earth, and now there are about four billion."

"Huh," said Evelyn.

"So there's that," said the priest. "Population growth."

◆

MAUREEN'S HUSBAND HAD A turkey fryer he could set up on their patio, but instead of cooking turkeys in it he deep-fried ham roasts. Bud's brine was big on brown sugar—so was his glaze—and his ham, after seventy-five minutes in a vat of peanut oil, got cut into slabs Maureen piled on a platter and served buffet-style with green bean casserole. If you wanted to, you could sit at their kitchen table, but if you didn't you could take your plate into the front room and eat on the sofa in front of the television, and in the summer you could take your plate outside and sit at a table with benches near the pool. Sunday dinner was served at two, which meant Sunday dinner was less like dinner and more the kind of eating that doesn't stop until the pie is gone.

Bud liked to say things like, "Cliff's hairstyle is pretty flaky," and share other opinions and observations about Cliff, the point of it all being Bud thought Evelyn was wrong about everything in life. Sometimes he called her Sister Golden Hair, and sometimes he called her "Bobby McGee," which was his way of saying he thought Evelyn was "a dog," which she knew was what he meant by "Bobby McGee" because more than once he'd said Janis Joplin was the definition of one. Bud's way was to say things he could walk back if someone called him on it, which no one did because then he'd get testy, and because arguing with him made things worse for everyone, and who needed that, Evelyn had decided.

"Hey, Cliff!" called Bud while cleaning out his deep fryer. "Whaddya think about getting your ears lowered?"

Cliff just looked at him. That was his answer. "Ears lowered," Bud said, "means a haircut."

Cliff went on looking at him. "Haircut," said Bud. "Whaddya think? You think you oughta get yourself a haircut?"

"Okay," Cliff said.

After pie and ice cream, Evelyn said, "Cliff, say goodbye to your cousins now, and to Uncle Bud and Aunt Maureen, cuz we're gonna have to go soon."

Cliff said his goodbyes. She got him in his coat. Maureen went with them out to the sidewalk. "Hey," Evelyn said to her. "I don't know why this jumped into my head right now, but remember you had a crush on the *Gunsmoke* guy?"

"Matt Dillon."

"And the *Tarzan* guy."

"Ron Ely."

"And Bobby Sherman."

"Bobby Sherman and Davy Jones. But that was earlier."

"I don't know why I thought of that," said Evelyn. "Take care, now, Maureen."

◆

HER FATHER'S IDEA WAS, meet at a restaurant in Bloomington instead of at his house, since his house, right now, was torn up on account of a remodel. What he had in mind, he said, was Cloverleaf, because at Cloverleaf you could get all-day breakfast, plus the menu had things for Cliff.

They took a booth. Across the way, an old couple ate in silence. The woman who poured water said, "Wow, cute guy. How you doing there, sweetheart? Wait here a sec, I'll bring you crayons."

When their food was on the table, Evelyn's father shook his head at his biscuits and gravy and said, "It's pretty much inevitable that as you get older you get fatter, but look at this, this is ridiculous."

Along the way eating he said, "Big picture twenty years or so we're gonna be dealing with China." "I don't know what's going to happen, but somewhere warmer in winter would be good." "Make a loop, go to Vegas, see Roswell, go to Sturgis." "The remodel will give me an open floor plan." "Diverticulitis. Fortunately it responds to antibiotics." "You're making a good dent in that plate there, Cliff, I like the way you're going at it."

Her father ate half his biscuits and gravy, then pushed the rest away and asked, "Why did I order that?" Next he fell silent watching Cliff, who was deep into a plate of chocolate chip pancakes. Evelyn's father put his elbows on the table and cupped his face in his hands. "Cliff," he said, "you make Grandpa really happy. I really like watching you eat those pancakes. It's just really nice for me to sit here and watch because there's nothing in the world like being your grandpa. Nothing. You're the number one best boy in the world."

◆

EVELYN'S MOTHER BEGAN AIRING grievances. She said that when Evelyn was seven and a half, her father fell into a pretty bad depression. His life became an act after that. He dragged himself around pretending he was fine. "Your father was ashamed," Evelyn's mother said. "If I brought up depression, he got irritable and started yelling. Claimed I was the problem, when all I ever did around here was everything for him and you kids. And that's not whining, by the way, Evelyn. That's just fact. I'm not complaining, I'm just telling you. *He* was the problem. What a coward! Making it my fault so he didn't have to admit to shortcomings. What a thing to do to someone! Using other people like that, especially your wife, who supposedly you're going to cherish till death do you part, and then being dishonest—with himself and everyone else. Too proud to get help. Which would be fine as far as I'm concerned if it was just him alone and his attitude didn't go and poison you children. Your father convinced you I was the problem and that's why you went up to Bloomington for high school.

"I'm not a whiner or complainer," added Evelyn's mother. "I'm just presenting you with the facts."

◆

LARRY AND ANNETTE WANTED more stuff moved, but first they had to talk a lot, as usual. They said they'd watched a movie called *Excalibur*—Excalibur being the sword of King Arthur—a not-bad movie, a pretty good movie, which Evelyn should pick up at the video store and watch too, but then, on the way home, Evelyn forgot the name *Excalibur*, and at the video store had to ask, "Got any movies about Arthur pulling a sword out of a stone?"

" 'Animated,' " the guy answered.

It wasn't *Excalibur*, but that didn't matter. While she and Cliff watched it she answered a ton of questions. "I don't know why they call him Wart." "No, owls can't talk." "Merlin wears that hat because the hat is a wizard hat." "The stars floating around like that means something magical is going on." "That's called a telescope. You can look at the moon and the stars with it." "I don't know why the dog's named Tiger." "He can pull the sword out of the stone because it's not about muscles, it's about being pure." "His crown doesn't fit because his head isn't big enough yet. He has to get bigger before it'll fit." " 'Discomboomeration' isn't a real word. Merlin is just saying that when you fall in love, you go off the deep end."

◆

EVELYN DIDN'T HAVE A license but drove anyway. Their first night they passed in a motel near Kansas City. On their second day they stopped in Hays, Kansas, so her mother could visit the Boot Hill Cemetery, which she was interested in out of sheer curiosity, and where it turned out there wasn't much to look at. On the other hand, her mother said afterward, the detour had a silver lining because they happened on a diner between Boot Hill and the interstate. "You gotta get off the beaten track," she said, from her place in the backseat next to Cliff, where she could turn the pages of his picture books for him and feed him orange segments.

On the third day they stopped at a grassland reserve where, if you hit it right, you might see buffalo. Probably about twenty degrees out, though, so Evelyn's mother sat in the car while Cliff and Evelyn walked along a ridge, where the thing that excited Cliff the most was that the moon was out in daytime. No buffalo.

On the fourth day, when they crossed from Idaho and got into Washington, Evelyn's mother said, "They're serious at prisons—

remember that." "Don't make a false move." "Do what they say." "Don't give them lip." "Control yourself, Evelyn."

They drove out into hills of brush. The first thing Evelyn noticed was how big they were on razor wire. They had it strung up in coils atop the fences. Other than the fences and the razor wire, the place was all concrete, watch towers, searchlights, and nothing else except the wind.

Jimmy was in because when he worked on the Tacoma waterfront he got caught pilfering, not exactly pilfering but telling people what was in containers so they could pilfer, and the racket he was part of got so out of hand that the Port Authority busted nineteen people for grand larceny. Which was sad, said Evelyn's mother, but on the other hand, you couldn't do that.

When they finally got to see him, it was in a room where the tables and benches were bolted to the floor. He came in wearing white pants and a red sweatshirt and the first thing he said was, "Hey, three of you!"

"Jimmy," said Evelyn's mother, and started to cry.

They sat down and talked. Like on Maureen and Bud and her kids and Gram and if anyone had gotten married or died. Then Evelyn's mother said, "How you doing, Jimmy?" and Jimmy said, "It's prison."

He had a job because they put together desks and chairs for offices—which was a scam, he said, but none of his business, because the main thing now was to keep his head down and ride out the rest of his time on good behavior. He looked kind of thin-faced and had his skull shaved close. His eyes were bulgy and his skin was real white. "Hey, there, little guy," he said to Cliff, "what I got here is chits for the vending machines there, so why don't we go over and get you something?" Soon he had Cliff on his knee eating potato chips. "They don't make guys like you anymore," Jimmy told Cliff, patting his back. "You're number one."

Cliff settled in. He got his head propped up on Jimmy's shoulder and went after the potato chips. He plucked them from his bag one at a time, and, with a slow hand, brought them to his mouth. There was a rhythm to his eating, which Cliff finally broke. He plucked a chip from his bag, but instead of eating it, peered up and poised it in front of Jimmy's mouth. "No," said Jimmy, "that's for you."

"You," said Cliff.

Jimmy opened his mouth. Cliff put in the potato chip. "Wow," said Jimmy. "Thank you."

✦

As SOON AS SHE was back in Evansville, Evelyn sent a letter to Jimmy, saying, among other things, "Hey, sorry I was such a jerk when we were kids."

He wrote back:

I don't remember you being a jerk. I remember we biked out to Blue Lake and you taught me how to swim. You also taught me how to catch a snake and how to recognize poison ivy. Same summer we went out looking for owls down by The Mounds. You had that dog Toby who could walk on his hind legs. One time on Halloween you showed me a dead raccoon full of maggots. Remember the guy who revved up his chainsaw whenever he saw trick-or-treaters coming? That guy was on my paper route. You and me went to see The Shining and after that if I was on my route in the dark and if I saw one of those little plastic trikes on someone's lawn like the kid rode in the movie, I dodged it and ran. Yikes. Nightmares. I got spooked.

I always thought it was cool in Bloomington when you were living at dad's and I always thought it was fun to hang around with you up there and drive around with that friend of yours, Kurt. That guy literally drove in circles. I didn't care because I got to sit in the back with his sister, which was okay with me because I had a crush on her. Never gave me the time a day, though. Three years older. Pretty.

I saw what was going on. You kept getting grounded.

They thought there was something wrong with you. But actually we had a pretty good childhood. The Catholic stuff and play by the rules. They gave us a shot, and what did I do with it? Anyway, four hundred and twenty-seven more days here. Love to you and Cliff from Jim

✦

THE THERAPIST EVELYN HAD seen a long time ago was still in business, and still had a lot of books. The biggest change was that her hair was silver now. The other change was that she had a new office, three buildings over from the old one, that was not so long and narrow and had a lower ceiling but more room.

"What do I think," the therapist asked, "of chanting, *Namu Myoho Renge Kyo*, to get what you want in life?"

"Yeah."

"Why do you want to know what I think about that?"

"Cuz you're smart."

"If I were to say chanting *Namu Myoho Renge Kyo* will bring you what you want in life, would it matter?"

"Just talk about it," said Evelyn.

"Some people will fight with a bear," said the therapist. "Fighting is their form of desperation. Some people will run—that's their form of desperation. Some will play dead—another form of desperation. And some will squeeze their eyes shut and chant, *Namu Myoho Renge Kyo*."

"Huh," said Evelyn.

"People have entrenched habits," said the therapist. "Are you thinking of chanting, *Namu Myoho Renge Kyo*?"

"No," said Evelyn. "Just learning about it."

"Right," said the therapist. "But if you're learning about it, you must be interested."

"Interested in a lot of stuff. Interested in those people in India who don't want to step on bugs accidentally, so they brush the ground in front of them when they go somewhere."

"Jains."

"Interested in whirling dervishes."

"Sufis."

"Reading about Zoroastrianism."

"Great."

"Things like that. Spiritual stuff."

❖

KURT JOHANSON CALLED OUT of nowhere. He said he was living in Chicago now, and working in security, but that "working in security" really meant he was a night watchman at a museum. He said he lived in a hip studio apartment in a hip part of town, which really meant the Elevated ran outside his window all night and on his street he could get Cuban food. He said his sister had three kids and lived in Indianapolis. He said he didn't exercise and had gotten chubby. He said he was learning slide guitar and listening to Ry Cooder and Taj Mahal.

Evelyn asked Kurt if he still drove around a lot. Then she asked if he still had a shortwave. She told Kurt that Jimmy had had a crush on his sister. She told him she'd always thought it was funny that every time they walked through the kitchen, his grandfather, the Captain, was listening in on the police. Kurt answered, "Everyone had a crush on my sister," and, "Guy didn't know what else to do with himself."

"Still around?"

"No. My grandma got put in a old folks' home, so now she looks like in Madame Tussaud's museum, which I can say because I'm a watchman at a museum and that makes me totally and completely an expert. Ever get married?"

"No. But I got a kid."

"You got a kid. Who's the dad?"

"A guy I met in a bus station."

There was no answer. "Hey, Kurt," said Evelyn. "Remember we went up on Weed Patch Hill and I told you you looked like Bobby Orr and you said I looked like Gertrude Ederle?"

"No."

"I was fishing for a kiss," said Evelyn.

"Sorry," Kurt answered.

❖

ON THE CAMPUS OF the University of Southern Indiana—according to an article in the *Courier*—there was a yogi who lay on a bed of nails, rain or shine, each weekday at twelve-thirty.

Evelyn took Cliff to see the yogi's performance. He was a small, pale guy with a wispy goatee, bare except for a cloth around his waist, who did his trick where students went in and out of a cafeteria. He lay there on his bed of nails, doing nothing, never speaking, for all intents and purposes asleep. Meanwhile, an assistant sat next to him, cross-legged, on a cinder block. Nearby, propped against a wall, was a second bed of nails. In front of the yogi was a box with coins in it.

At 12:35, the assistant rose and spoke. He said that lying on a bed of nails was a feat originating in India with health benefits similar to acupuncture. Lying on a bed of nails healed the body and the mind, released mental and emotional blockages, and paved the way for spiritual enlightenment. In the midst of his monologue, without missing a beat, he picked up the second bed of nails and set it atop the yogi, who, now sandwiched between thousands of nails, showed no ill effects.

Next the assistant picked up his cinder block and set it in the middle of the top bed of nails, the weight of which must surely have caused hundreds of sharp points to pierce the yogi's skin. A martial artist, the assistant said, might now split the cinder block with a karate chop, but he, not being a martial artist, couldn't perform that trick, and besides, if he did, he'd have to buy a lot of cinder blocks. "No," he said, "I'll be performing a different trick, watch this, please, watch this ancient marvel," and with that he maneuvered himself into a headstand on top of the cinder block, which you'd think would finish off the yogi on the bed of nails. "Voilà," he declared, while upside down. "I'm actually amazingly comfortable right now. As is my friend, Yogi Bill."

Yogi Bill turned his head, opened his eyes, and winked at the audience. "By the way," he said, "if any of you feel that the feats of amazing skill we've displayed for you here today are worthy of a contribution, contributions would be appreciated."

Evelyn put a dollar in the collection box, then said to Cliff, "So what do you think?"

"Magic trick," he answered.

◆

EVELYN TOOK CLIFF ACROSS the Traction Line and into the creek bottom, which had been turned into a junkyard and a garbage pit. It was like since the easiest and least expensive thing to do was to leave dead machines in a forgotten place where no one cared if they sat there forever, that's what the farmer did. And then, as long as the place was opened up like that, he might as well toss in leaky oil drums, rusted wire, broken irrigation pipe, skewed trailers, cracked cisterns, smashed culverts, mucky catch basins, ragged tarps, and whatever else was in the way of his farming. Cliff loved it. He got up inside the cockpit of an old thresher and tried to operate its dead controls.

They got to where she'd put Toby in the ground, and sat where they could look out over The Mounds. Really, thought Evelyn, if you didn't know The Mounds were Mounds, you wouldn't think much of them because they just looked like hills. "See those hills?" said Evelyn. "There, there, there, and there? Those are special because those hills were made by people. A long, long time ago."

"People make hills?"

"And no one knows how they did it," said Evelyn. "But somehow, they did. A long time ago."

"Ants make hills," said Cliff.

Cliff studied ants whenever he came across them. He said on the inside they were just like people. When he saw ants, he squatted to watch. When they got in the kitchen, he followed their trails. He looked at ants through a magnifying glass. He blocked their paths with his hand or his foot and watched them consider which way to go next. He got excited when he saw an ant carrying a load or clinging to a blade of grass. Cliff knew facts about ants—they had six legs, they had antennae, they had eyes, they had queens, they had soldiers, they had workers, they drank water, they pooped, they didn't have ears, they collected sugar. Cliff also made up facts about ants. Like ants talked in ant language and had meetings at night and flew without wings. Like they could see through walls and breathe underwater. He said they didn't get cold and climbed mountains without getting out of breath, and that the queen always did whatever she wanted. The other ants gave the queen all their sugar, the other ants all worshipped the queen, they bowed to her, they put their heads down when she went past, they piled up the sugar where she could reach it, the ants had to feed the baby queens sugar, if the queen wanted to she could banish an ant. Ants didn't sleep, ants didn't feel pain, ants didn't have names, ants loved each other, none of them hurt other ants. For ants, everything moved slowly. Everything that happened, happened in slow motion. Everything that happened had rainbow colors around the edges. Things looked round to ants. If you left a piece of candy in the sun, infinity ants would crawl all over it. There were ants that liked adventures. They went into the forest and wandered. Some learned magic tricks. Some became invisible. Some could turn into rocks or flowers. Some snuck onto boats and airplanes. Some rode in spaceships. Ants could talk with people, if they wanted to. They didn't.

◆

EVELYN TOOK CLIFF TO the library. He sat on the floor in the children's section, examining the pages of picture books without looking up or away. It was like when he played with his snap-together train tracks—complete absorption, fixated, rapt. His long, thick hair fell like privacy drapes. His hands cupped his book softly.

When he turned a page, he reared up a little before disappearing into the next; then he became intent again, bent toward his book. Sometimes Cliff swayed side to side; sometimes he bobbled forward and back; sometimes he put a finger on a page as if underscoring something or making special note of it. Or his finger moved from point to point, as if he might be counting like-objects or finding or making relationships or tracking causes and effects. The books he chose had densely drawn pages—crowded pages with a carnival air. The more chaotic and frenzied, the better; anything filled with celebration. Pages with busy people or thronged with animals. Cats in feathered caps on unicycles, dogs on ice skates with their hands behind their backs, skirted elephants parading along high wires, piglets on surfboards, rabbits in spacesuits with their ears poking out of their helmets, turtles in running shoes, rhinos in tutus, bears in pajamas riding in cable cars. Skiing pandas. Monkeys playing badminton. Hippos working in a flower shop. Leaping dolphins with apples on their snouts. An airplane factory. A fair. A concert. A stadium. A beach. A parade.

Finally, without looking up, Cliff said, "Mom?"

"What?"

"Why are there so many books here?"

◆

THE LIBRARY HAD JUST one book about Tibet called *In Search of the Abominable Snowman*. Evelyn thought that if someone ever asked her why she read it she'd just say it was entertaining. Besides looking for but never finding the abominable snowman—known in Tibet as the yeti—the author nearly died in an avalanche, nearly drowned in a coracle, walked across swaying rope bridges over canyons, crashed in monasteries—one of which was built into a cliff—ate tsampa, drank chang, and got interested in folklore about yetis. There was a moral, it turned out, to yeti stories: stay away from dangerous places and don't go looking for trouble. Someone told the author a story: People on the far side of a pass, feeling harassed by yetis, make a plan to get rid of them by portering loads of chang into the mountains and intoxicating the yetis with it so they can kill them. At first their plan fails because the villagers drink a lot of chang themselves, and end up arguing and fighting with each other. Then the yetis come out of hiding and bolt down the rest of the chang.

There was another story. A hunter falls asleep in a cave and wakes up captured by a female yeti who gives him a fur quilt and makes his breakfast, lunch, and dinner. The hunter and the female yeti do the deed. *She's better*, thinks the hunter, *than my wife in the village*, so he goes on living with her and they have a good time together. Then an earthquake causes the cave to collapse and the hunter and the female yeti run to the village, where the hunter decides he's going to sleep with his wife now. The female yeti withdraws into the mountains, where her sadness turns into hatred for human beings. So the moral was you should play it safe because you never know about yetis.

◆

EVELYN WATCHED A SHOW on the Learning Channel. "Every year on the Fourth of July," a lady scientist in a lab coat said, "on the street where I live, the children have fun running around with sparklers."

On the screen appeared children running around with sparklers.

"They twirl their sparklers," said the scientist, "and their sparklers make mysterious and wondrous rings of light."

On the screen now, a child twirled a sparkler and made a ring of light.

"That's interesting," said the scientist, "because actually there is no ring of light. Shouldn't we just see the sparkler going around in a circle?"

Suddenly the scientist was gone, replaced by a photographer with a camera hanging from a strap around his neck. "As a photographer I work with exposures," he said, "so I think I can explain what's going on here, Dr. Mullins."

On the screen there appeared a diagram of a person's eyes, brain, and optic nerve. "You see," said the photographer, "when we human beings look at a twirling sparkler, the light it makes arrives at our eyes, and the perception of that light passes from our eyes to our brains. However, before our brains can make sense of what we're seeing, there's another perception of light in a different place, because the sparkler is twirling and the light it makes is moving."

On the screen a twirling sparkler made a ring of light. "Since each perception follows the one before it rapidly," said the photographer, "the brain doesn't have time to cut them up into individual perceptions."

Dr. Mullins appeared in her lab coat again. "It's like a flip book," she said, rippling the pages of a flip book showing a ballerina doing a pirouette. "Things look continuous."

"That's right, Dr. Mullins," the photographer said.

The camera pulled back to reveal him standing beside her in the studio. "It's the flip book phenomenon converging with what photographers call 'afterimage,'" he said. "Are you familiar with afterimage?"

On the screen now was a very bright light bulb. "You shouldn't stare at a light bulb," the photographer warned. "That would not be good for your eyes. Sometimes we do, though, and what do we experience? After looking at a very bright light bulb, we can turn our heads left or right—really anywhere—and still we'll see the afterimage of a light bulb." On the screen, bright light bulbs were everywhere.

"Why is that, Dave?" Dr. Mullins asked.

"Well," answered Dave, "our eyes aren't perfect, so even after we turn away from a bright light, our eyes erroneously keep telling our brains that the bright light is still in sight."

A twirling sparkler made a ring of light on the screen again. "I see," said Dr. Mullins. "The flip book phenomenon, light exposure, our imperfect eyes, and the brain's maximum processing speed—these things together explain scientifically why a twirling sparkler appears to us as an amazing, mysterious, and wondrous ring of light!"

She paused. "When we come back," Dr. Mullins said, "we'll look at echoes—how they're produced, the mysteries they present, and how science can help us understand those mysteries."

◆

IT WAS HARD TO find. No one she'd asked could say where it was. Pretty soon the side lanes were gravel. The ditch beside the road verge ran with water. The houses sat in the shelter of shade trees. The radio was on because Cliff liked it that way. Liked the station that played classical music, liked his window rolled down all the way, liked the wind in his face on the passenger side, liked to wear his sweatshirt hood up with the drawstrings tight.

The sun was in the east. The shadows of the power poles stretched across the road. They passed a cottage with a crumbling chimney. Someone had built a little roof over its door. Bricks had fallen off the facade. Underneath were tar paper and plywood. There was one more house after that, on the right, and then, on the left, flags strung between two trees, and an open gate.

No cars were in the lot. The man in the foyer said it didn't matter—they were there, she and Cliff, they'd come all this way, so the tour could begin right now, he said. "Welcome," he said. "People are often surprised to find a Tibetan cultural center in the middle of Indiana, but there is a good reason why it happens to be here. Are you familiar with His Holiness The Dalai Lama? Most of our visitors have heard of the Dalai Lama because he is the leader of the Tibetan people, but not many know that the Dalai Lama's brother—or more precisely, one of his brothers—lives in Bloomington and is a professor at Indiana University. He's known as Tagster Rinpoche. My name is Thubten."

They left the foyer and went into the temple. "There is so much to see here," Thubten said. "But beginning on the left, this is what is known as a thangka painting. Here we see the Wheel of Existence. It is very detailed and there is a lot I might say about it. You will notice that it has three circles. In the innermost we see three animals—a pig, a hen, and between them, a snake. These are at the very center of the wheel and represent ignorance, hatred, and attachment. There is more to say, but we have much to look at. Ahead of us now, is an image of the Path of Mind Training, an image depicting Dependent Arising, an image of the Nine States of Mental Development—and so much more, all still to come. I don't want to shortchange any of it, but let me assure you that when our tour is concluded, you are very welcome to return to what interests you and spend more time with it."

"That's a pig?" said Cliff.

"Yes," said Thubten.

"It looks like a dog."

"That's true," said Thubten.

"The hen looks like a duck."

"It does," said Thubten.

"See that?" Cliff asked.

"Yes," said Thubten.

"Those people are walking on a rainbow," Cliff told him.

When the tour was over, Thubten said, "Many of our visitors are practicing Buddhists. We say to them, and to all our visitors, please feel free to look around on your own. Please feel free to ask me questions. I'll be right here if you need me for anything. And please feel free to sit anywhere on the grounds, or in the temple, if you wish. This concludes our tour of the Tibetan Cultural Center. Please refer to your brochure as you look further. And be sure to visit, outside, the Prayer Wheel, the Kora Trail, and our Kalachakra Stupa, which symbolizes world peace and harmony."

They stood in front of the Kalachakra Stupa. "What do you think?" Evelyn asked Cliff.

"No one is here," Cliff answered. "Just us."

◆

WHEN THE PLANE TO Seattle began to move down the runway, Evelyn said, "We're gonna fly now."

In answer, Cliff tapped her shoulder three times. "Do you know how flying happens?" he asked.

"No, I don't."

"Magic," said Cliff.

They left the ground. He watched out the window. Everything went white—whiteness streamed past. "Look," said Evelyn, "we flew into the clouds."

Above the clouds was sunlight. Cliff went on watching. Eventually Evelyn got out his "fun bag"—crayons, race cars, food. She put on his tray a packet of gummy worms, and a little book with pictures in it of animals in alphabetical order. Cliff went straight for the gummy worms. He was totally absorbed and had nothing to say. For him it was all about looking out the window while stuffing his mouth in a daze.

Later, Evelyn walked Cliff toward the bathrooms. He was slow going down the aisle. They waited because the bathrooms were in use. After a while Cliff tapped Evelyn's leg and when she leaned down said, "You're tall."

"So are you."

"How come?"

"Some people are tall."

He took his time in the bathroom. He sat on the toilet like it was just another chair and asked, "Are we still flying?"

"Yep."

"Our bathroom is flying?"

"Yep."

Cliff hopped down and pulled up his pants. "Do I have to wash hands?" he asked.

"Yep," said Evelyn.

They went back to their seats. Cliff ate more gummy worms. Evelyn gave him paper and crayons. When he was done drawing he said, "Guess."

"Rainbow."

Cliff followed the rainbow's arc with a finger. "You can walk on it," he pointed out.

"Really," said Evelyn.

"Up here," said Cliff, putting a finger on the white space above the rainbow, "this is where people live, and when they want to they just come down onto this rainbow."

"How?"

"On ropes."

"Wow," said Evelyn.

"They walk down the rainbow and then they're here."

"Huh," said Evelyn. "Then what do they do?"

"Magic tricks," said Cliff.

◆

WYNN KENT LIVED IN an apartment building where, outside its front door, you could call people who lived there from a phone in a nook after figuring out which apartment they lived in by scrolling through a list. "Excuse me," said Evelyn into the phone. "The person I'm looking for is named Wynn Kent."

"Who's this?"

"Evelyn Bednarz."

"Say that again?"

"Evelyn Bednarz, mother of Cliff Bednarz, who got recognized as the reincarnation of your lama."

"Say that again?"

"Reincarnation of your lama."

"Okay," said Wynn Kent. "I'll buzz you in."

Standing in the hallway outside his apartment, Wynn Kent put one hand up like a stop sign. "Who are you again?" he asked.

"Lama Gendun knocked on our door and said this guy here is the reincarnation of your lama."

"My lama?"

"Yeah."

"Norbu Rinpoche?"

"Yeah."

"The Norbu Rinpoche born Tsering Lekpa?"

"Yeah."

"Okay," said Wynn. "Come on in."

They went in. Wynn was big and had a beard like Scott Widera's, but he wore something Scott never wore, and wouldn't wear—a button-up Mr. Rogers sweater. He had a ground-floor apartment with a galley kitchen, wall-to-wall carpets, and Buddhist stuff on all his walls and shelves—pictures and paintings, statues like the ones Tommy had in his mining camp, and an altar with bowls on it.

They sat in his front room—Evelyn and Cliff on his sofa, Wynn in a chair in front of Cliff. "Cliff," he said. "Do you know who I am?"

"Yes," answered Cliff.

"Who?"

"The guy."

"What guy?"

"The guy Mommy said."

"Have you been here before?"

"No."

"Do you see anything you recognize?"

"The TV," said Cliff.

"Nothing else?"

"No."

Wynn scratched his head. "Cliff," he said. "Want orange juice?"

He went for the orange juice. When he came back there was a straw in the glass; he also had with him a tin of butter biscuits. "Let's sit at the table," he said. "I'll make tea."

He poured it from a pot. He said he always put milk and honey in his tea before he served it. Since more than one person returning from India over the years had presented him with gifts of tea he used that, whichever tea it was, and then he slid a cup of it across his table toward Evelyn.

Yes, he said, when Evelyn asked, the woman who was kind to Norbu Rinpoche on that hot day when he passed away looked like her. Yes, he said, he had the written-up description of the dream about frogs and crickets, but not in his apartment. He'd send it to her.

"Norbu Rinpoche," Wynn said, pointing, "used to sit on the floor by that heat register over there." Next he pointed at a photo on the wall. "That's him," he said. "Underneath him, that's the first Norbu Rinpoche. The next one's the second, then the third, the fourth, the fifth—the third knew eight languages. The fourth was a scholar. The fifth passed half his life in retreat. The one I knew, what he really liked to do was roam around and talk to people. Talk to people one-on-one. Just have long and slow, quiet talks. Otherwise, he really didn't talk very much, and when we went to dharma centers he never gave lectures. He answered questions. He liked to go for walks in the park and he was really good at sitting on a park bench." Wynn smiled. "If I came in while he was sitting in his spot there," he said, "which happened all the time, I tiptoed so I wouldn't bother him. He thought that was funny. Every time I tiptoed in, he laughed."

Evelyn took Cliff to look at the photos. The Norbu Rinpoche who'd once lived in this apartment had furrows in his forehead. His brow was an overhang. The line at the bottom of his chin was long. His nose looked like it had been mashed in multiple times during boxing matches, and there was a lot of space between his eyes. He was either not smiling at all or smiling only a little; with the way things were lit it was hard to tell. He had his elbows on his knees and his fingers laced—except for his thumbs, which he pressed together at the tips. The arrangement of his hands was such that his thumbs and forefingers formed a diamond. With his head tilted down and his eyes cast up, he looked like he was waiting for the photographer to adjust something. "What do you think?" Evelyn asked Cliff.

"Old grandpa man," he answered.

✦

WYNN SENT THE DREAM with a note attached. "Greetings," it said. "After you left I got in touch with Lama Gendun. I told him you and Cliff came to see me in Seattle. He asked for my assessment. I told him I had no assessment. I told him that your purpose in visiting me was to ask the sort of questions a person asks when they are evaluating the credibility of an assertion. I told him that your inquiries focused on evidence, and that you wanted to read the text of Norbu Rinpoche's dream, and that I had agreed to send it to you. And so, here it is, translated:

> *A monastery. I walk under a stone lintel, and up narrow stairs. I go through a curtain and into an assembly hall. In the hall is my teacher, but he doesn't see me. He pays no attention to me. I want to speak but don't. He's facing an altar where butter lamps are lit. Then I'm outside and can see a great distance. The sky is cloudless. I am looking to the south. In front of me, children play in a street.*
>
> *I look out over a stone parapet. Below is a slow river stretching away in curves. On the near bank are smooth, round hills. Between the monastery and these hills is a footpath. It makes a straight line, like railroad tracks.*
>
> *I hear frogs and crickets, and then I wake up, and outside the noise is from more frogs and crickets.*

"Hey," said Evelyn.

"What?" said her mother.

"This is the dream the lama wrote down."

"What lama?"

"The reincarnation lama."

"Evelyn," said her mother.

" 'Below is a slow river stretching away in curves,' " Evelyn read aloud. " 'On the near bank are smooth, round hills. Between the monastery and the hills is a footpath. It makes a straight line, like railroad tracks.'" Evelyn looked up. "That sounds like the Ohio River and The Mounds and the Traction Line," she said.

"Evelyn," said her mother. "You're going off the deep end."

◆

YOU COULDN'T JUST DRIVE forever with Cliff, but she figured they could make it to Peace Mountain by car, which was better because it didn't cost like flying. Best way was goof off a lot, drive at night him sleeping in the back, give him food he liked, give him orange soda, say yes when he wanted to stop, don't make a big deal about things, don't try to force anything. Some people thought if you're like that you spoiled kids, but Evelyn didn't agree with them. It was half the country, one thousand seven hundred miles, nobody liked it, driving forever isn't fun for anyone so obviously it wasn't fun for Cliff—but actually, in her opinion, Cliff was good at it, good at looking out the window for a long time without having to say or do anything, good at going along, good at living.

There were cabins at Peace Mountain now. Each had a name. Theirs—Tara—was made of adobe and had a woodstove and a roof deck. To get onto the roof deck, you climbed a ladder and pushed on a skylight shaped like a bubble. The skylight was on a hinge, so it moved out of your way.

On the rooftop deck, Evelyn blew soap bubbles for Cliff, and the wind carried them out over the desert. Someone walking on a path between the cabins stopped to watch, then called up to Evelyn and Cliff, "It's like in the Diamond Sutra!"

"What?" asked Evelyn.

"Like at the end of the Diamond Sutra!"

"Oh!" called Evelyn.

"Where it says everything is like stars, dewdrops, dreams, or bubbles!"

"Diamond what?" called Evelyn.

"Sorry!" called the woman on the path. "I promise not to bother you again!"

In the morning Evelyn took Cliff to the base of the mountain. The road had been widened and paved, and the pile of limestone had been replaced by a staging area where a tanker sat loudly running its pump. A hose ran straight up the mountain flank. There was a new path now, with switchbacks.

Evelyn carried Cliff a lot, but he also climbed on his own in spurts. On top of the mountain, a plinth was in the ground. Stacked nearby were bags of mortar mix. Fourteen courses of stone had been laid, the sixth and seventh stepping inward and the thirteenth and fourteenth stepping out again. Masons were busy laying the next course. Three passed stones and bags of mortar up the scaffolding. Two mixed mortar on the scaffolding in buckets. The last, who had to be the oldest, troweled and placed stone. "Hey!" Evelyn called to him.

He looked down, waiting. "Did anyone say anything to you," said Evelyn, "about skipping one life on the way to nirvana?"

The mason spoke to another mason in Spanish. Then he called, "No."

"Well, I don't know if it's true or not," said Evelyn, "but that's what somebody told me!"

◆

EVELYN AND CLIFF WENT to see Lama Lobsang. He still looked stove-in, grizzly and disheveled. He still wore the maroon skirt, the yellow shirt with the cap sleeves, the black stockings, and the clogs, and he still had prayer beads wrapped around his wrist. The main thing different was that he had a better chair now, a more comfortable chair with armrests and cushions. "You got a new chair," Evelyn observed.

"Boy," answered Lama Lobsang.

"This is my son. His name is Cliff."

"Yes, new chair," said Lama Lobsang. "Very bad back. Also, hips. Remind me of your name."

"Evelyn Bednarz."

"Obstacle," said Lama Lobsang.

Evelyn nodded in agreement with that. "So," she said. "Do you know a Lama Gendun?"

"Who?"

"Lama Gendun."

"I don't know Lama Gendun."

"He said he talked to you."

"Yes. On the telephone."

"Did you know Norbu Rinpoche?"

"Yes. He died."

"But you knew him," said Evelyn.

"Long time ago. Very little."

"I ask," said Evelyn, "because Lama Gendun says Cliff is the reincarnation of Norbu Rinpoche."

Lama Lobsang looked hard at Cliff. Then he said, "Reincarnation of Norbu Rinpoche."

"Right."

"What do you think?" asked Lama Lobsang.

"Could be," said Evelyn. "Or, could not be."

"Agree," said Lama Lobsang. "Could be or could not be."

"You're a Buddhist?"

"Yes, Buddhist."

"Don't Buddhists believe in reincarnation? Like when a person dies, but then they come back again?"

"I don't know," said Lama Lobsang. "Person dies, maybe they don't come back."

Evelyn didn't answer. "Your son is Norbu Rinpoche," said Lama Lobsang.

"That's what they say," answered Evelyn.

"Norbu Rinpoche!" Lama Lobsang yelled at Cliff, who didn't give an answer or change his expression; instead he just stood there staring at Lama Lobsang. "Hah!" said Lama Lobsang. "Norbu Rinpoche doesn't answer."

"Lama Lobsang," said Evelyn. "What do you think?"

"Good!" said Lama Lobsang. "No more obstacle!"

✦

SHE WENT DOWN INTO the ditch with Cliff, up the other side, and onto the Traction Line. The farmer had sowed sweet sorghum. Already its canes had been whacked down to stubs. There was fresh broken glass on the rail ties. Ahead of them, as they walked, sparrows wheeled off. A thunderstorm that morning had put a sheen on the brush, but it left as they walked, drawn out by the sun, drawn off.

They sat above The Mounds again where Toby was in the ground. Cliff rolled around in the grass a little. Finally he flopped in beside her, gasping. "Say you could wish for anything," said Evelyn. "What would you wish for?"

"Fly around and look at stuff."

"What stuff?"

"The universe."

"If you could live anywhere, where would you live?"

"The buffalo place."

"Why?"

"The moon is out in daytime. When I was flying around looking at stuff, I could go inside a mirror."

"Good idea," said Evelyn.

"Not the buffalo place," said Cliff. "A cave."

She put a hand on his head. "A cave inside a mirror," said Cliff. "Where I could fly around and look at stuff."

✦

EVELYN TOLD HER MOTHER straight-out, "Me and Cliff are going to Nepal."

"Evelyn," said her mother. "Oh, Evelyn, Evelyn. Evelyn, Evelyn, Evelyn, Evelyn. Evelyn," said her mother. "You were doing so well."

"I know," said Evelyn.

"Oh," said her mother, "this is bad. I was so, so sure you were doing better. But especially, especially—honey—you've got Cliff! Little Cliff is embroiled in this! Poor little innocent Cliff! Evelyn, you can't do this to him!"

"I know," said Evelyn.

"This is mental illness, dear. It's like you're in a cloud. A cloud! A cloud!"

"A cloud?"

"Of course you think you're fine. Of course you do. That's my whole point." Her mother rubbed her forehead with her fingertips and massaged her eyelids with her palms. Then she sighed and said, "Ugh."

During all of this, Cliff sat on the sofa with a blanket over his legs, eating a bowl of cornflakes and watching cartoons. He paid no attention to what they were saying. His cartoons and his cereal had him rapt, as usual. "Look at him," said Evelyn's mother. "Just look at him! Cuz this isn't only about you, Evelyn. This is about Cliff. Cliff and his life."

◆

BUD AND MAUREEN WERE at the door with no kids, and as soon as she opened it, they barreled toward the sofa. Maureen plopped down and tried to look unreadable, but Bud leaned forward and dove right in: "What's this about hauling Cliff off to Tibet?"

"Nepal," answered Evelyn.

"Mom," Maureen called. "Maybe you should take Cliff to the den."

Evelyn's mother took Cliff to the den. Then Bud said, "You're mentally deficient."

"Bud," said Maureen, "that's not what you mean. You don't mean mentally deficient, Bud. Mentally deficient means 'retarded.' You mean not able to care for Cliff because of poor mental health." She turned toward Evelyn now. "Evelyn," she said. "We love Cliff and we care about him."

"Likewise," said Evelyn.

"And we love you, too," said Maureen. "We don't want anything bad to happen to you, and we don't want anything bad for Cliff, either."

"Me, too," said Evelyn.

"We just want both of you to have good lives," said Maureen. "That's why we don't think you should move to Tibet and put Cliff in a monastery."

"It's Nepal," said Evelyn, "not Tibet."

◆

SHE ASKED THE REPORTER how he'd heard about it. "Evansville is a big small town," he said.

"That doesn't explain it," answered Evelyn.

"I know," said the reporter. "But I'm new on the job, so I do what they tell me."

"All right," said Evelyn. "Come by, then."

On the phone he'd sounded timid, but in person he turned out to look like an FBI agent—crew cut, horn-rims, tie, short-sleeved dress shirt, hairy forearms, rangy, monotone. "May I come in?" "May I sit down?" "Is this all right?" "Are you ready to begin?" "Do you mind if I use this little tape recorder?" All of it staccato but none of it rude. All of it standard, none of it personal. Someone with a deadline.

He took pictures of Evelyn in the backyard, beneath the tupelo. He took pictures of Cliff in the front room with his toys. He took pictures of Evelyn holding Cliff's hand on the front porch, and of Evelyn and Cliff at the kitchen table. "I have everything I need now," he said, putting his camera in its case. "Anything at your end?"

"Nope," said Evelyn.

"We'll put a bow around it, then."

The article appeared in the Sunday *Courier* on the front page of the B section. It was called "Evansville Boy Is Little Buddha," and alongside it was the porch picture with a caption reading, "Evelyn Bednarz and Cliff, the little Buddha, at home in Arcadian Acres." Its first sentence was, "Things like this just don't happen in Evansville," and it ended with Evelyn's mother remarking, "Cliff is very special to us. We don't want to lose him. We don't want to see him go. To us he isn't a reincarnated Buddha. He's Cliff, our boy, our loved one."

❖

A MANILA FOLDER CAME from the *Courier*. Inside of it were three letters written to Evelyn. The first read:

To: Evelyn from the article in the *Courier* paper
From: Carol Jones

Reincarnation is one of Satan's biggest lies. Reincarnation says a person has many lifetimes to work on their salvation, and that's false. There is one lifetime, and I stress that to you.

Satan is so, so clever. He has minions doing his work all the time. His minions are immortal and can possess human bodies. When they do that, they stay until a person dies unless they are driven forth by an exorcism. Over time, they move from a dead body to a live body, without forgetting details about people before. That's why there's people who "remember past lives." Don't believe what they're saying. It's demons talking.

Satan will do anything to lead people away from God, even plant the idea in their heads that they can sin in this life and make up for it in the next. But that's not so. Hebrews 9:27 and 28, man is destined to die once, and after that to face judgment. That is a direct quote from the Bible.

I am worried and concerned for you and your son. Please don't make a terrible mistake. I am praying for you.

Sincerely,
Carol Jones

The second letter read:

Dear Evelyn Bednarz,

Perhaps you've heard of the Canadian psychiatrist Ian Stevenson, whose body of work on reincarnation has been shrugged off by mainstream science, even though Stevenson is himself a scientist at the University of Virginia School of Medicine. I would like to refer you to his many case studies, and in particular to his book entitled *Twenty Cases Suggestive of Reincarnation* (University of Virginia Press, 1966). In this systematic and very scientific book, Stevenson exhaustively and rigorously investigates reports of instances where people spontaneously, and in astonishing detail, recall past lives. In particular Dr. Stevenson finds credible cases of responsive xenoglossy—that is, those very rare people who are capable of speaking languages outside their purview, which is unexplainable without recourse to reincarnation.

Take, for example, Dolores Jay, who, while under hypnosis to treat severe backache, spoke fluent German. In his report on Dolores Jay, Dr. Stevenson recounts his exhaustive efforts to determine if she had previously learned German during her upbringing in Clarksburg, West Virginia, or somewhere else along the way in life, finally concluding no, she hadn't. It was with great interest then, that Stevenson observed Dolores Jay, under hypnosis, state that her name was Gretchen Gottlieb, that she lived in Eberswalde in northeastern Germany, that her father Hermann Gottlieb was the mayor of Eberswalde, et cetera, et cetera. While all of those details were of interest, of greater interest was the incontrovertible fact that Dolores Jay delivered them in German.

I very much deplore how Stevenson had been castigated, and deplore as well the aspersions leveled against him by mainstream scientists who lose objectivity in the face of quote, the paranormal. I am scientifically trained in the field of chemistry and have thoroughly digested the principles of science, but such has never prevented me from bringing genuine objectivity to each and every phenomenon.

Sincerely,
Willard Heldmore

The third letter read:

Dear Evelyn,

My name is Genevieve Wolbach. I live in the Riverside neighborhood, so not far from where you are in Arcadian Acres.

As a former social worker specializing in child welfare, I read the article about you and your son with interest. It was an informative article that laid out the who, what, when, where and why very clearly, and I appreciated that, as it is not always so in the world of journalism.

I am writing to you now in the sincere belief that children do best when they are raised in loving homes by loving parents. I personally would have a difficult time placing my own young child in a monastic setting where he will not experience the many advantages that come with growing up in his parental home.

Over and over in the course of my work I saw again and again how children who lack a loving home and loving parents suffer saddening consequences. I can not imagine what it would be like for your son to leave behind his home in Arcadian Acres and pass the rest of his youth in a faraway monastery, but when I think about it, I am filled with trepidation, both as a parent myself and as a former social worker.

Again, I enjoyed reading the article. In the picture your son reminds me of the Dutch boy on the paint can!

Respectfully,
Genevieve

◆

SOMEONE CALLED FROM A radio station in Indianapolis and said they'd seen the article in the *Courier* newspaper and it was fascinating to her, and now if Evelyn could come on up there to talk with Elaine Ridger on *Outside the Box* they would put her up at the Severin Hotel, and pay transportation by the mile for her car, and she could put her dinner and breakfast on their tab because they understood it was three hours each way, so she ought to enjoy the good food at the Severin. "Huh," said Evelyn. "I'd rather get cash."

They couldn't do that, but they could tack on a gift certificate for Kroger.

The show started with music featuring a xylophone before Elaine Ridger said, "Okay, welcome back to *Outside the Box*," and then told listeners that, one day not long ago, a Tibetan Buddhist in robes knocked on the door of a house in Evansville and informed the woman in residence there that her young son was a reincarnated lama. "And not just any old reincarnated lama," said Elaine Ridger, "but the reincarnation of a highly respected lama with a lineage going back hundreds of years."

She paused. Then she said, "The woman who opened that door was Evelyn Bednarz, and she's with us today in our studio. Welcome."

"Hey," said Evelyn.

"Let me put this in context," Elaine Ridger said. "There's an ancient institution in Tibetan Buddhism known as the tulku system. In the tulku system, positions of status and power in the Tibetan Buddhist hierarchy are transferred from generation to generation by means of reincarnation. A great lama dies, a search is initiated, and a child is identified as that lama's successor—literally so; his reincarnation. Now, Evelyn Bednarz's son Cliff has been identified among Tibetans as the seventh incarnation of a lama named Norbu Rinpoche, the first of whom was born in the sixteen hundreds. Is that your understanding, Evelyn? Has your son Cliff been identified that way?"

"Yes."

"Help us," Elaine Ridger said. "You were born in Evansville, attended high school in Bloomington, and then what did you do?"

"I bopped around a lot."

"You picked fruit with migrant workers, gathered forest floral greens in Washington State, spent a year at a meditation retreat center known as Peace Mountain, and worked at an Alaskan gold mine."

"Stuff like that," said Evelyn. "I bopped around a lot."

"And along the way, you found yourself pregnant. What can you tell us—if you would—about Cliff's father?"

"He's a guy who never even knew I got pregnant."

"So in no way a part of Cliff's life. Or yours."

"Right."

"Okay," Elaine Ridger said. "So you found yourself pregnant and returned to Evansville. Lived a quiet life. An ordinary, everyday American life. And then, one day, the knock on the door we mentioned earlier. And the news that your son is the seventh incarnation of a highly respected Tibetan Buddhist lama."

"Uh-huh."

"So then what? What did you think?"

"I thought, okay, maybe Cliff's a reincarnated lama."

"You think that's really possible?" Elaine Ridger asked. "Because until now, this was unheard-of. This would be totally unexpected, right? That a child growing up in Indiana could suddenly, out of nowhere, be proclaimed a lama?"

"I know," said Evelyn.

"So how does it work?" Elaine Ridger asked. "How does your son go from, I don't know, riding a tricycle on a sidewalk in Evansville to doing what a lama does?"

"He goes to Nepal and gets trained in a monastery."

"And you're okay with that? You accept it? Tell me, Evelyn, are you a Buddhist?"

"No."

"As commonly understood," Elaine Ridger said, "reincarnation is the moving of a soul from one life to the next. Do you accept that?"

"No."

"But you consent to this. To your son becoming a lama and living in a monastery in Nepal?"

"I just feel like, hey, if Cliff has the chance to live a spiritual life and grow up to be a spiritual person, that's worth checking into."

"The telephone lines are heating up," Elaine Ridger said, "so let's take a call. Listener—go ahead."

"Hi," said the listener, through mild phone fuzz. "Thank you. Good morning. This is fascinating. I think it's a really captivating story. But as the mother of two children ages eight and five, I can't help thinking it would be painful for you to put your son in a monastery and say goodbye. Wouldn't that be absolutely heartrending?"

"Nope," answered Evelyn. "Cuz it wouldn't be goodbye. And also I'd be happy for him."

✦

SHE SAID SHE WORKED, so it was hard to get away. They said they could give her money to make up for that. She said she didn't have the money anyway. They said she wouldn't have to spend one cent because everything would be taken care of by them. They would buy her plane tickets, they would make her hotel reservation, they would send cars, she could eat meals in one of the hotel restaurants or order room service at their expense. She said maybe; it sounded like a hassle. They said the hassles would be taken care of and that the point person for hassles was Leah Sloan.

Leah Sloan called. She said that a driver would come to her house to get her to the Evansville airport. She said that when she got off in New York another driver, holding a sign with her name on it, would meet her in baggage claim. She said that at the hotel she had billing established and that the hotel had workout facilities on its ninth floor and nice beds. You'll sleep well at this hotel, Leah said, and the next morning we'll meet in the lobby at 7:50. Wear wrinkle-free clothes. Pick clothes that complement your skin. Bring picture ID. First they would go to the makeup department, then to the greenroom. There would be muffins, croissants, pastries, fruit, and yogurt in the greenroom.

The driver in New York wore shiny cuff links. No, she told him, she didn't have baggage. "Follow me," he said, and started walking. At his car he opened the rear passenger door. It was a black Cadillac with black leather seats. She sat in the back; he drove, saying nothing. Maybe he didn't want to talk, or maybe he wasn't permitted to talk. Hard to say. His car was quiet. There was a newspaper and a bottle of water on the seat beside her. Everywhere they went there was major traffic. The driver didn't care, though. He'd been in traffic a million times, he expected traffic—traffic was normal for him. It caused him no stress. It was what it was. He changed lanes politely but on the other hand, he tailgated. Everyone did. They thought nothing of it. Tailgating was the norm, so to them it wasn't tailgating. What was cutting someone off in Evansville wasn't cutting them off here. In its way, it worked, and actually, she liked it. Get with the program.

The hotel had a doorman dressed like he was English. Over-the-top English, like the Beefeater's gin guy—high stockings, poufy sleeves, puffy collar, loud shoe buckles. There was a shiny spittoon out front for cigarettes. She hadn't seen a spittoon like that since the Lincoln Hotel in Evansville at Christmas season. This one was five hundred times bigger than it needed to be, with perfect sand and almost no butts in it. In the lobby they had trees in pots and blown glass on pedestals. Evelyn's room was on the twenty-seventh floor. The view was of another building but the street was eight lanes wide, so that helped.

Around five she went to the first floor and found the bar. "Okay?" she asked the bartender.

"Of course," he answered. "What can I bring you?"

"Okay to eat?"

"Let me bring you a menu."

"I'm a loner, so why hog a table?"

"You're welcome to a table if you prefer it," said the bartender.

"No," said Evelyn. "I like a bar."

They had a list of whiskeys. "I'm gonna have one," said Evelyn. The bartender asked did she have a preference, single-grain or blended, if blended, blended grains and malts or pure malts? "Pure malts," she answered. "Pulling from a hat." "This section," said the bartender. "These four are all good pure malts." Evelyn picked one and said that, as far as food, fries worked. "Start a tab?" the bartender asked.

"Room two seven eight seven."

"Name?"

"Bednarz."

"ID?"

She showed it to him. "Excellent," he said. "Welcome."

There were other people at the bar, all down the way some. The bartender came back and poured the whiskey. "Cheers," he said, putting it in front of her.

She decided he was handsome. They'd decked him out in a gold vest and satin bow tie. He wore his hair slicked down real tight. Evelyn said, "Like your tie, pretty sharp." He smiled at that and said, "Costuming." She didn't let him go. She said, "Wear a bolo?" "I'm a clueless guy, so I don't know what that is." "You're not clueless." "I'm actually pretty clueless." "You know about whiskey." "What brings you to New York?" "I'm gonna be a guest on a television talk show." "Which?" "I forget the name of it."

She watched television on her hotel bed for three hours. Surfed channels. Fell asleep that way. Woke up at two and thought about the bartender. Scott Widera seemed far away now. Life happened quickly. In the middle of the night it was depressing to be alive. Just kind of a down feeling. So dumb to think someone else could change things. If something was missing you wouldn't find it with a love partner. Guy in a Wyatt Earp tie, you get a feeling, it goes nowhere even if it goes somewhere. People were scared. Biting it for good was scary, but worse was feeling you didn't exist in the first place. There was nothing underneath. Whatever you held on to was connected to nothing. The city kept going anyway, even at two in the morning. Most of the sounds were muffled and vague, but not the sirens on the police cars and ambulances. She'd seen a guy blow a conch shell once. It was like that. Always.

✦

THEY GOT IN A taxi. Leah Sloan said reincarnation interested her. Last year she'd moved from a nine-month internship to her current position, the show was taped five days a week, she'd seen tons of programming. Reincarnation was a departure from the norm. The norm was celebrities, self-help, relationships. On the other hand, Buddhism was growing in popularity, Hollywood and Buddhism were forging a nexus, so having Evelyn on the show made perfect sense. They liked to be topical. A lot of thought went into it. Meanwhile, a few details: The show is taped before a live audience. Susan Orloff is a seasoned professional, good at setting guests at ease. The taping will take forty-five minutes. Audience capacity is 225. Every seat will be filled. Questions from the audience are vetted. The show is scripted but since it's taped it can be edited.

Leah was from Wisconsin and was enjoying New York, but she didn't plan on staying in New York forever. Didn't want to live in Wisconsin again, but definitely, in five years, she wouldn't be in New York. Where next was up in the air, kind of depended on a lot of things, actually—mainly on who she ended up with for a partner—but for now New York was great, she liked New York, it was a vibrant place to live, she felt alive here and in the middle of things, there was so much going on all the time, she was never bored here, but New York wasn't a good place for children and Leah wanted children. Wanted to be married by thirty-three at the latest, wanted two children by the time she was thirty-eight, wanted to raise them somewhere safe. "Of course," she said, "I'm jumping the gun here, because so far I haven't met Mr. Right!" Leah's eyes twinkled. She was normal-looking; it was going to work out for her. "Who knows?" she said. "We'll see how it goes."

"Just walk right up and say, 'Hey, cowboy!'" Evelyn advised. "That way, from then on, it's your rodeo."

◆

SHE FELT KIND OF stiff with her hair sprayed into place and with makeup on her face and with all the encouragement people were throwing at her, like the makeup person Claudia, who said, while dabbing her cheeks, "You're going to be great, I can see it in your eyes," and the producer, who said, "I love your stage presence." Also Susan Orloff, who came in while Evelyn was tilted back in the makeup chair with a barber apron draped across her and said, "You're looking excellent, I'm still disheveled. I absolutely love you, you know that, right? See you soon, 'bye!"

There was a mirror in the greenroom bathroom like the ones in movies where they show actors in dressing rooms—up one side, over the top, and down the other, lights. 'Worse with makeup,' thought Evelyn. 'All it does is cover up the moles.' She had a joke in her head, something she thought she'd say to a hairdresser if she ever decided to go to a hairdresser. The hairdresser would rotate Evelyn's chair toward a mirror, put her hands on Evelyn's head, plump her bad hair and say, "What did you have in mind?" Evelyn would answer, "What I want you to do is make me look different from how I really look. Keep cutting until I have a different face."

They had a screen built into a wall of the greenroom. It was live, and right now it showed the show's set. When you watched one of these types of shows on television, you didn't think of a set—even though you should—but now, obviously, it was just like in a theater play. That's what it was. A real thing that was fake.

The breakfast food was on a counter. Leah pointed out a refrigerator, a coffee urn, a hot water urn, and a tea bag assortment, and said she'd become partial to green tea lately, had learned to appreciate green tea, but of course Evelyn was welcome to any tea she wanted, or coffee, or anything else. "This is funny," answered Evelyn. "I never wear makeup."

"You look great," said Leah. "You're going to do great."

＋

THEY WERE ABOUT TO start the show. Evelyn watched on the greenroom screen. A guy was working the audience up. He told them that when Susan came out they should get more excited than they'd ever been in their entire lives, that they should go nuts. Stand up, clap, smile, root, cheer, raise your arms over your head, give each other high fives, jump around—go crazy. "Let's practice," he said, "on my signal, ready?" The audience did it and the guy used his hands after a while so they would know to take it down to total silence. "That's perfecto," he said, making an O with a thumb and forefinger. "We'll do it like that." Someone offstage yelled, "Are we ready?" and the guy who led the cheers said, "Ready, go ahead."

Susan Orloff walked in. Not onto the stage but right into the audience. On cue, the entire audience went nuts. Susan Orloff waved to people, came down in front, and watched as if shocked that everyone was going nuts. "Oh my!" she said. "Oh yeah. Here we go. Let's party. We're doin' it. We're on fire. Are you ready? Are . . . you . . . ready!" At which point the noise wound up even higher and there were even more arms raised and high fives and whoops before, with Susan Orloff's help—with Susan Orloff making the right faces—it finally settled down. "Wow," said Susan Orloff. "Wow, wow, wow!"

She straightened her clothes, primped her hair, posed. "How do I look?" she asked, and curtseyed. Immediately, more craziness, more whooping, Susan Orloff putting up her hands as if to say, I don't deserve this, please quiet down, like she was playing the part of someone conceited and therefore wasn't in real life conceited, which made Evelyn think she was probably conceited, but so what, people did what they did because things were what they were, she herself included, it was all equal in the end, probably when Susan Orloff woke up at two in the morning and couldn't sleep she had the same thoughts as anyone else, things like the bartender with the satin tie and how dumb everything is.

The set was two big armchairs, a glass coffee table with flowers on it, and a screen with one big word on it, REINCARNATION, followed by a question mark, and underneath that, in smaller letters, A BOY AND HIS MOM. Susan Orloff stood in front of the armchairs and said, "Today we're going to be doing a show that's off the charts. We're going to be talking to a woman who has been told that her five-year-old son is the reincarnation of a Buddhist lama, and who has decided she believes this. What will she do now? She will take her son to Nepal, a poor country in the Himalaya Mountains, and leave him there to live in a monastery for the rest of his life. We're going to talk to this mother about this, but before we do, I want to show you something. Take a look at this."

On the screen behind Susan Orloff there now appeared a picture of Richard Gere standing beside the Dalai Lama. Then a picture of Cindy Crawford standing beside him too, and then of Tina Turner in front of a meditation altar. During all of this, upbeat music played, and over the top of it Susan Orloff said that Buddhism had now entered American culture and become hip and fashionable. Steven Seagal, Uma Thurman, Courtney Love, Sharon Stone, Goldie Hawn, Phil Jackson, and even Adam Yauch of the Beastie Boys—all had taken an interest in Buddhism. "There are even Buddhist products now," she said. "Just look at what it says on this bottle of cold tea: 'Please recycle—I deserve to be reincarnated too.' Buddhism is everywhere these days, it seems. America is fascinated by Buddhism."

The upbeat music ended. The camera closed in on Susan Orloff. "In a moment," she said, "we'll meet today's guest. Stay with us. Right back. Stay with us."

◆

THEY SAT IN THE armchairs. Susan Orloff told the audience that Evelyn had been born and raised a Catholic. That she lived in Evansville, Indiana, with her mother and son. That she had worked at many jobs in her life, including as a migrant fruit picker and a dishwasher, and currently was employed as a house cleaner. That her son was a normal, everyday little boy who liked to ride a tricycle and play with Legos. "All normal," Susan Orloff said. "Ordinary, everyday American lives. But then, one day, a knock at the door, and when Evelyn opens it she finds standing there three Tibetan lamas in flowing robes. Take a look."

On the screen was a picture of a Buddha statue. Next, a monastery. Next, monks chanting in a temple. Monks blowing horns and crashing cymbals. Monks bowing at an altar. Monks eating out of bowls with their hands. Monks walking through a courtyard. Monks hanging laundry on a line. Monks working in a kitchen. Monks sweeping a corridor. Monks studying. Tutor monks teaching boy monks. A boy monk getting his head shaved. A group of boy monks prostrating in a courtyard. A boy monk stretching his back and yawning. A boy monk peering into a book, scratching his head, pulling his ear, rubbing his forehead. Meanwhile, Susan Orloff's voice: "Welcome to Thaklung Monastery in Nepal, where very soon Evelyn's son will come to live. The monks here rise at four o'clock every morning. They lead rigorous lives of study and prayer. The young monks are held to high expectations. The curriculum they follow is very intense. Evelyn's son will have his head shaved like them. He'll wear a robe like them. But—the life he will live will be different from theirs, because Evelyn's son is a very high lama. In Tibetan Buddhism, high lamas are revered." Now, on the screen, was an image of a golden throne—a very high throne on which sat a high lama who was twining his hands in a ritual pattern while below and in front of him sat a throng of monks with legs crossed. Over blaring horns and crashing cymbals, Susan Orloff's voice remained calm: "Evelyn's son will eventually sit here, on this golden throne at the front of this temple. He is expected to study long and hard so that one day he can lead this monastery as its abbot."

Now on the screen was a picture of Tsering Lekpa—the lama Wynn Kent had interpreted for, the lama who'd sat by the heat register in Wynn's apartment, the lama who'd had a déjà vu from heatstroke, the lama with all the furrows in his forehead. "Evelyn's son will rise to this position because he is said to be the reincarnation of this man, a highly respected Tibetan Buddhist lama who died ten months before Evelyn's son was born. He was revered by many, and now that same reverence will be shown to a little boy from Indiana—Evelyn's son, Cliff River Bednarz. Am I saying that, right? Bednarz?"

"I can't even say it," answered Evelyn.

There was laughter from the audience. Susan Orloff raised her eyes. "Cliff River Bednarz," she said. "Not Clifford River Bednarz?"

"Cliff like a cliff," said Evelyn. "That goes with 'River' cuz I like nature names."

"Cliff River Bednarz," said Susan Orloff. "Let's meet Cliff River Bednarz."

A picture of Cliff appeared on the screen—Cliff on the floor with his toys in the living room, wearing his overalls and his Dutch boy haircut. "There he is," said Susan Orloff. "What a little cutie!" Next was the picture of Evelyn and Cliff on the porch, the one that had been in the *Courier* newspaper. "And there they are," said Susan Orloff. "Mother and son, at home in Evansville." Another picture—Cliff in the backyard, standing on the maple stump in front of the tupelo. "The beautiful boy with the beautiful name," said Susan Orloff. "And you're his mother and you love him."

"Right."

"And your mother, Cliff River's grandmother, both you and Cliff River live with her, and she loves Cliff River."

"Right."

"And an aunt and an uncle and two cousins nearby, all of whom love Cliff River."

"Right."

"And your grandmother," said Susan Orloff. "So Cliff River's great-grandmother. Also nearby, also loves Cliff River."

"Right," said Evelyn.

"So, Evelyn," said Susan Orloff. "The plan is for you and Cliff to go to Nepal and for you to help him make a transition from living with his mother and his grandmother and his family to living in a far-off monastery."

"That sounds right," said Evelyn.

"The purpose of living in a monastery," said Susan Orloff, "would be for Cliff to get an education there and be trained as a religious leader."

"Right."

"So that's huge," said Susan Orloff.

"Huge," said Evelyn.

"Out-of-this-world huge," said Susan Orloff. "We're talking about a new life seven thousand miles away from here, in a country on the other side of the world. A completely different universe for Cliff. Watch this."

Now on the screen there was a picture of a dusty beggar with a gray beard and a gray topknot, naked but for a cloth around his waist, sitting on a rock with a staff in one hand. Then a porter on a dusty street with a stick across his back so he could balance loaded gunnysacks. Then a little boy in ragged clothes rolling a bicycle tire who knows where. Then three women squatting with their heads down in front of begging bowls. Another porter, this one with his hands locked behind his head and bent beneath a load way bigger than he was. Once again, Susan Orloff narrated. "This is Kathmandu," she said, "the capital of Nepal, a landlocked country between China and India. This is where the little boy from Indiana will live, an exotic and beautiful country in the Himalaya Mountains, but a poor one too, in fact—one of the poorest on earth.

"So let me understand this," Susan Orloff said to Evelyn. "You're going to ease Cliff into this new life, give him a last kiss and hug, a big final squeeze, say goodbye, and be on your way?"

"I don't know," said Evelyn. "We'll see."

"But ultimately you'd have to leave Cliff there. Leave him to be raised by others in a monastery seven thousand miles away from you. Maybe talk to him by phone with some regularity, maybe visit with him now and then, but ultimately, leave him to be raised by others."

"I guess that's how they do it," said Evelyn.

"Evelyn," said Susan Orloff. "I have to ask now. Where is Cliff's father in all of this? How does Cliff's father feel about this?"

"I'm a single mother," answered Evelyn.

"His father has no say in the matter?"

"His father has no involvement in his life."

"So the decisions are all yours," Susan Orloff said. "You're responsible for everything when it comes to Cliff."

"Maybe," said Evelyn.

"Evelyn," said Susan Orloff. "It was a dream, for the most part, as I understand it, that led to the conclusion that Cliff is the reincarnation of an important religious leader. We asked around a little, getting ready for the show, and learned that it was this religious leader himself who had this seemingly significant dream, and that he had it while visiting your home state of Indiana, wrote a description of it, and gave that description to his American interpreter. Our producer obtained a copy of this dream description. Our creative team here on the show is the absolute best—let's take a look and see what they did."

What they'd done was blurry animation. A monastery in snowy mountains. A monk standing on a parapet. Below, on a street, children playing kickball. The monk scratches his head, then turns his eyes toward a valley where a river stretches away in curves. On its near bank are hills. Then comes the noise of frogs and crickets. The monk wakes up in a bed by an open window, beyond which frogs and crickets can still be heard, and then the blurriness gets more blurry and the screen goes white.

"So that's the dream," said Susan Orloff, "that led lamas to your door. That led them to you—that led them to Cliff. That's how they interpreted it. That Cliff is the dreamer's reincarnation."

Evelyn shrugged.

"You believe—I assume you must believe—that your son is really, truly, actually, and factually the reincarnation of a Buddhist religious leader?"

Evelyn shrugged again. Susan Orloff looked at the people in the audience. She didn't say a word, and neither did they.

"When we come back," said Susan Orloff, "we're going to hear from you, our audience, with questions you have about all of this. So stay tuned, stay with us, what a story. Right back."

The microphones went off. "This is so weird," said Evelyn. "Television."

◆

THEY DID THE WHOLE clapping thing, like the people in the audience were happy that commercials were over and the show was under way again, and then Susan Orloff said that she was looking forward to tomorrow's show because her guest was a woman everyone would want to meet, a psychiatrist who specialized in love and addiction, in the connection, sometimes, between love and addiction. Sometimes, said Susan Orloff, love has a dark side.

The questions started. A woman in the audience was pissed off. She said, "This whole thing sounds contradictory to me. Here Buddhism is supposedly about compassion and being loving and kind all the time, but then you decide you won't do any of that and instead ship your son off like he's being put up for adoption. Like maybe you don't want the responsibility, because let me tell you,

I'm a mother myself, I have three children, and being a mother is a big responsibility. A mother's love and support is everything. There isn't any substitute, I can tell you that. What I think is, you want your freedom. It's convenient for you, this miracle in your life. These guys come to your door and, guess what, we're going to take Cliff off your hands, and now you can do whatever you want. It's like shipping them off to boarding schools. Or keep them home but let the maids raise them. So just shame on you for being like this. Shame, shame, shame, shame, shame!"

"Evelyn?" said Susan Orloff.

"I mean," said Evelyn, "my whole life, ever since I was a little girl, like as far back as I can remember, from my earliest memories, I've felt like something's wrong, something's missing, something isn't right about, you know, this. Not just because, let's face it, I'm a giant. Not just because I look like—I don't know. Even if I looked normal I'd feel this way. When I was growing up and they talked about Adam and Eve at church and how they got kicked out of the Garden of Eden, I was like, exactly. We got kicked out! And the reason I didn't stay Catholic is because they said that's right, something missing, it's missing because we're sinners, and if you want to get it back, too bad, you have to wait until you get to heaven, or wait for the day when Jesus comes back. Okay, that works for people, I don't have any problem with that—something's missing until you get to heaven—that's fine, it works, great, whatever, just depends on how you're put together, but I'm not put together like that. And then you talk about freedom like freedom means being an individual and going around doing whatever you want, but that doesn't work for me either, I know because I tried it, and the more I did whatever I wanted, the more it felt like something's missing, cuz now I couldn't blame society anymore. Here you are free, you thought that would do it, but no, it doesn't, so now it's worse. And then there's this, television, getting dressed up, wearing makeup, all those famous people, like whoever they were, movie people, nice hotels, good cars, stuff like that—for me, the problem is, something's still missing. You see what I mean? I bet you see it. I bet deep down inside you see it. So that's my answer. You have children and you love them and I respect that, and I have a son and I love my son and I just keep thinking I don't want him to grow up and be like, you know, something's missing."

◆

EVELYN'S FATHER SAID BOTTOM line he wasn't in charge of anything anymore, so what he'd like to do is take Cliff to The Carousel and get him fiddlers and a hot fudge sundae. "Cliff ever had fiddlers?" he asked.

"No."

"Well, better late than never," answered Evelyn's father.

"Right," said Evelyn. "But to tell you the truth, I don't think Cliff's gonna go for fiddlers."

"It doesn't have to be fiddlers, then, but really he ought to try fiddlers, Evelyn. If he doesn't like fiddlers I'll get him something else."

"Kids don't like fiddlers."

"Sure they do. When we used to go to The Carousel when you were little, you went to town on fiddlers."

"No, I didn't. I hated fiddlers."

"You didn't hate fiddlers. When we got you fiddlers, you downed 'em fast."

"No," said Evelyn. "I hid them in napkins."

"You what?"

"Same thing at Stockwell with their gross fried brain sandwiches."

"That I can understand," her father said. "That I can't blame anyone for. But fiddlers? Come on, now."

"Yep. Wrapped them up in napkins."

"That's kids for ya," her father said. "I did stuff too when I was a kid. People came out of the movie theater, me and my friends sidled in, backwards."

"Huh," said Evelyn.

"Geez," said her father. "Remember your paper route?"

"Yeah."

"Remember you used to cream people swimming? Absolutely destroyed the field. I mean, lapped people—put them to utter shame."

"I was the champion of the world back then."

"Remember you used to mow the lawn? I come home from Mesker's and step out of the car, it looks like someone took barber tools to the grass."

"I mowed with the best of 'em. No one mowed like me. So, yeah," said Evelyn. "Memory lane. Remember Joanie Weston whaling on Ann Calvello?"

"Wailing on her merciless. Hey, Evelyn, remember when I stopped going to church?"

"Yeah."

"Well, that was because I joined the Shriners, and if you join the Shriners you can't be Catholic."

"What?"

"Oh, you know," said her father. "The Shriners are Freemasons."

"So?"

"Freemasons have temples and stuff like that. You know the official name for Shriners? The Ancient Arabic Order of the Nobles of the Mystic Shrine. With secret handshakes and oaths and rituals. Your mother didn't like it."

"Huh," said Evelyn.

"Yeah," said her father, "so I had to decamp. I didn't want to live that way anymore, with your mother breathing down my neck about religion."

"I can see that," said Evelyn.

"And yet here you are, for some reason," said her father, "going in for reincarnation. Anyway, I'm gonna take Cliff to The Carousel. If he don't want fiddlers, he don't want fiddlers. I'm not gonna make Cliff eat fiddlers. Cliff can eat whatever he wants."

MAUREEN RIGHT NOW HAD to wear a knee brace on account of tendonitis from aerobics class, and with the knee brace on she hobbled some, and with hobbling she got short of breath, and with shortness of breath she felt depressed because at her age she shouldn't have shortness of breath, and also right now she was eating too much so she was putting on weight in her hips and butt and that was making her more depressed. People like her could do Weight Watchers all they wanted, she said, but the shape of your body is determined by genetics. Same with getting fit—determined by genetics. And the problem with aerobics was, aerobics made you hungry, like after aerobics you really need to eat.

But that wasn't the real subject, Maureen said out of nowhere. The real subject was that Evelyn was leaving again. Just like when she moved to Bloomington. Just like when she ran off after high school. Evelyn was leaving again because that was just how Evelyn was, and Maureen had decided she could completely respect that. It used to be she didn't respect it but now she could totally see how a person is what a person is and some people are restless and some people aren't, for whatever reason. So if Evelyn wanted to go to Nepal, then Evelyn should go ahead and go to Nepal, and if Evelyn wanted to put Cliff in a monastery, that was totally within her rights, end of story, period. And now Maureen felt really sorry that she hadn't been nicer to Evelyn when they were younger and had ignored her and made fun of her. Just like trying to separate from Evelyn and be like one of the popular kids, which was so ridiculous—the popular kids!

"Anyway," said Maureen. "I really, really love you. I do, Evelyn. And I'm really, really, really gonna miss you. So this is just hard for me. This is just . . . I mean . . . goodbye."

"Hey," said Evelyn. "It's not like I'm going to Mars or something."

"Still," Maureen answered.

◆

EVELYN TOLD HER MOTHER to go ahead and give Cliff the haircut she'd been wanting to give him before he could even walk. Immediately her mother turned off the television and went in search of her barbering kit, which eventually she found on a high shelf in a closet. On the heels of that, she got her sewing machine stool and set it in front of the mirror in her bathroom. Then, with Evelyn, she went to the den, where Cliff was on the floor, lining up dominoes. "Honeybunch," she said, "guess what?"

"What?"

"Your mama's gonna let me give you a haircut."

"Watch," answered Cliff, and pushed his dominoes over.

In the bathroom Evelyn's mother stripped Cliff's shirt off. "Honeybunch," she said. "Just look at you!"

She cupped his shoulders and shifted him toward the mirror. "Look at you," she said. "What a big boy!"

He was indeed big—and soft, like a marshmallow. Cliff swelled up his doughy gut and said, "Look at me, Gra-mah, I'm fat now!"

"No, you're not fat at all," Evelyn's mother said. "Cliffy, you're not fat, honey."

"Oh yes I am."

"Besides," said Evelyn's mother, "even if you were—even if you were the fattest boy in the world!—it wouldn't matter one little bit, because we'd still love you forever and always!"

"I'm fat now!" repeated Cliff.

Evelyn hauled him up onto the stool. "Can we go into mirrors?" he asked.

"Into mirrors?" said Evelyn.

"Cuz on television a girl jumped right into a mirror."

"That was just television," said Evelyn's mother. "That doesn't happen in real life, Cliff."

"Oh," he answered.

She started in front of his right ear, trimming up, using the tines of a comb in places where his hair insisted on lying flat, then worked her way to the nape of his neck with a hand on his head so she could tilt him. Head down, Cliff lifted his eyes to watch in the mirror while his familiar Dutch boy locks disappeared. He looked docile. One hundred percent willing to let his grandmother twist his head around. A little bit troubled and a little bit pouty. His lower lip protruded. A stoic look came over his face. "Okay, now," said Evelyn's mother, "I'm gonna trim your whorl. Whatever you call it. Where your hair makes a whorl. Good thing about this type of haircut—even I can't mess it up."

When she started working back from Cliff's forehead, he squeezed his eyes shut with the same intensity he used in the bathtub for bubble-blowing. Evelyn's mother winked at Evelyn in the mirror. "Good boy," she said. "Don't get hair in your eyes!"

When she was done with the haircut, Cliff looked stark, the Dutch boy on the paint can resemblance was gone, and suddenly, thought Evelyn, he looked like her father. Cliff leaned in and assessed himself. "So whaddya think?" asked Evelyn's mother.

"Mirrors are backwards," answered Cliff.

◆

EVELYN STARTED THINKING ABOUT it. They'd get off the airplane and come out of the airport, and a bunch of lamas would be waiting for them, and the lamas were going to take one look and think, Uh oh, the new American Norbu Rinpoche's mom's a yeti. Definitely don't give her a ride to the monastery, and if she finds it on her own, make sure the gates are locked. "I can't show up like a slob," thought Evelyn, "that would just be disrespectful. I gotta get clothes."

She went to the mall. She got Cliff red pants, red sneakers, a red jacket, and a yellow T-shirt; between that outfit and his buzz cut he'd at least be in the ballpark. Then she went to the plus-size place, where for the first fifteen minutes nothing looked right, because once again if you imagined those lamas, what were they going to think about these outfits? "Semiformal," said the helper lady. "Nice, airy sundress." "Casual wear." "Safe and conservative." "Wedding-guest attire." "Special occasion." "Good look for you—a hundred percent rayon." "Three-quarter sleeves." "A nice shirred velvet." "Maxi-dress in polyester." "Fit and flared." "Tiered." "Breezy."

Now what? She thought of surrendering. Except that at another shop there were house dresses for $21.95. Really simple, with hook and loop fasteners. One was called "The Cutie Dress." Lightweight and breathable cotton fabric. Came in triple-large and red. Covered everything except half your arms, a little of your legs, and some skin below your throat. 'Well, those guys show an arm,' thought Evelyn, 'on account of the way they wear their robes, so probably this so-called Cutie Dress is fine. Cutie Dress,' she thought. 'Me?'

◆

THE DAY BEFORE THEY were going to leave, she took Cliff to see Gram, who said, "Looks like someone got a beautiful haircut." "Little Mr. Handsome gonna turn some heads." "Now you can see what I mean—he's a Crabtree." "Over yonder on the table's your orange soda, Cliff." "You mean to say you're going there on a trip? That ought to be a great big adventure, traveling up into the snowy Himalayas where they gong their bells or whatever they do, and eat rice I guess and ride little yaks. Little itty-bitty people dressed in costumes and cooking up meals on cow-pie fires—ever smell a cow-pie fire? Some of 'em with hair grows down to their toes, and some's got fingernails longer than a ruler, and some's dressed up in finest silk, and some is lepers with their skin falling off, and some is always smoking that old opium. You know, it used to be we had opium here, but the only thing was, we called it laudanum. And there was a place in Hammond called Frank S. Betz made Tincture of Opium in quarter-pint bottles, and that was good for whatever you had, right off the bat it's like a miracle happened. Lotta people used it for rheumatism, but me I got kicked in the shin by a stallion and my leg swelled up so bad it got infected and all I could do was take that Frank Betz quarter-pint Tincture of Opium to make my way through. And oh my, I saw stuff. I laid around half 'tween sleep and wake and flew out the winder, and after a while I didn't wanna get better because taking that Frank Betz Tincture of Opium was like going to heaven where the angels sing and you float on clouds."

"Well, hey, now," Gram said, when it was time for them to leave. "Now, don't the two of you be strangers here, cuz I'm planning to live to a hundert 'leven." And then, when the door was open and they were going out, Gram leaned over her walker and called, "Evelyn, you're off to the snowy Himalayas, where everything is shrouded in mystery! God works in strange ways, don't He?"

◆

THEY SAT ON THE sofa in the front room together—Evelyn and her mother, with Cliff between them—and it was kind of like her mother had said once about babysitting: that things should be clean when the parents got home, and you ought to be waiting in the front room on the sofa because that was how you got a reputation.

Evelyn had vacuumed first thing that morning. It was hot out now, so the drapes were closed. The overhead fan whirred and the cuckoo clock ticked. Their suitcases stood waiting not far from the door, each with a name tag her mother had filled out and snared to the handles with key-chain rings. There wasn't a whole lot in Evelyn's suitcase, but as far as Cliff's went, her mother'd gone whole hog. Like a dozen pairs of new, colored underpants and a big jar of baby aspirin and a fat tube of antibiotic cream and a can of purple Band-Aids and a hat she'd knitted and mittens she'd made and brand-new patrol boots and seven pairs of wool socks. A red long underwear onesie and a snow parka with a cowl like he was going to the North Pole, and three sets of pajamas. His deck of Uno cards and his box of dominoes and a little bag with a drawstring full of marbles and a little tub full of jacks and a Slinky and a wad of Flubber and a book he'd beaten up and ripped some pages in called *Busy, Busy Town*, by Richard Scarry. And a lot of new clothes he would never wear, because from now on Cliff was going to wear robes.

The clock struck noon. This time Lama Gendun didn't bring the other lamas or the driver in street clothes with the Econoline van. Instead he had with him a driver dressed like the villain in *Goldfinger* who threw a bowler hat to murder people; at the curb sat a black Oldsmobile Cutlass Supreme with a huge trunk and huge doors. The driver didn't make a peep, just lifted the suitcases six inches and waddled out the door with them like a mason carried bricks, while Lama Gendun stood by with his hands behind his back, sweating in his burgundy robe.

Evelyn's mother had her arm around Cliff and got him pulled in now so he was pressed against her good—squeezed in tight and mushed against her housedress. "Well, now," she called to Lama Gendun, giving him the side-eye, throwing him shade. "For the record, anyway, I don't approve, but what can I do—just little old *me*? What could I ever do about *anything*?"

There was no good answer. There was nothing to say. They went out to the curb like funeral mourners. Arcadian Acres looked still and sunbaked. The lawns had all been burnt to a crisp. No one was around—just cars and houses, a stage set: it seemed so to Evelyn. "Honeybunch," rasped Evelyn's mother. "Listen here, Cliffy. Even though you're big now I can still pick you up, you know." And then she did, and rubbed his back, and kissed him on one cheek a bunch, and said, "Oh my, what ever will I do?" and started in crying the loud way she did when she didn't care what people think and couldn't help it anyway, at which point Evelyn wrapped her mother and her son in her arms and said, "We gotta go now, Mom. Me and Cliff."

Epilogue

I FIRST MET EVELYN BEDNARZ ON THE BOUDHANATH Stupa near Kathmandu. I was there as a tourist, though primarily in Nepal in my capacity as a professor of Buddhist Studies.

I first met Evelyn's son Cliff in St. Paul, Minnesota, where he lives with his wife Nancy and their daughter, Christine, and where he works as an urban planner. There's more than one story to be found about him online among the bevy of stories about Western tulkus who for whatever reason didn't stick with the program. In Cliff's case, he made it through nine years in his monastery in Nepal and two years in a monastic college near Darjeeling before hanging it up as "not who I am." He was seventeen at that point.

Today, Cliff enjoys cross-country skiing and runs long distances for exercise. He likes the poet Adam Zagajewski and the philosopher David Loy, and follows the Minnesota Twins, Vikings, and Timberwolves. Nancy is an associate professor in mathematics at Hamline University. Christine is enrolled in a French immersion school.

In his life as the seventh Norbu Rinpoche, Cliff told me, he grew "tired of the kowtowing." He asked if I knew what a khata was. "It's a ceremonial scarf," he said. "People lined up by the thousands with these scarves. They draped them across their forearms and dropped their heads. When they got to me, I tossed the khatas around their necks. Over and over and over again. It's too much. But that's not what you asked. You asked how I felt about ending the lineage. I didn't end the lineage. They still think I'm him. It doesn't matter what I do. When I die they'll look for the next Norbu Rinpoche.

Who knows, maybe I'll have a dream or something. Help it along, add to the mix."

As for Evelyn, the reason I talked to her in the first place was because she talked to me. I wasn't looking to talk to anyone, but I fell while walking on the Boudhanath Stupa, "on account," as Evelyn might have put it, of looking at my phone. I had just gotten done looking at mountains that seemed to hang like a mirage, and after sidestepping someone with my phone poised in front of my face, hit uneven ground and lost my footing. Fortunately, a retaining wall broke my fall, and I made a good enough save to absorb at least some of my embarrassment, and in the end the only thing that hurt was one shoulder, but not too badly. Really I was okay and my phone was okay, but the episode, I have to think, had a quality of slapstick, so it was probably due to that that a number of people halted to take me in for what I was: a buffoon who'd paid for his lack of piety. While people were still grinning at my come-uppance, I pretended not to see them and stuffed my phone in my pocket. That broke the spell. My phone lost its power as a font of condemnation. People moved on and forgot about me. I sat on the retaining wall thinking that I should not be sitting on the retaining wall and then stood quickly, rubbed my shoulder, and tested my legs for steadiness with a couple of knee bends. "That's right," someone said. "Get loose before you walk." The speaker of those words was a mountainous robed Buddhist nun, maybe sixty-five, with a shaved head. Evelyn Bednarz.

Acknowledgments

I AM INDEBTED TO Sallie Tisdale, Richard Wakefield, Mike Drake, Paul Bogaards, and Ani Sakya for reading this novel in draft form; to Adrienne Chan, co–executive director of the Sakya Monastery in Seattle; and to my agent, Emma Parry, and my editor, Alane Mason. I also owe a debt to David L. Jackson's *A Saint in Seattle*, without which I would not have been able to imagine the life of Tsering Lekpa.

Finally, I would like to express my gratitude to Carolyn Massey and Dezhung Rinpoche III for their disparate and converging inspirations, and to the Sakya Khon family for the many gifts it has bestowed on me over the years.